'Father—' Adam's clear voice halted him on his way out. 'You didnae see him towards the end. Tell him, Elizabeth, what it was like.'

'Adam – let it be!' She caught at his sleeve, shaking his arm, but his blue gaze raked her mercilessly before returning to his father.

'Since he's got his own opinions he should know more about it. You'd as soon hide away from the truth about sickness, wouldn't you, father? You know nothing of the cramps, and the convulsions, and the pain that's like a sword being drawn through the body – handle and all—'

Rab's turkey-red face too⬚ ⬚⬚ grey tinge. He went into the hall, and Ad⬚⬚ ⬚⬚⬚⬚g Elizabeth's tugging at his sleeve, ⬚⬚⬚⬚⬚ ⬚⬚⬚. ⬚⬚e surgeon stood at the top of ⬚⬚⬚ ⬚⬚⬚⬚⬚⬚⬚⬚ the illness in detail, raising ⬚⬚⬚ ⬚⬚⬚⬚⬚ ⬚⬚ sure that his father heard e⬚⬚⬚ ⬚⬚⬚ ⬚⬚'t stop until the front door s⬚⬚⬚ ⬚⬚⬚⬚ d Rab.

A Stranger to the Town

Evelyn Hood

WARNER

A *Warner* Book

First published in Great Britain in 1985
by William Kimber & Co. Limited
This edition published by Warner Books in 1999

A CIP catalogue record for this book
is available from the British Library.

ISBN 0 7515 2519 7

Typeset by Derek Doyle & Associates, Mold, Flintshire
Printed and bound in Great Britain by Clays Ltd, St Ives plc

Warner Books
A Division of
Little, Brown and Company (UK)
Brettenham House
Lancaster Place
London WC2E 7EN

To the people of Paisley,
past and present

Prologue

The Town Hospital had been built in 1752 to house Paisley's poor. It seemed to Elizabeth, as she tried in vain to scrub the scuffed parlour floor in 1828, that nobody else had attempted to clean it in the intervening seventy-six years.

The scrubbing brush was a poor mess of bristles and wood, the water she worked with cold and scummy, adding its own dirt to the filthy floor. The soap, harsh yellow stuff made in the hospital kitchen, had vanished.

'Teenie!' She sat back on her heels, pushed lank hair from her eyes, glared at the elderly woman kneeling beside her. 'Give me that soap!'

Teenie worked on, scrubbing as though intent on wearing her way through to the foundations of the building. But Elizabeth's sharp eyes had seen the yellow lump in Teenie's almost-closed fist. The woman was a known thief. She took everything she saw, and if she couldn't sell it for a few pence, she hid it in the garden.

'Give it to me!' Elizabeth launched herself at Teenie, who was caught by surprise. The two of them rolled on the wet, dirty floor, Teenie squawling in childish outrage, Elizabeth silent, fighting with tooth and nail, feet and fists. If the soap went missing it would mean yet another punishment. This time, surely, she would be made to spend an hour in the cells where the insane folk were kept. The thought of it made her skin crawl, and redoubled her efforts.

She had just gained hold of the precious soap when fingers dug into her scalp, dragging her head back as tears flooded into her screwed-up eyes. The soap slid from her hand and she and Teenie were separated.

'Elizabeth Cunningham!' Mistress Jamieson, matron of the hospital, glared down at her. 'I might have known it! Get to the kitchen this minute and wait for me!'

'She stole the soap, and—'

'I never did!' Teenie shrieked, then fled to the corner of the empty, gloomy parlour as Elizabeth rounded on her.

'That's enough!' the matron rapped, then another voice, low and calm, spoke from the doorway.

'And how old is this lassie?'

'Fourteen years, Mistress Montgomery.' The matron released her grip on Elizabeth, who stood where she was, Teenie forgotten.

'Old enough to go into service.' Mistress Montgomery came further into the room, lifting her skirts to keep them away from the muddy floor.

'She's of some use in the kitchens and with the younger children. And most folk feel she doesn't have the looks or the proper manner to be a servant.'

Elizabeth's cheeks flamed and she opened her mouth to protest that she wasn't an animal to be discussed as though she had no feelings. Then she remembered the cells, and closed her lips. Two hours at least, for a girl who had the audacity to answer back before a visitor.

Instead, she tilted her chin defiantly, determined that she wasn't going to lower her head. To her surprise, her brown gaze met grey eyes filled with warmth and interest. There was even sympathy there, though it was an emotion she hadn't seen often before.

Mistress Montgomery wore a fine dark red silk gown and a feathered bonnet. Greying brown hair framed a pretty face that looked as though it smiled easily. About her shoulders was one of the beautiful, intricately-patterned shawls woven on Paisley looms and famed throughout the world.

'Is your mother in the hospital?' The question was directed at Elizabeth herself, subtle reproof to the matron, who drew in her breath with a faint hiss, but said nothing.

'She's—' Elizabeth swallowed hard. 'They – died of the smallpox, my mother and father and – and—'

And Davie, and the laughing baby. In the seven lonely years since, she had demanded of Mistress Jamieson's God, over and over again, why she had been made to stay alive without them.

Her face coloured again as she saw the woman's eyes travel over the scar that stretched from one corner of her mouth to the angle of her jaw. Many people in Paisley carried smallpox scars, but Elizabeth felt as though the uneven, puckered groove she bore was the ugliest ever seen.

'But you survived it. You were meant for a long life,' Mistress Montgomery said gently. 'Tell me, Elizabeth Cunningham, would you be willing to work for me?'

Mistress Jamieson moved forward swiftly. 'I really think you should see the girl I've selected for you—'

Mistress Montgomery held up an elegant hand, her eyes still on Elizabeth's face. 'I require a girl who can learn to manage a household, and perhaps become my companion. Would you like that?'

'Aye.' The word was no more than a strangled gasp, but it spoke volumes. A smile told Elizabeth that the woman understood.

'Someone of a more placid disposition—' the matron tried to intervene, and the smile deepened.

'My dear woman, a more placid disposition would be quite bewildered in a household of men,' said Mistress Montgomery crisply. 'I require someone with some spirit – and I think we'll both be well pleased. You can send her to the High Street tomorrow. And I think, under the circumstances, that it would be a kindness to forget today's misdemeanour.'

She swept out with a rustle of silk, followed by Mistress Jamieson with a clank of keys. The soap vanished within the folds of Teenie's greasy, shabby gown and she gave the bucket a sly kick, setting the floor awash with spilled water, soaking Elizabeth's worn shoes. Elizabeth didn't care.

On the following morning she stood in the Town Hospital's front hall, her face scrubbed until it glowed painfully, her hair washed and screwed into plaits and hidden beneath a respectable white linen cap. Her sole possessions, a change of clothing and a Bible, were in the bundle she held.

Mistress Jamieson surveyed her from every angle before coming to a standstill before her.

'I want you to know, Elizabeth Cunningham, that Mistress Rachel Montgomery is the wife of one of Paisley's most important manufacturers. You must never, never—' a large-knuckled forefinger wagged before Elizabeth's nose '—never do anything to anger her or her man. If you bring shame on this Institution by your bad behaviour or disobedience or impudence, the Lord himself will strike you down. Do you mind me?'

Elizabeth, too overcome to speak, nodded violently.

'May He go with you,' the matron finished, in a voice that said plainly that she was sure He had more to do than go with the likes of Elizabeth Cunningham, orphan and trouble-maker.

The hospital doors opened. Elizabeth took a firm grip on her bundle, and walked out to face a new life.

I

Rounding the corner from New Street into High Street, Elizabeth staggered and gasped as the wind caught at her cloak. She staggered again when an elderly woman pushed by her roughly, intent on getting out of the gale – in some ale-house, to judge from the smell that hit Elizabeth's nose in the passing.

The summer of 1831 was whirling itself out of existence with ill-tempered grace. Well it might, for it had been a bad summer for Paisley. Scotland's most successful weaving centre had too many looms lying idle and too many hungry weavers seeking work.

'Mind the stour, lassie—' A plum-coloured arm with lace at the wrist swept out to hold Elizabeth back from the gutter, which swirled with filthy water. The man smiled down at her as she regained her balance and stammered thanks, then he disappeared into the tide of folk sweeping along the High Street in both directions. The footpaths were packed with housewives, bare-footed children oblivious to the cold, plump businessmen with gold chains looped securely across ample stomachs. The narrow roadway too had its traffic – carts and carriages, mail gigs, men on horseback swearing at pedestrians who crossed beneath the very noses of the horses.

It was just as well, Elizabeth thought as she looped the basket more firmly over her arm and battled on her way, that she hadn't much further to go. And there it was – the fine solid oaken door proclaiming in the gleam of its handle and knocker that it belonged to a prosperous man.

It swung open under her hand then closed behind her, shutting out the noise and the wind. As always, she felt a faint thrill of pleasure when she stood in the hallway of Rab Montgomery's fine house. It had an air of opulence that she had never known until three years before. Normally she would have scurried down the narrow passage that led down the side of the house to the back door. But now and then, when she knew her employer wasn't at home, she permitted herself the luxury of using the front door and pretending that the house belonged to her.

In reality the only part that could be said to be hers was the kitchen. Elizabeth enjoyed her moment of pride then crossed to the door set in the shadows beyond the staircase.

The kitchen of the Montgomery house was a large room, stone-flagged and, at that moment, rich with a mixture of aromas from pots bubbling on the range. The big scrubbed wooden table that took up most of the floor space was packed with platters carrying crisp golden tarts, sugared cakes, cold meats and loaves crusty and hot from the oven. Such a banquet had to be prepared for that night that several neighbours and one of the baker's shops nearby had been called on to lend their ovens for the occasion.

It was a sight guaranteed to gladden the heart of any housewife. But Elizabeth's attention was immediately taken from the table by the noise of Tibby's scolding and Jean's sobs.

'What's amiss?' She found a stool to hold her laden basket, and unfastened her tartan cloak.

'Well you might ask!' Tibby, a small shrew of a woman, rounded on her, hands tucked into her skinny waist. 'It's thon stupid big lump of a lassie. Why you keep her on here's beyond me!'

Jean, huddled in a chair with her apron over her face, howled like a banshee. Cold terror caught at Elizabeth's heart.

3

'She's gone and let the beef burn! Jean, did I no' tell you time and again to keep your eyes on that beef!'

'It's no' the beef.' Tibby made it sound as though burning the beef counted as a very small sin.

'What then?' Elizabeth anxiously studied the table as Jean bayed to the smoky ceiling like a dog serenading the moon. 'The puddings! What happened to the puddings?' The perfect house-keeper, she was more concerned over her employer's favourite foods than anything else. Rab Montgomery had spent days ordering this meal and he was a hard taskmaster if he was crossed.

'The puddings havenae come from Mistress McNair's kitchen yet. This daft gowk – you cannae leave her to do anything!' Tibby nudged Jean, bringing another howl from her. Elizabeth, now almost beside herself with worry, dragged the apron down and revealed a swollen, turkey-red face.

'Then what's she done? In the name of reason, Jean, will you just tell me what's gone wrong?'

'Oh, Miss Eliza – lizabeth!' Jean gulped, sniffed, and was about to slip into a fresh bout of keening when a look at Elizabeth's face made her change her mind. 'I c-cannae mind if I salted the b-br-b-broth or no'!'

'Is that all?'

'All?' Tibby squawked self-righteously. 'And me standing at that table for near on two hours chopping and cutting so that they'd have the best broth ever put on a table to welcome a wanderer home?'

'Did you think to taste the broth?'

They stared at her blankly and Elizabeth found a wooden spoon, dipped it into the huge pot on the 'swee' that held it over the range, and blew the soup cautiously before tasting it.

'Aye, you salted it, Jean.' She waited, unkindly, for the first look of relief to spread over the scullery maid's face before going on, 'Twice. Now see here—' she added swiftly as Jean's face screwed up again and Tibby opened her mouth for another scolding '—crying'll no' cure it, tears are salty too. Away and get more water for the kettle while I see to this.' She seized a cloth, lifted the heavy kettle that was always simmering on the range, and tipped some of it into the broth pot.

'You'll ruin it!' Tibby danced about the kitchen in a frenzy. Elizabeth tasted the mixture again.

'It's still got a good flavour to it, and there's enough to drink if the salt makes them thirsty. They'll no' complain.'

Tibby jerked a white-capped head in the direction of the open back door. 'Why you keep that

5

lassie on here's beyond me. She hasnae got as much sense as would fill a flea!'

'She can manage well enough when she's no' being hurried,' Elizabeth raced to the maid's defence. The truth was that Jean, like herself, had been brought up in the Town Hospital. Orphan must help orphan. Elizabeth knew well enough that Tibby, who worked in her brother's butcher's shop, would have preferred Jean's job and never missed the opportunity, when helping out, to show up the girl's shortcomings.

Jean staggered in from the darkening night with a stoup of water from the outside well in each hand. Elizabeth directed her to refill the kettle and to wash her tear-stained face, then hurried to the parlour, rolling up her sleeves as she went, to make sure that everything was prepared for the evening's celebrations.

The room was a flickering patchwork of light and shadow in the firelight. She drew the heavy curtains, lit a taper at the fire, and attended to the lamps. The parlour was large and well furnished with good pieces chosen by Rab Montgomery's late wife. The carpet, soft underfoot, was in muted shades of blue and green and brown. Elizabeth crossed the hall and peeped in at the door of the dining-room, nodding her satisfaction over the big table's snowy starched covering and the discreet glitter of glass and silverware. This room was hardly ever used; since Rab had been widowed almost a year before, he and his sons preferred to take their morning meal in the kitchen and their evening meals at the small table in the parlour.

The knocker rattled importantly and as soon as Elizabeth answered it Christian Selbie swept into the hall on a gust of cold air and a handful of rain. She divested herself of her fur-trimmed cloak, revealing a lilac silk dress with a lace-edged ruff about the neck, and full lace-trimmed sleeves.

'Well, Elizabeth—' She unfastened her bonnet strings and took the hat off, patting the fine lace cap that hid most of her grey-streaked dark head. 'Is everyone at home?'

'Mister Montgomery's gone to meet the coach.'

Christian tutted and smoothed the skirt of her gown with a beringed hand. She was a small plump active woman, warm-hearted and generous, quite unlike her dour cousin, Rab Montgomery.

'No doubt he'll catch the pneumonia and Adam'll find he only came home to attend a death-bed. Mind you, he'll probably be cosy enough in Sadie's tavern, waiting for the coach in comfort,

7

with a drink in his hand. What about Matthew and James?'

'Not home yet.' Elizabeth allowed her fingers the luxury of a swift wriggle in the thick fur that lined the cloak Christian had handed to her. It would be dreary in the big warehouse by the river on a stormy night like this. She could picture the lamps casting weird shadows in the corners and on the high ceilings above the bundles and bales. Matthew and James Montgomery would be the last to leave as usual – Matthew with his brain buzzing over the figuring he hated, James in a dream of his own, working out a new poem or a new design in his head.

Christian brought her back to her own business with a bump when she said briskly, 'Well, we'd best be seeing to things—' and bustled off to the kitchen.

'Ma'am – Mistress Selbie—' Elizabeth scurried after her. 'Would you no' be more comfortable in the parlour?'

Christian tutted. 'Lassie, mebbe I'm here to preside over this party for Rab, but you'd surely never expect me to sit alone in the parlour till the folk come?' She threw the kitchen door open. 'Good evening to you, Jean – you're here too, Tibby?—' In a moment she had cast an eye over the table, swung the broth pot out from the fire and peeped inside, muttering to herself all the time.

Born to money and widowed by a well-to-do husband, Christian had inherited the character of her grandmother, a weaver's wife. She was used to servants, but she had no time for a woman who knew nothing of the workings of a kitchen or the right way to apply a poultice or darn a stocking. Her father had been a surgeon, her brother a lawyer, her husband a banker. It was Christian's belief that she could have bettered any of them if she had not had the misfortune to be born a woman.

'I see the fatted calf's been killed for the prodigal son,' she observed dryly, unfastening her sleeves and rolling them back to expose rounded, capable forearms. 'Elizabeth – a clean pinny, if you please!'

A rap at the back door heralded the arrival of Mistress McNair's small maid with the sweet puddings. Suddenly all the last-minute arrangements became essential and by the time everything was ready Elizabeth had reason to be grateful for Christian's calm, efficient organisation.

'You're on the young side to be giving orders to the likes of Tibby.' Christian brushed words of appreciation aside as she led Elizabeth back to the parlour, fastening her sleeves again. 'She's lazy and she needs someone who's ready for her. It's foolish of Rab to expect you to see to everything. He should have had the sense to employ an older woman.' Then, realising that her words sounded critical, she added kindly 'After all, poor Rachel engaged you to be her companion, not the housekeeper.'

Rachel Montgomery, Rab's second wife and mother to James and Matthew, had died several months earlier, and Elizabeth missed her warmth and her guidance bitterly. But there was no time to think of that now. The front door opened and closed and Christian, tidying her hair in the mirror above the mantel, whirled round.

'They're here! Rab? Adam—?' Then her voice flattened with disappointment. 'Oh – it's you, James.'

James Montgomery, youngest of Rab's three sons and twenty-one years of age, blinked in surprise at his cousin.

'Are you here already?'

'Already?' she screeched at him. 'The guests arriving at any minute and Adam late? Have you no idea of the time? James Montgomery, get upstairs this minute and get yourself into a decent coat and cravat, else your father'll have something to say when he gets home!'

Placid James, who always gave the impression that his thoughts were elsewhere, gave her his sweet, warm smile and turned away obediently.

'Wait – where's Matthew?' she rapped, and he looked around as though slightly surprised to realise that he had come home alone.

'Oh yes – he's calling in at Shuttle Street,' he remembered.

His kinswoman raised her eyes to the ceiling. 'Does he have to go courting tonight of all nights? Off you go, James—' she added, shooing him across the hall as though he was a stray chicken. Then she bustled back into the parlour. 'Mind you, I see no reason why Isobel couldn't have been invited here tonight with Matt. Nobody ever ended something by pretending it wasnae there. Isobel's a fine lassie. Rab's a fool – his son could find a worse wife.'

The knocker banged and Elizabeth hurried to the hall, rushed back to the parlour in answer to Christian's squeak of horror, caught the rejected pinny as the older woman tore it off and threw it to her, then ran back to open the door.

She returned to the kitchen just as the back door opened, frightening the life out of Jean, who had been leaning against it.

'Beth!' Matthew seized her hands in an icy grip, his nose red from the cold wind. 'Are they here yet?'

'No, but due any minute. Your cousin Christian's entertaining the Blairs in the parlour. You're awful late, Matt—'

His light brown hair was windswept. 'I saw the Blairs at the door, so I came down the side passage. I'll get upstairs and get ready.'

He picked up a pastry, ignoring her angry 'Matthew Montgomery—!' and slid like a shadow through the inner door. Tibby, stirring the broth, sniffed.

'That's no way for a young gentleman to behave. Stealing through his father's back door like a thief. Mind you, there's some say that he's no' keeping the right company these days—'

'You can see to the potatoes now.' Elizabeth found a new hardness in her voice to make the woman subside. Christian was right, Tibby did need to be bullied before she would mind her sharp tongue. Elizabeth had a soft spot for Matt, for she knew he was unhappy working as his father's warehouse foreman. And Isobel Gibson, Matthew's love, was a friend of Elizabeth's.

Isobel's father was a silk weaver, now old and unable to do much work. Isobel herself worked for the Montgomerys, trimming shawls for one shilling and threepence a day. Rab had made it clear that he didn't consider her a good match for his son.

The door knocker thumped again. And again, and again. Matthew and James, both neat and well groomed, appeared among the guests. The parlour was full, the meal ready, but still Rab Montgomery and his eldest son, Adam, the guest of honour, were missing.

'I mind Adam was never good at arriving anywhere on time,' Christian remarked to Mrs Andrew Blair as Elizabeth went into the parlour for advice. 'He took three days to his own birth, and his mother never survived it, poor flower. What's amiss, Elizabeth?'

The meat was amiss, beginning to sizzle ominously in its own shrinking fat. And the potatoes were ready for eating.

'Could I serve the meal now, ma'am?'

'You cannae put the food on the table before the master of the house is here, no' to mention—' Christian's head lifted sharply 'Did I hear the front door? They're here!'

Her shrill voice caught everyone's attention. It was too late for Elizabeth to slip back to the kitchen, so she had to stay with the others and await Adam Montgomery's entrance. He had been away from home for some years and Elizabeth had never set eyes on him. She would have preferred to be well out of the way for his re-introduction to Paisley.

13

All heads turned towards the door and Rab Montgomery, arriving on the threshold of his own parlour wet, cold and in a very bad temper, found himself the centre of some two dozen pairs of eyes.

'You can all stop staring,' he informed his guests curtly. 'He's no' here.'

'No' here?' Christian, a miniature Moses, divided the throng with little effort, clawing a path to her cousin. 'The stage didnae arrive?'

Rab let his damp coat fall to the floor and scowled at the gathering. Mrs Andrew Blair gasped and fluttered a hand to her throat. She was known to be a highly-strung lady.

'Here? Of course the stage is here, woman!' Rab snarled. 'A good hour late, and with Adam's boxes on board.'

'Mercy,' quavered Mrs Andrew Blair. 'He's fell off!'

Rab gave her a withering glance and pushed his way to the small cupboard where the whisky was kept. Ignoring the buzz of speculation that rose about his ears he poured himself a generous glass-ful and drained half of it before speaking.

'He left the coach on the outskirts of the town. It seems that some drunken fool of a man let himself fall under the horses and Adam undertook to tend

14

him. As to where he is—' His small blue eyes, bloodshot and bright in his round red face, were like glass as he looked at them all over the rim of the tumbler. When he lowered it again he went on '—I have no idea. And damn me if I care!'

'We'll have the dinner now,' Christian's voice cut decisively across the babble of shocked, alarmed voices. 'Elizabeth—'

Everyone turned with relief towards their hostess. Everyone except Rab, who emptied his glass and picked up the bottle.

'Aye, off you go to the trough,' he told his guests with his customary surliness. 'That's what you came for, was it no'? For myself, I'll just have a wee dram—'

His arm was seized by a plump, determined fist. Its partner took the glass from his hand.

'You'll just come through and sit at the table with the rest of us, Rab,' Christian ordered. 'For you're more in need of hot food than of drink on a stormy night like this.'

She was the only person, now that his wife was dead, who could make Rab Montgomery do anything against his will. The two of them warred whenever they met, but Christian kept Rab's household going, and his life in order. Muttering beneath his breath, he allowed her to lead him to the dining-room, followed by the people who had come to welcome Adam home.

The meal was more like a wake, with Adam's empty chair reproaching them all. Some of the guests, who had indeed come for the food, gave a good account of themselves. Rab, a big man who had never been known for his cheerfulness, and who had become even more soured since Rachel's death, picked morosely at the contents of his plate and devoted more time to the wine, not opening his mouth to anyone. He had planned this evening to the finest degree, and by missing it Adam had spurned him.

Matt, deeply disappointed by his brother's absence, also picked at his food. As she bustled round the table, serving people and making sure that all was in order, Elizabeth caught his blue eyes, and was rewarded by a smile. She knew that Matt was wishing that Isobel could be at his side.

James worked valiantly to entertain the guests, though all he wanted was to get away to the peace of the small room he shared with Matt. He, too, had dreams; in James's case they were about books of poetry, or fine shawl designs. Like Matt, he found that his ambitions were scorned by his father.

The guests didn't stay for long once the meal was ended. Christian was the last to go.

'I have it in mind to hold a wee gathering for some of the younger folk soon,' she murmured to Matt as he escorted her to her carriage. 'I'd like fine if Isobel would come to it.'

His face flushed and he beamed at her gratefully. 'I'd – she'd – that'd be fine!' Gratitude hampered his tongue.

Rab and James were in the hall with Elizabeth when Matt went back indoors. 'I'll wait up – mebbe Adam'll come home tonight.'

Rab rounded on him. 'You'll go to your room and get a good night's sleep! There's plenty to be done at the warehouse in the morning and I'll have you ready for it, no' sleeping over the books because your laggardly brother saw fit to go off with some drunken fool. He can sleep at the house-end till the door's open in the morning!' Rab locked the door firmly. 'That might teach him a lesson – if he troubles himself to come home at all!' And he stumped upstairs, dragging the leg that had been injured during the riots eleven years earlier. Matt and James, exchanging looks, followed him.

Tibby and Jean helped Elizabeth to clear the table and set the house to rights. A great deal of food had been left over and Tibby went off home with a bundle beneath her shawl, her shrill tongue sweetened at last. As Elizabeth shut and bolted the back door behind her she thought of the missing Adam Montgomery. The wind was still strong and it was raining heavily.

She sent Jean off to sleep in the cupboard-like bedroom off the kitchen and decided, tired though she was, to sit up for a little longer just in case Adam Montgomery arrived home. She couldn't bear to think of him having to huddle in the shelter of a wall till morning. After all, Rab Montgomery hadn't forbidden her to stay up.

The rest of the house was in darkness now, but the kitchen was lit, and cosy. The kettle simmered quietly on the range. Rain tapped now and then at the window and the wind howled round the trees in the garden. Elizabeth's lids drooped, lifted, drooped, and settled.

She woke with a start, bewildered to find herself in the kitchen, confused by the noise that identified itself, as she blinked drowsiness away, as a thunderous attack on the front door. Still not fully clear as to why she wasn't in her bed she snatched up a lamp and scuttled into the hall, the light chasing shadows before her.

Someone was pounding the solid oaken door with determined fists, and adding a kick now and then. Elizabeth, hurrying to answer, recalled the fiasco of a few hours before and the missing man. She set the lamp down on a carved straight-backed chair and reached up to slide back the bolt at the top of the door.

As soon as the bolts were drawn and the latch lifted the door was thrown back, Elizabeth staggering with it. Then the handle was torn from her fingers as the door was slammed shut again, closing out the wind and rain. A large shape, a man in heavy coat and tall hat, his chin tucked close to his chest, and his coat collar pulled well up, surged into the hall.

'God's teeth!' boomed an angry voice as the door slammed shut, 'is everyone deaf in this place? Must a traveller take the very walls apart before he's heard?'

Flickering lamplight stilled and grew as the air settled again. Its glow illuminated Rab Montgomery's slippered feet and bare ankles below his night-shirt as he stopped on the third bottom step of the staircase. His own candle, held high, lit his face and his night-capped head. Behind him Elizabeth could hear Matt and James in the shadows.

'Adam!' Matt whooped, but Rab's sturdy body blocked the way down as he stood still, glaring at his errant son.

Adam Montgomery took his hat off and tossed it onto a table, peering up into the candle-lit area above. 'Matthew. Father. James,' he acknowledged his family crisply.

In the uncertain light Rab's face was drawn into a malevolent scowl. 'So you found your way back home after all,' he said sourly, making no move to come down the last few steps.

'I was – detained.'

'We heard. No doubt I'll see you in the morning – if you've nowhere better you'd rather be,' Rab sneered, and turned to go back to bed. When Matt and James stood back to let him pass, he barked at them, 'I'll have no family reunions at this time of the night – get to your beds! You can speak to your brother in the morning!'

Reluctantly, the two were driven before him to the upper floor, leaving Elizabeth and Adam in the hall.

'Well – do you mean to let me stand here all night?' he turned on her. All she could see of him was a face set in lines as uncompromising as Rab's, and broad shoulders that shone wetly. Hurriedly, she bobbed a curtsey and led the way to the kitchen. He ducked his head to follow her through the door, then looked round as he unfastened his caped travelling coat.

He let it drop to the floor, in a gesture similar to his father's earlier, and went to spread large, long-fingered hands before the range, shivering.

'Is there food in this place?'

She realised that she had been standing gaping like a fool.

'Of – of course. There's broth I'll heat for you, and some cold fowl, and—'

He tore a handful of bread from a loaf on the table, delved into the butter crock, and spread the bread liberally.

'And hot water – I'm in sore need of good hot water,' he ordered thickly through a mouthful of food.

Nervously Elizabeth fetched a piece of her own soap and a basin, which was promptly tossed into a corner.

'A decent wash, woman, not a dipping of my fingers!' he barked at her. 'Is there no bath in this God-forsaken house of my father's?'

She opened a door and dragged out the tin hip bath, struggling with it to the door.

'Now what are you doing?'

'I'm – I'm taking the bath to your r – room—' Her tongue wouldn't shape the words properly.

'You'd have me wash in a cold room on a night like this?' The bath was taken from her and deposited before the fire. The steaming kettle was emptied into it, followed by a pot of water that had been sitting on the range. There was about two inches of hot water in the bottom of the bath.

'God save us – there's enough for a sparrow!' he said in disgust.

'There's the water heating in the wash-house for the morning's washing—' she ventured, hanging the soup pot on the iron swee and swinging it over the fire.

'Then hold the light for me—' Adam opened the back door and plunged out into the night, Elizabeth close behind him. The wash-house, which held the big copper boiler, was built at right angles to the back of the house and had its own door, close to the kitchen door. He picked up two buckets, scooped warm water from the boiler, and returned to hurl their contents into the bath.

By the time he was finished the boiler was almost empty and the kitchen was fragrant with the aroma of hot broth. Adam grunted with satisfaction as he surveyed the hip bath, half-filled with warm water.

'Will you eat first?' Elizabeth had set a corner of the table with cutlery and food. He studied it hungrily, then looked down at his own untidy, mud-splashed figure.

'I'll take the edge off my appetite, for the hunger's gnawing at me,' he decided, flicking a contemptuous finger at the bottle of his father's prized brandy she had set out for him. 'You can take that away. Get me a jug of good Scots ale, woman!'

She ladled out broth, fetched the ale jug, and ran to put a warming pan in his bed. Adam was to use the small room at the far end of the upstairs passage.

When she returned with towels he had emptied the soup pot and the jug. He indicated to her to bring more ale, then she retired to a chair by the fire, waiting for his next instructions.

He ate swiftly, greedily, with his eyes fixed on his plate, and after a moment she dared to look up at him. His clothes were good; a dark red coat, a yellow satin waistcoat, fawn trousers and sturdy boots, with a black cravat at his throat. The boots and trousers were covered in muddy streaks, the coat splashed with darker stains which could have been blood. His dark hair was neither dressed nor powdered, but left free to curl strongly about his forehead and the nape of his neck.

His face was square, rugged, handsome, though set in forbidding lines, his eyes—

His eyes, she realised with sudden confusion,

were looking straight into hers. Flustered, she fluttered her fingers together in her lap.

'And what do they call you?'

'Elizabeth.' Her voice came out in a gasp.

He pushed his chair back and stood up. 'Well now, Elizabeth, you may have saved my very life with your broth.'

He moved to the fire, leaving her free to go to the table to begin gathering up the used dishes. 'You sleep here in the house?'

'In the attic.' She nodded to the door of Jean's little room. 'The scullery maid sleeps in there.'

He dropped his stained coat onto a chair, began to unfasten the buttons of his waistcoat. 'She must be a heavy sleeper tonight – if she isn't dead.'

'Once her eyes close Jean wouldnae know if the house fell down about her ears.' Elizabeth attempted a laugh, but it died before the unsmiling scrutiny from the man who stood in the kitchen as though he owned everything in it. The cravat dropped from his nimble fingers, followed by the waistcoat.

'Mebbe it's time you were going to your own bed, Elizabeth.'

'But—' It didn't seem right. This was no welcome for a man who had been away from home for so long, and had travelled so far. But

Adam, it seemed, was as uninterested in convention as his father. He was unfastening the pleated cuffs of his shirt, popping buttonholes from neck to waist – then the shirt, too, was tossed carelessly to the chair. His smooth, muscular torso gleamed in the lamplight as he let the garment fall and straightened up again.

'Unless—' he suggested as his fingers moved unhurriedly, but with purpose, to the buttons at the waistband of his tight-fitting trousers, 'you have some notion of giving me your own welcome home? You must forgive me if I devote myself to my bath first. Or are you gifted like those famous geisha girls of Japan—?'

Elizabeth didn't wait to hear any more. With a scandalised gasp, realising that he had no intention of letting her presence prevent him from stepping naked into the tub, she scooped up a lamp and fled to her room.

She tiptoed up the main staircase to the first floor, then up the second, narrower flight of stairs to the attics high above the street. One room was used as a store-room, the other was Elizabeth's – her first private room and her pride and joy. Here, on a shelf Matt had made for her, stood a few books that Rachel Montgomery and Christian Selbie had given her. There on the wall was a picture painted by James. This was where Elizabeth kept her few clothes, her hairbrush, her mirror.

It was the middle of the night. In a few hours she would have to be up again. She swept the lawn cap from her light brown hair and let the long, heavy tresses tumble down her back. She brushed it out as she used to brush Rachel's hair, then took off her apron and gown and underclothes, putting them away neatly before slipping into bed in her shift.

She knew that she would never be able to sleep. There was too much to think about.

She blew out the lamp, then opened her eyes to the sound of the first risers moving about in the street below. It was time to get up.

II

The house was silent as Elizabeth hurried down to the ground floor. She was always first up and it was her duty to have the housework started and breakfast ready before the men of the house arrived in the kitchen. She and Jean would normally have started work on the washing first thing, but the copper had been emptied for Adam Montgomery's bath. This meant that work would be behind-hand all day.

Trying to reorganise the day in her mind she went into the kitchen, put the lamp on the table by the remains of Adam's meal, then turned and caught her breath. He was still there, fast asleep by the range, which now glowed dully. He had dressed himself again in his shirt, open at the neck to expose a strong throat, and his trousers. The stained jacket was thrown over his shoulders and his bony bare feet sprawled untidily on the mat before the range. The hip bath had been put out of sight.

She lit a second lamp and put it on the shelf above the fire. Its light fell across his face but didn't disturb him. He looked, she thought, very uncomfortable. His long frame spilled over the chair, his head lolling on one shoulder. Even in sleep the set of his mouth was uncompromising, though the dark lashes brushing his cheeks were surprisingly long and silky. His hair was disordered, and she saw in the light that there were threads of silver among the black curls over his temples. One arm lay across his body, the other was over the wooden arm of the chair, his fingers dangling in mid-air. He had fine hands, she thought enviously, aware of her own work-reddened fingers. But then, Adam Montgomery was both a physician and a surgeon, where she—

She suddenly realised that it was almost six and nothing had been started. She was torn between reluctance to wake him and the urgency of her work. Nervously she spoke his name but he didn't stir. Her hand reached out towards his arm, hesitated, withdrew, and finally settled. His body was strong and hard beneath the soiled material of the shirt.

She shook him slightly, saying his name in a

louder voice, and his dark blue eyes suddenly flew open. For a moment he stared uncomprehendingly at the hand on his arm, then he said sleepily 'Who—?' and lifted his chin to look up at her.

'Oh – it's you.' He rubbed a hand over his face. 'What is it?'

'It's nearly six, sir. I have to clean the range and get the meal ready.'

He brushed her aside and got to his feet, yawning, stretching till his knuckles almost touched the ceiling, then looking with distaste at the clothes he wore.

'Did my boxes arrive?'

'Aye, sir, they're in your room.'

He nodded, picked up his jacket from the floor where it had fallen, and went to the door. Then he turned, supporting himself with one hand on the frame.

'How do you address my brothers?'

'By their given names.'

'Then you'll call me Adam,' he said, making an order of it, and walked out.

Jean was buried in blankets, her hair a rumpled black mass on the pillow, mouth open, eyes tightly shut. Elizabeth shook her awake with a lot more vigour and a lot less sympathy than she had used on Adam and dragged her, protesting, to the cold floor. Then she hurried back to the kitchen, where she scooped up the remains of the late meal, cleaned out the grate with noisy speed, and set the fire. Jean shuffled in, sleepy-eyed and yawning, and was ruthlessly ordered to wash her face in a bowl of cold water.

'And stir yourself, girl, for there's the porridge to make and the front doorstep to clean – and see you get a good polish on that door knocker! Set out the dishes first – I'll have to see what can be done about the washing!'

The flurry of orders set Jean in action, and Elizabeth hurried across the yard, still dark and cold. As she whirled through the wash-house door she realised with surprise that the place was warm. Someone had stoked up the fire beneath the boiler during the night.

She lifted the top of the boiler and found that it had been refilled, and the water was steaming gently, ready for the morning's wash.

When Adam joined the family for breakfast he had changed into dark trousers, strapped beneath the foot, and a clean white shirt under a red patterned satin waistcoat. He looked as though he had enjoyed a good night's sleep.

Rab was distant towards him at first, obviously still angry at being forced to return home alone to face his guests. If he had hoped to shame his son into an apology he didn't succeed. Adam greeted them all cheerfully, and launched into answers to his brothers' clamoured questions without giving his father a second look.

Elizabeth, apparently busy about her work, listened avidly. Adam had been a naval surgeon for the past six or seven years, and the stories he had to tell filled her with astonishment. She was vaguely aware that there was a world outside Paisley, but never before had she heard a first-hand account of beaches of white sand, dark-skinned peoples, continuously blue skies, tremendous heat, or the sight of the sea stretching to every horizon. She could visualise each picture as he described it.

'And where did you get to last night?' Rab finally asked.

'The coach knocked a man over in the dark. I saw to it that he got home, and dressed his injured leg.'

'A drunken fool, I've no doubt.'

'Aye, he was drunk. But a man in drink can bleed and suffer as much as an abstainer once he's been hurt.'

'And I was left to explain your absence to your friends!'

Adam raised those compelling dark blue eyes

from his plate. 'Your friends, father,' he corrected calmly. 'I'm sure you managed fine without me.'

'You're as ill-mannered as ever you were. Have you learned nothing in those seven years?' Rab barked at him.

'I learned that no man's my inferior or my superior unless he can prove it to my satisfaction.'

There was a brief silence as he and his father eyed one another, Adam serenely, Rab cautiously. Then the older man said, 'You've picked up a fancy English way of speaking, I hear. Too proud to use your good Scots tongue?'

Adam shrugged. 'We've to learn to speak the way they do, else they'd never understand what they're being told. And a surgeon has to be understood.'

'I can follow the English tongue well enough,' Rab said shortly. As a shawl manufacturer he visited London markets now and then. His eldest son darted a glance at him from beneath thick black brows as he concentrated again on the food before him.

'Aye – but that's because we've got a sharper ear for a turn of the tongue than the English.'

'What was life like on board ship?' James butted in, unable to keep silent any longer.

'It wasnae pleasure trips I was on. I saw little of

what went on above decks. As for between them –
I saw sights I'd as soon no' have had to face.'

'What about India—' James urged, then
coloured as Matt dug him in the ribs. Adam's
face, Elizabeth noticed, tightened slightly, though
his voice was still calm. She had heard that the
girl he was to marry, the daughter of an Army
officer, had died in India before the wedding
could take place.

'Hot and barren, what I saw of it. And folk are
folk wherever you are, even if they do speak differently.'

Rab pushed his chair back and got up, moving
awkwardly to get past the table. A big-boned man,
he had put on weight in middle age. His bad leg,
the souvenir of his hot-headed younger days,
when he was quick to support political activities,
made him awkward in confined spaces.

'You'll be coming to the warehouse, Adam.'

'I've things to see to first, but I'll be down when
I can.'

Rab's ruddy face took on a deeper hue at the
casual words, and he turned on the other two.

'I'd appreciate it if you'd break your fast as soon
as you can. There's plenty of work waiting for you.
A shipment of silk yarn's coming in, and the
weavers are waiting for it!'

'Father—' Matthew half rose. 'Will you see John Gibson today?'

'How often do I have to tell you I've no time to listen to Gibson's fancy plans?'

Matthew reddened. 'But I've seen the new yarn. It's good. All he needs is a manufacturer who's willing to commission enough for one shawl!'

'Aye – a fool that'll throw his money away on a daft ploy, when there's trouble enough making ends meet. And we know good and well why you're favouring the likes of John Gibson,' his father sneered. 'I'll be no party to it – and let that be an end to your arguing. I dinnae pay you to encourage the likes of John Gibson!'

Elizabeth winced as she went ahead of Rab to the hall, where she waited with his coat, his tall hat, and his silver-knobbed stick. This time, she hoped, Matt would realise that there was no sense in calling his father's anger down on his head by persisting. John, Isobel's brother, was partner in a small thread and silk factory, and Matthew wanted his father to commission work using a new thread that John had spun.

Rab's mouth was still tight with anger as he came into the hall, checked that his spectacles were safely in his pocket, took his coat, hat and stick from her, and went off with a brief nod.

'And James has drawn a fine design – we could manufacture a shawl that would be the envy of the town,' Matt was telling Adam when she went back to the warm kitchen. 'But he'll try nothing new. The order books are busy, and that's all he cares about. Now John'll have to find another manufacturer and we'll lose the chance of getting that new yarn.'

'And the chance of pleasing Isobel and her father,' James put in slyly and Matt's fair skin, a torment to him, flushed rosily.

'James, it's time we were off. There's more work waiting than I can manage as it is, and the London shipment due in—'

Adam tipped his chair back, thumbs hooked into his waistcoat. 'You sound like father. Have you turned into a money-minded creature as well?'

The flush deepened. 'I have not! Damn it, I'm a silk weaver, and no notion to be anything else. But thanks to you and your physicking I'm the one that's going to have to take over the business one of these days. I'm the one who's had to give up his trade and spend his time sitting in a draughty office working with numbers!'

'James has to work there too,' Elizabeth pointed out and Matt gave his younger brother a withering glance. 'Ach, he's happy enough designing his patterns and scribbling poetry when he thinks nobody notices. It's me that was born to work with my hands, no' my head!'

Adam, unruffled by the outburst, unfolded his long body from the chair and followed the other three into the hall. 'Then it's time you told father that you want to get back to your trade, surely?'

'Man, the hot sun and all that salt water to look at must have addled your brain,' Matthew said flatly. 'When did you ever know my father listen to reason? And he's got worse in the past twelve-month. James, will you put your hat on and come with me?'

James stopped at the open door, his eyes fixed hopefully on his half-brother. 'Did you read those poems I sent you?'

'I did, but I could make nothing of them,' Adam said bluntly, and the younger man's face fell. 'James, we all see things differently. For Matt here, beauty's in his Isobel's smile—' Matt's face, now bobbing outside the door in the lightening September morning, flamed again. '—for Elizabeth it might lie in a copper of hot water, ready for the washing—' Adam's eyes glinted blue fire at Elizabeth. '—for you it's words, for me it's the sight of a clean, healthy stump I've operated on.

But I left the poems in London with a man I know. He's sending them to a publisher of his acquaintance,' he finished, and the disappointment in James's dark eyes flowered into delight.

'Come on, James!' Matt crowed impatiently, reappearing behind his brother.

'Come with me to the theatre tonight, Adam—' James asked.

'I will, if I havenae caught my death from standing at this open door.' Adam slammed it shut in his brother's face. 'God's sakes, Matt's going to be as dour and difficult as my father in another ten years' time if this Isobel of his doesnae save him.'

Elizabeth couldn't stand by and let Matt be criticised without taking his part. 'Someone's got to run the warehouse – mebbe he's dour because he's no' happy!'

Adam looked fully at her for the first time in an hour. 'You sound more like a sister than a servant lassie.'

Colour rushed to her face and she scurried to the kitchen, teeth sinking deep into her lower lip. She had defended Matt against his arrogant brother, but as he had just reminded her, they were in his father's house, and she could not defend herself.

If he knew that he had hurt her he gave no indication of it, following her into the kitchen instead of going to the parlour, or his own room.

'How did you come to work here?'

Busying herself as a pointed reminder that she had better things to do than talk – and also taking the opportunity to keep her face hidden from his gaze – she explained briefly that Rachel Montgomery had found her in the Town's Hospital, had seen to it that she was educated at Hutcheson's Charity School, and had brought her to High Street to become her companion.

'It can't have been long ago. And instead of being a lady's companion you found yourself acting as nurse in her last months.' She could feel his eyes on her, but refused to meet them. 'I mind now that she mentioned you in her letters. What are you doing working in the kitchen when you were meant to sit in the parlour and talk about ribbons and scandal?'

The man was a fool! Without realising what she was doing she looked up, straight into those penetrating blue eyes.

'Your father didnae have much need of a lady's companion,' she said tartly, 'but he did require someone to see to the running of the house.'

He laughed, but persisted, 'Are you content with – this?' One hand indicated the range, the sink, the dishes she was taking from the table.

'Content enough.' It was all right for the likes of him, she thought resentfully as she swept crumbs from the board. It would never enter his head that if his father had put her out of the house after his wife's death she would have had nowhere to go, nobody to turn to. She was grateful for the rough kindness that had allowed her, young as she was, to take over the running of the big house. Nobody knew how often she longed for Mistress Montgomery, with her humour and her wisdom and her ability to soften her husband's hard ways.

'I'd have thought—' He stopped, then went on briskly, 'Is there plenty food in the house?'

'A lot left over from last night.'

'Put some into a basket – a big basket – and put your bonnet on. I've work for you elsewhere.'

'But my work's here!'

'The lassie can see to that, can't she?' he asked impatiently, on his way out of the room.

'Jean? She cannae lift a hand without me telling her how to go about it. There's the washing and the rooms to be seen to, and the parlour fire to be set in case you want to sit in the room—'

'I've more to do with my day than sit in a parlour, woman! It's time the girl learned how to manage. Where is she?'

'In the wash-house. But I cannae—'

He caught her hand, dragged her, protesting, behind him as he strode out of the back door and into the wash-house. Jean, wreathed in steam from the hot water, blinked uncertainly as the two of them burst into the small room, and the clothes she had been sorting fell from her fingers.

'Jean, you're to listen well to what you're told, for you're to see to things on your own this morning,' Adam said firmly. 'Elizabeth, it'll take no more than half an hour to instruct her and get yourself ready.' He consulted the watch on its chain across his flat stomach. 'I'll expect to see you in the hall in thirty minutes' time. And make sure there's nothing but good nourishing food in that basket.'

Jean squawked as the door closed behind him. Elizabeth began to marshal her thoughts and decide what Jean must manage on her own and what could be left until later. She had no liking for Adam Montgomery's ways. They might be all very well on board a ship, but they were not going to do in Paisley.

There was something about him, though, that made it impossible for her to defy him. Exactly thirty minutes after he had left her in the wash-house she was in the hall, wearing her cloak and bonnet and carrying a basket filled with Rab

Montgomery's food. Adam, dressed for the street and carrying a shabby leather bag, came downstairs as she arrived, and cast a critical eye over the basket's contents before nodding.

'It'll do. Come on.'

He forged a way ahead on the busy footpath, putting a hand beneath her elbow now and then when the crowd was thick. The previous night's rain had stopped but the weather was still unseasonable, with the sky heavy and the air damp.

As they hurried west towards the fringe of the town the crowds thinned and the going was easier. Down Maxwellton Street Adam strode, Elizabeth hurrying after him, the basket bumping against her hip. They were going to Maxwellton village, she realised. It consisted of a huddle of weavers' houses, formerly built for men employed by manufacturer Humphrey Fulton. Until fairly recently the hamlet had been separated from Paisley by grassy land, but now the two were linked and Maxwellton was being drawn into the town's claws. Many of the inhabitants of the cottages now worked at the thread manufactory built at nearby Ferguslie by the Coats family.

Moisture dripped from a row of low thatched cottages and the aroma of wet, rotting straw tickled Elizabeth's nose. She divided her attention between Adam's broad back and the narrow path she walked on. A step too close to the houses meant drips landing on her from the thatch; a step too far away from the walls risked the greasy puddles edging the road.

When Adam stopped and thumped at the door of one of the houses she almost bumped into him. The door opened a crack and he swept it wide with one hand, taking off his hat with the other, not so much from good manners as from a need to bend his head as he went into the house. Elizabeth, clutching her basket and quite bewildered, bobbed in after him.

The smell of rotting straw was in the cottage, mingled with the stink of people living in close, insanitary conditions. She recognised it from her dimly remembered babyhood and tried not to wrinkle her nose against it. Not that it mattered if she grimaced. There was little light allowed into the room through the dirty, patched little window, and the people already in the house were watching Adam, not her.

'Have you no candle?' he wanted to know, taking his coat off and tossing it over a rickety chair. There was a scuffling in the shadows then a small wavering flame helped to brighten the place as the stump of a candle was set on the table.

'Right, man, let's see how the leg is—' Adam seated himself on the edge of a wall-bed and Elizabeth saw that there was a man lying there, propped against a sagging, split pillow. His face was grey, his eyes suspicious as he watched the visitor. Adam pulled the blanket aside, unwrapped the man's leg, and moved his fingers over it gently. The sick man flinched.

'As I said last night, you're fortunate the bone wasnae broken.'

'Aye, but look at the size and colour of it.' The man's voice was a thin whine. 'And me no' able to put a foot on the floor.'

'You're able enough,' Adam said dryly. 'It's whether you're willing enough that matters. It'll take a while to mend properly, but you'll no' be crippled, be grateful for that.'

The only furnishing in the room was a table, two chairs, and a truckle bed. The fire was unlit and the earthen floor thinly scattered with straw. A woman near the bed watched patient and physician anxiously. Her clothes were patched and her apron, the good housewife's emblem, was dirty and torn. There was a baby in her arms and two small children held tightly to her skirt.

'What about my loom?' the weaver was asking.

'You'll no' get back to it for a day or two. The

next time you take a fondness for ale you'll mebbe watch what you're about on your way home. Though I'm thinking the silver would be better spent on caring for those bairns of yours,' Adam told him. His accent, Elizabeth noticed, had lost its slight English flavour. He spoke to the weaver in the broad Paisley tongue.

'A day or two? How are my family to live in the meantime?'

There was faint disgust in Adam's voice now. 'You're a wee bit late in thinking about their comfort, are you no'?'

He got to his feet and reached for his coat, while the sick man raised himself on one elbow.

'D'ye expect them to live on air while I'm away from my loom? Or on the charity of neighbours? We're none of us rich folk in Maxwellton, mister. Nobody's got food to spare for another man's weans. Would you stand by and watch—'

'Elizabeth—' Adam cut across the lament, his voice like the crack of a whip. She had moved obediently forward before she could stop herself. 'The lassie here's brought some food to help you out, and there could be more if you do as I tell you instead of lying there pitying yourself.'

He swung the basket to the table for her then turned away and left her to unpack it. The woman, her fear forgotten in wonder, edged forward, eyes gleaming in the candle's light. They widened as she looked at the bread and meat and cheese being lifted from the basket. A long-nailed dirty hand reached out to touch a quartern loaf.

'Oh – God bless you, mistress!' she whispered, and to Elizabeth's embarrassment her hand was caught and carried to the woman's lips.

'Stop havering!' Adam barked. 'See to your bairns and make sure your man gets onto his feet before that leg goes stiff.'

The door opened, bringing a welcome waft of cold damp air and a glimpse of daylight to the stuffy room. A child backed in, dragging a bundle with it. It turned out to be a girl, in clothes that had obviously once belonged to an adult. They bunched around her, trailing on the ground. Her wrists and ankles poked out like dry sticks and her head was a tangled mess of hair, probably alive with vermin. She let the bundle go and turned, blinking in the light, seeing but not understanding the food on the table. Her face was gaunt but her eyes were enormous, reflecting and throwing back the light, as brilliant as diamonds.

Adam, putting on his jacket, stopped.

'What's amiss with this wee one?'

'Nothing,' the weaver's wife said swiftly, too swiftly. 'She's fine!'

Adam lifted the candle and moved round the table to the child, holding the light so that it illuminated her. When his fingers touched her shoulder she jumped, seeming to waken from a trance, and cowered away, one arm thrown over her face.

'I'm not going to harm you, lassie.' It was a voice Elizabeth had not heard from him before, gentle and reassuring. 'See, come over here for a minute and let me look at you.'

Reluctantly, eyeing her mother's expressionless face, the child allowed him to lead her to where light filtered through the window. He pulled a chair towards himself and sat down, drawing the girl forward to stand between his knees, talking gently to her all the time. Suddenly the flint and iron were gone, and Elizabeth watched, astonished, as the child began to relax under that voice, and his touch. Even the blue gaze, so penetrating, so quick to sharpen in anger or exasperation, bathed the dirty little girl in its warmth.

Elizabeth had never known anyone as different as Adam Montgomery. His step-mother and her sons had spoken highly of him, and she knew a little from them, but nothing that had led her to expect this strange, outlandish man. Adam, born to Rab's first wife, had been apprenticed to a Paisley apothecary, had then studied at a Glasgow medical school, and had opted to finish his medical training in the best way, as a surgeon with the navy.

He had recently left the service, and his visit to Paisley had originally been planned to introduce his new wife, the girl who had died in India.

'There's nothing wrong with her!' The weaver's shrill voice broke into Elizabeth's thoughts as she watched Adam. 'Look at the lassie – she's got better colour than the rest of us!'

'She has that,' Adam agreed under his breath, smiling at the nervous child as his eyes noted the red patches high on her cheeks. 'D'ye keep well enough, lassie?'

'Whiles she has a cough – but nothing to fret over,' the mother said anxiously. It was clear to Elizabeth that the man and his wife wanted Adam out of the place.

'And how old are you, my wee bird?'

The child whimpered deep in her throat and it was left to her mother to supply the information that she was seven years old.

'What sort of work does she do?' Adam persisted. His voice was still soft, but now Elizabeth recognised steel beneath the velvet tones.

'She helps to pay her way. That's only right, is it no'?' The weaver was getting angry, twisting round in the bed to glare at this interfering stranger. 'The lassie runs errands and helps with the cleaning in some of the big houses. And she helps her mother with washing for the big houses too. And some mending.' He nodded to the bundle she had dragged in. 'If we sent her to work in one of the manufactories the way some do, she'd work harder than that – and have the walk there and back too.'

'What food does she get? And what caused these?' Adam turned the child round to face her parents, holding the candle so that it lit her. Elizabeth could make out dark stains beneath the general dirt on her face and neck.

'You've done what you came here to do, mister – now get back to your fine friends and leave us be!' the child's father flared, his voice cracking in its pathetic attempt to bluster and bully. The child shivered violently and would have run to hide in her mother's skirts like the others if Adam hadn't kept a restraining hand on her shoulder. He got to his feet, his head almost brushing the smoky ceiling.

'The bairn's overworked, and it's my suspicion that she's had some ill-treatment as well. No doubt

I could find bruising on the others if I looked for it.'

The woman shrank back, her grip on the baby tightening, her free hand pressing the other two children against her legs. Her husband raised himself up in the bed. 'It's no concern of yours!'

Instinctively Elizabeth moved to stand by Adam, putting a hand on the little girl's arm. She could feel a frantic pulse banging beneath the hot dry skin. And she could sense the effort that the man beside her was making to guard his tongue. The weaver was right; there was little Adam could do, and the man's anger would probably be taken out on the children later.

When Adam spoke again, it was in a level, reasonable voice. 'Listen to me. Your daughter's sick and she has to rest for a while. She needs good food to build up her strength.'

The weaver sneered at him openly. 'And where do the likes of us get good food from? How can we live at all while I'm unfit to work and she does nothing to earn her keep?'

'I told you I'd see to it that your bairns would have food till you were back at your loom—'

'If there's any work to be had,' the man interrupted sullenly. 'There's plenty waiting to be taken on in my place.'

A muscle jumped in Adam's jaw. 'Then you'll

need to make sure that you're back at work as soon as you can instead of lying here making yourself out to be an invalid. You can begin by getting out of that bed and putting the lassie into it. And she's to stay there until I tell her to get up, d'you understand me?'

He slipped a hand in his pocket, leaned forward, and flipped a coin onto the table. The dull ring of it on the scored wood brought an immediate change in the weaver's attitude. He scrambled from the bed, dragging his bandaged leg behind him, and the bewildered child found herself taking his place. She lay with eyes wide and body rigid with fear, obeying her elders without understanding what was happening.

'I'll be back often to see her,' Adam warned as he and Elizabeth left. The woman hurried out of the cottage after them and clutched at his sleeve.

'We've no money to pay for a physician,' she said anxiously.

'For God's sake, woman, d'you think we all worship silver—?' He stopped as she flinched under the barrage of angry words, then went on gently, putting a hand over the fingers on his arm, 'There'll be no payment needed, however many times I visit the bairn. If there's an account, she's already paid it in full herself. Now – go back inside and see to her.'

'I've no doubt the lassie'll be dragged from her bed in the morning and put to work,' he added bitterly as he and Elizabeth walked towards Broomlands Street. 'I'd have dearly liked to lift her and carry her away from that place to where she could be looked after.'

'What's wrong with her?' This time Elizabeth didn't have to run to keep up with him. He walked slowly, eyes on the muddy ground.

'Consumption. A destruction of the lungs. I thought it would do you no harm,' he added with a return to his former arrogance, 'to see for yourself how these folk have to live. A far cry from my father's fine house in the High Street, is it no'?'

Anger sharpened her voice as she retorted 'You've no need to complete my education – I was born in a cottage like that, and raised in the Town Hospital as a pauper.'

He spun round, dark eyebrows climbing. She had never noticed people's eyebrows before but Adam's were thick, well-shaped, and strangely attractive. 'You?'

He waited for more information, and she regretted having spoken. But it was too late.

'We moved to the hospital when I was small,

after my father lost his work as a farmhand and we had to leave the cottage.'

'Where do your family stay now?' They had reached Broomlands Street.

'I'm the only one left. There was smallpox in the hospital one year and they – they—' It was still difficult to talk about it.

'They died of it,' Adam said crisply. 'And you lived – although it left its mark on you.' His fingers, surprisingly warm against her cold face, lifted her chin. His eyes studied the scar from her mouth to her jawline and she felt herself redden under that gaze.

'How old are you, lassie?'

'Seventeen.' She tried to pull away but those firm fingers forced her to stay where she was, face raised to his.

His brows tucked together thoughtfully. 'You've nothing to be ashamed of in a wee scar like that. You're bonny enough with that pretty brown hair and those wide brown eyes of yours.' A faintly teasing note crept into his voice as she closed her eyes against his look. 'Long dark lashes, too. Many a lovely lady would like to steal those lashes from you. And many a young gentleman would try to steal a kiss if you fluttered your lashes at him like that.'

She opened her eyes at once, started to indignantly deny any such ploy, and was unable to speak because he refused to release her chin. He grinned at her embarrassment.

'There's gold flecks to those eyes—'

She tore herself free with undignified haste and turned to hurry on, the basket bumping against her hip.

'We all carry scars,' Adam caught up with her. 'Whether they're on the skin or below it, they're there. Paisley's scar is that family we've just left and others like them. D'you know what I mean?'

When she shook her head he sighed and walked on, lengthening his strides so that she was forced to run to keep up. She was shocked to hear that he was misquoting the Bible when she reached his side. Furtively she looked around, worried in case he was overheard.

'Lord, forgive them,' Adam was declaiming as he passed through the crowd as though it was made of mist. 'For they know fine what they're about.'

III

A carriage passed, throwing muddy water from its wheels. A voice screeched from within and the coachman drew the horses to a standstill. A bonneted head emerged from the small window and the screech was heard again.

'Adam! Adam Montgomery! And Elizabeth,' Christian Selbie added with some surprise. 'I've just been to the house to look for you, Adam.'

He kissed the gloved hand she held out to him. 'Well, cousin, I'd have known that voice if I'd heard it in an Indian bazaar,' he drawled.

'So you found your way home after all. Not that I ever doubted you would.' The door swung open. 'Come and take tea with me – both of you.'

Elizabeth began to shake her head, thinking of the housework and Jean's lack of efficiency. Without looking at her Adam said, 'We'd be pleased to—' and bundled her into the carriage, while Christian moved along the well-padded seat to make room.

Adam, opposite them, had to take his tall hat off in the confined space and rest it on his knee. Christian immediately demanded to know what had happened on the previous night, and Elizabeth left it to Adam to talk to his cousin while she herself gave her attention to the window. She had not been whirled through the town in a carriage since Rachel Montgomery's illness had confined her to the house, and this short journey was something to enjoy and treasure. The horses turned to take the steep climb up Hut Brae to Oakshawhill and she clutched nervously at the strap, certain that the harness would break, catapulting the carriage backwards down the narrow hill.

But the leather held, the horses managed the climb without difficulty, and they disembarked before the large, square house where Christian Selbie lived.

Adam eyed the building fondly. 'You're still rattling round in a house that's far too big for your needs, I see.'

'Only because I'm too busy to find somewhere more suitable – and I'm no' one to rattle, I'll have you know,' she told him severely. 'Though the window tax alone fair destroys me. The Council seems to think I've nothing to do but pour good silver into their purses.'

'It must be a sorry plight, having so much wealth to fret over,' her kinsman agreed solemnly, eyes twinkling. It was already clear to Elizabeth, following Christian into the entrance hall, that Adam and his cousin shared a deep affection, well smothered in sarcasm.

In the handsome drawing-room Adam declined tea from the fine silver tea-service, and chose to pour himself a generous helping of brandy from a crystal decanter.

'At this time of day?' Christian clucked. He took his place before the fire, glass in hand.

'And why not?'

'You've learned some strange habits abroad. But all the same—' her faded blue eyes travelled over him with open approval '—you've grown into a fine figure of a man.'

He returned the scrutiny. 'And you're as you've always been – a fine figure of a woman.'

She smoothed her skirt, tidied a strand of hair back beneath her lace cap. 'I've worn well,' she agreed smugly. 'Go on with your story about the man that was hurt by the coach – but keep the nasty bits out of it, for I cannae be doing with talk of blood when I'm at my tea.'

Adam gave her a graphic description of the cottage, the poverty, the sick child, turning to Elizabeth now and then for confirmation.

'It seems to me, cousin,' he finished, 'that you could take on the task of helping the family, for Elizabeth here's doubtless got enough to do looking after my father's house and trying to get some work out of that lassie in the kitchen.'

'So you think time hangs heavy on my own hands, do you?' Christian snorted. 'You've been away too long, my lad. I could show you a dozen families living in the same misery, not a stone's throw from here. We cannae molly-coddle each and every one of them. Have some sense!'

His hand tightened on the glass he held and his brows knotted together. 'You could do more for them – you and my father and all the other well-to-do folk in this town.'

'We're no' exactly unaware of the need for improvements,' Christian told him stiffly. 'But it's the way of the world, Adam. There's aye been folk that find it harder to make their way through life than others. Mebbe some of the fault's their own. Mebbe they just don't strive in the way our family did.'

'Don't try to confuse me with words,' he told her bluntly. 'I'm talking about the one lassie. Seven years in this world, just – that's twenty-three years less than me, and she's dying of old age. She's been starved and beaten and worked till the heart's gone out of her. She'll no' live to see eighteen thirty-two – though some might say that that's no loss to her. All I'm asking you to do is to see that the last few weeks of her life are made a bit easier than the first seven years!'

Christian looked thoughtfully at him. 'I could see about getting her into the House of Recovery.'

His laugh was harsh. 'And have her die of fear and loneliness within two days? Mebbe her family's no' much, but it's all she's had. Poor wee soul, she should at least end her days with those she knows.'

Elizabeth's cup rattled slightly as she set it in its saucer. 'Adam, I'll keep an eye on the bairn for you—' she began, but Christian interrupted her.

'Tuts, lassie – you've enough to do. I'll see to the child and her family. And that's the thing decided. And you needae smirk like that, Adam, I'm no' saying you've won, I'd have done it anyway.'

The smile on his handsome face widened. 'I know that. I was counting on it.'

'In return I'll expect you to attend a wee gathering I'm planning.'

He paused in the act of putting his empty glass on the table. 'Ach, I was never good at those social fripperies, Christian.'

'James and Matthew and Elizabeth'll be there,' she went on, ignoring him. 'And Isobel, of course. And Helen – you have mind of Helen, surely? Rab never forgave you for going off to sea instead of marrying her.'

Exasperation clouded his eyes. 'We were never more than friends, me and Helen, and my father knew it.'

Christian shook a forefinger at him. 'I have a feeling Helen herself would have been willing to marry you at one time. But now she's Mistress Alec Grant and living in his parents' big house in Barrhead. As bright and bonny as ever, for all that she's got a wee girl of her own. You should meet Helen again, now that you've come back to Paisley.'

'I'm only here for a visit. For a few weeks, mebbe.'

Her brows rose. 'They must have paid you well in the Navy if you can afford to live like a gentleman of leisure for all that time. Surely you don't expect Rab to support you while you're here? He'll put his hand in his pocket for nobody.'

'I know that. I have the money I earned those

past years. There's little use for money on board one of His Majesty's ships, unless it's spent on gambling or drinking, and I never cared for either of them as a pastime. I can pay my way for a wee while, then I have it in mind to settle in England.'

'There's a good living to be made by a surgeon in Glasgow. My own father did well enough for himself in this district.' Christian looked complacently about the fine drawing-room. The house she lived in had once belonged to her parents, Margaret Montgomery and Gavin Knox.

'Your father pandered to the society folk. My work's with those who might have most need of me. I've no interest in money.'

Christian shrugged off the insult to her father. 'So Paisley's no' good enough for you?'

'I've no quarrel with it. I just don't care to live in the place. That's why I wouldnae take up the loom as a trade.'

She barked a laugh at him. 'Man, it was the loom that refused you, no' the other way round. Highlanders are all thumbs, and you inherited your hands from your Highland mother, God rest her soul.'

The smile caught again at his wide mouth as he held out his broad, capable hands. 'So I turned to surgery because I was too handless to be a weaver?'

'Weaving,' Christian told him crushingly, 'is an art, and don't you forget it, Adam Montgomery!'

The delicate clock on the mantelshelf tinkled out a peal of bells indicating the time, and Elizabeth jumped, her mind flying at once to the work that waited for her at the High Street house. Christian's sharp eyes caught the movement.

'But no doubt I'm keeping you both from your business,' she said, making it possible for Elizabeth to get to her feet.

They were at the front door when Christian put a hand on Adam's arm. 'Adam, I was right vexed to hear about your Caroline's death.'

His face stilled suddenly. 'My father and my brothers did me the service of not mentioning her,' he said flatly. 'I'd be obliged, cousin, if you'd do the same.'

'Men—' said Christian as the door opened to reveal the coachman waiting to take them back to the High Street, 'have never learned to handle bereavement.'

At dinner that evening Adam asked his father abruptly 'Do you know of a man named Patrick Hamilton?'

Elizabeth, who usually dined with the family,

felt her stomach constrict beneath the blue silk of her gown. Rab, supping his broth, shook his greying head.

'He knows of you, father.'

'There's no' many folk hereabouts havenae heard of me.' It was a simple statement, not a boast. Matthew scraped his bowl clean and pushed it away.

'I know the name. He's a weaver. He's worked for us.'

'I want you to offer him work again,' Adam said bluntly.

'So—' Rab surveyed his eldest son. 'You're giving orders to the warehouse, are you?'

'I'm asking you to give a man work. He has need of it.'

Rab laughed. 'Man, if we offered work to everyone in Paisley who needs it this day, we'd have more webs than we could sell.' He turned his attention to Matthew. 'What d'you know of him?'

Matthew looked embarrassed. 'He's a slow worker and we found him to be unreliable.'

'You see? There's plenty of good skilled men ready and grateful for work without entrusting it to the likes of that. I've neither the time nor the money to spend on a man who'll no' do his fair share. Find some other manufacturer to look after your lame dogs for you,' Rab told Adam, and went back to his food with an air of dismissal.

Elizabeth saw Adam's jaw stiffen. 'Why should I go cap in hand to another manufacturer when my own father's one of their number? Mebbe the man's no' one of the best workers, but he's got a family to care for and a dying child that's been forced to earn her own keep from the time she could toddle.'

'Be damned to that, sir,' Rab's irritation was growing rapidly. 'You seriously expect me to squander hard-earned money on a useless worker just to please you?' One thick thumb stabbed at his own chest. 'Look at me – I served my time at the looms and so did my father before me. I'd be a weaver yet if I hadnae been crippled while I was marching in the name of better conditions for working men. I could have given up then and let you and your brothers live in poverty in some hovel—'

'I know well enough how hard you've worked!' Adam interrupted. Everyone knew of the struggle Rab had had to rebuild his life after his leg was shattered. He had clawed his way into the manufacturing industry, and had finally raised enough capital to start his own business.

'Then let Hamilton stand on his own feet and support his own bairns, as I did!'

The soup bowls were empty. Elizabeth gathered them together and helped Jean to serve the meat course. Then she despatched the girl back to the kitchen and sat down again, nervously picking at the food before her. Rab had started on a well-worn lecture about independence and laziness. The words rolled about Elizabeth's down-bent head. It was foolish to challenge him when he was in a mood like this, but Adam had either forgotten that, or didn't care about tact.

'You're forgetting something,' he cut into his father's lecture at last. 'When your father and your grandfather were making a good living as weavers a man could hold his head high and shape his own life. But it's different now that the manufacturers have a grip of the weaver by the back of the neck. They're the ones that make the money now. How much can a weaver expect to earn today?'

Rab spluttered, and glared over cheeks bursting with blood when Matthew supplied the information.

'If he's in steady work he can make about six shillings a week. A year ago it might have been seven or eight shillings in the week.'

'You see, father? The weaver's dependent on the manufacturer to advance the cost of setting up his loom now. And he's got rent to pay, and the use of

64

the loom if it's in someone else's shop. Is the fine lady paying less for her shawls? Oh, no – it's just that the manufacturers – you and the others – are never out of pocket. It's always the weaver who has to take the loss and worry about how he's going to make ends meet until he gets his money from the manufacturer. And there's no assurance of that, either. There's lazy manufacturers, and there's truck trading—'

Rab's fist crashed onto the table and dishes clattered. A potato rolled from James's plate but nobody except Elizabeth noticed it.

'There is no truck trading done by my warehouse!' Rab said thickly, his eyes almost bursting from his head. 'And no son of mine is going to accuse me of it, by God, or I'll—'

'Nobody,' Adam told him coldly, 'said such a thing, and you know it. I just asked you to find it in your heart to give work to a poor man with sore need of it!'

'Now here's a bonny man for you!' Rab sneered, and Adam's lids drooped to half-cover eyes that had darkened with anger, Elizabeth noted. 'He thinks himself too grand for the likes of Paisley, and yet he's more than ready to make use of the folk that helped to give this town its proud name. The day I tell you how to do your bleeding and your cutting, mister, you can tell me who should bring their webs to my warehouse!'

His anger, almost out of control, was a frightening sight. Matthew started to speak, but Adam put a restraining hand on his brother's arm.

'Finish your food, Matt.' He had been holding his knife in a white-knuckled grip; he put the utensil down carefully beside his untouched plate and stood up.

'I have your answer, father, and it seems that the matter's closed. James – I'll meet you at the Saracen's Head later. Elizabeth—'

He nodded briefly in her direction and turned towards the door.

'Sit down, man, and finish your meal!' Rab barked, rising.

'I have no appetite for it. And I'm no company for the rest of you tonight,' said Adam, and walked out, straight-backed.

In the silence that followed Rab Montgomery reseated himself and glared belligerently round the table. Matthew's lips parted, and his father's hand immediately swept up to stop the words.

'There'll be no more talk at this table!' he said harshly, adding after a moment, 'It seems that travel's done little for your brother's manners!'

Elizabeth would have been happy to escape to

the kitchen as soon as the meal was over, but for some reason of his own Rab insisted that she should keep him company. James went off to meet Adam and go with him to the theatre, Matthew disappeared, no doubt on his way to Isobel's house. Elizabeth fetched her sewing and spent the next few hours working, while Rab stared morosely into the fire.

When his sons had returned home for the night, Rab signalled to Elizabeth to bring out the big family Bible, which was read every evening. Tonight he chose to read from Paul's epistle to the Colossians exhorting them to obey their parents in all matters. As Elizabeth listened to his deep, rich voice rolling the phrases around the room she thought, as she had thought before, that surely Paul himself must have lost some of the beauty of his own words, being unable to deliver them in Rab's good Scots tongue.

When the Bible was closed, Rab wished everyone goodnight, in the same doom-filled tones used during the reading and limped upstairs. Jean, who had started one of her interminable colds, sniffed her way to bed, and the three brothers, freed from their father's presence, noticeably relaxed.

'My God!' James threw himself into Rab's special armchair, eyes dancing. 'Did ye hear the way his voice rose over that passage about paying heed to parents?'

'And the way it dropped right down when he reached the bit about how fathers shouldnae provoke children?' Matthew grinned. Adam shrugged and poked at the coals in the grate, sending a final burst of flame leaping up the chimney.

'It was in my mind to quote the Good Book right back at him,' he said dryly. 'Thon bit about supporting the weak, and it being more blessed to give than to receive. But since I near brought him to apoplexy already today, I thought it better to hold my tongue. Matthew – surely you can find some way to give Hamilton work?'

'Nobody tells father what business the warehouse gives out. He knows each and every one of the folk we use, and nobody else has the power to give out work.'

'You could talk to him about it.'

Matthew flushed. 'Adam, it's no' that easy! I'm trying to find the right time as it is to tell him that I want to wed Isobel.'

'For any favour, man!' Adam exploded at his younger brother, 'Are you so afraid of the man that you cannae even choose your own wife? What's amiss with the lass? Her father's been a respected weaver all his adult life, and her own brother supplies silk for the Montgomery house, does he no'?'

James sighed with exaggerated impatience. 'You never learn, Adam. It's no' a question of man marrying woman with the Montgomerys now. Matt's going to take over the warehouse one day. He's expected to find a wife among his own sort. A warehouse marries another warehouse – a London agent's daughter would be even better.'

'You're no' serious!' Adam stood tall before the fireplace and Elizabeth, finishing off the hem she was stitching, realised how unlike his home-based brothers he was. Adam had gone out into the world and his values were completely different from theirs. He found it hard to understand how they could meekly accept their father's rules; unlike him, they were conditioned, and so was she, to a life that was now alien and out-dated in his eyes.

'I mind the days when my father was a weaver himself, like old Gibson. And he'd no' have allowed any man to consider him inferior,' he said.

'That was before the riots and before he lost his trade trying to get better conditions for his fellow-workers,' Matthew pointed out. 'It wasnae just his leg that mended wrong, it was his faith in folk. He's crippled inside as well as outside.'

'That sounds like some of James's romantic thinking,' Adam sneered at him, and Matt's round face flushed. To her surprise, Elizabeth found herself saying hotly, 'It's no' romantic nonsense! Unhappiness can twist folk up inside.'

She blushed as they all looked at her, James and Matthew with warmth, Adam with amusement.

'Elizabeth's right,' Matthew defended her. 'I know that if I lose Isobel it'll break something inside me. And as for you, Adam—'

Adam's face was suddenly expressionless, as though smoothed over by an invisible hand. 'I've no' forgotten the bitterness the old man must have felt,' he said swiftly, his voice harsh. 'But I see no reason why he should let it warp him for the rest of his life.'

'He's fair enough with the workers,' James spoke up in his father's defence. 'He doesnae try to break the table of wages like some. And he'd never go in for truck trading. There was one manufacturer in court for it no' that long ago. A man by the name of Dunn. He was charged with paying a weaver a shilling only, and the rest of the payment in potatoes. The case was found to be not proven.'

'Justice is the same as anything else,' Matthew added bluntly. 'You get it if you can afford to pay for it.'

Adam surveyed his brothers. 'And you accept that?'

'We cannae alter it.'

'You can have a damned good try,' Adam said forcefully.

'And have our legs broken and our hearts twisted?' Matthew asked in a rare burst of cynicism. He yawned, stretched. 'I'm away to my bed. It's too late to start trying to change the world.'

Elizabeth made sure that the doors were locked and the kitchen range banked so that it could be poked into life in the morning. When she went back to the parlour to rake out the fire and put a screen before it she found Adam there, frowning down into the embers. He blinked at her, then rose from his chair.

'Sleep well, Elizabeth.'

'Adam—' She stopped him as he was leaving the room, lamp in hand. 'Adam, what were those lassies you talked of last night – from Japan?' The name of the country, so pretty and so alien, had been echoing in her head all day.

He raised an eyebrow. 'The geishas?'

'That was it. What do they do?'

'I've only heard about them, for I've never had the fortune to visit their country. But it's said that their work consists of singing and dancing and – pleasuring the menfolk.'

She was confused. 'With the singing and dancing, you mean?'

A slow smile curled his wide mouth at the sides. 'That – and all manner of other ways, I've heard.'

'Oh!' She felt her face burn.

'Mind you,' said Adam thoughtfully, 'I never did find out the truth of it for myself – I'm vexed to say.'

As he went into the hall, she caught the faint sound of a chuckle.

It was left to Christian Selbie to find employment for the weaver with the sick child. She called in one afternoon to report to Adam and Elizabeth on her visits to the Maxwellton cottage. She settled in the parlour like an exotic bird, in her beribboned bonnet, bright blue gown, and colourful Paisley shoulder shawl with its deep borders of blues, scarlets, and greens.

'As far as I can tell the man's attending to his work well enough. That poor stick of a wife he's got fairly glows with pleasure about it.'

'What about the bairn?' Adam was drinking tea today, but Elizabeth was sure that it was in order not to hurt her feelings rather than an honest interest in the beverage.

Christian put her bonneted head thoughtfully to one side, emphasising the similarity to a bird. 'She's been in bed each time I've called,' she admitted, 'but since there's aye a right scuffling about the door when they see me coming it's my belief that she's up and working most of the time, and they push her into that bed as I step through the door. Her mother tries to do the right thing by the bairns, but she's just no' what I'd call a good manager.'

'I suppose we're doing all we can,' Adam said absently, frowning at a bunch of flowers on the wallpaper behind his kinswoman's head.

'Well, I'm certainly doing all I can,' she told him. 'And I'm expecting you to keep your side of the bargain. Next Friday evening at my house – and you can escort Elizabeth there, just to make sure you don't forget!'

When the appointed evening arrived, though, Elizabeth went to Oakshawhill with James. Adam had gone off in the morning to visit friends in Renfrew, promising faithfully to be back in time.

'Aye – well, he'd better arrive soon, or he'd better stay in Renfrew out of my reach,' Christian said when Elizabeth reported his absence. 'There'll be trouble for Master Adam if he thinks he's going to stay away from my gathering! Come in, come in, the pair of you, and don't look so guilty, Elizabeth. You're no' responsible for the big useless lump of a man.'

Without doubt the most beautiful woman in Christian's parlour that evening was Helen Grant, Elizabeth decided with admiration rather than envy. Helen alone had dared to spurn the pastel shades that were in vogue and had dressed in a deep red gown cut in the latest fashion, with off-the-shoulder puffed sleeves and a daringly low neckline. The dress emphasised her full bosom and tiny waist. Her large brown eyes sparkled and rich auburn hair blazed round her lovely face. She looked far too young to be the mother of a toddler.

Elizabeth knew that she looked well enough in her home-made pink muslin gown, with her brown hair pinned up and allowed to curl at each side of her face. Her figure was pleasing, she assured herself in a hasty glimpse into the mirror while going through the hall to collect something from the kitchen. Her small breasts, not nearly as fine as Helen's, rose with becoming modesty from the square neck of the gown and her flushed cheeks gave her added beauty. But – her hand went up to the scar on her face, then was pulled down out of sight as her sharp eyes registered the rough red skin and broken nails – she could never match Helen for looks or for charm.

Alec Grant complemented his wife perfectly. Since their marriage he had left the army to work on his father's estates, and had put on weight. His handsome face had rounded and taken on a rosy tinge that spoke of fondness for the bottle rather than fresh air. Some said that he was too fond of the gaming tables, and evenings spent with his cronies, but there was no doubt, seeing them together, that he and Helen were deeply in love with each other. Alec wore a silk jacket of the same shade as his wife's dress, with a yellow waistcoat and white cravat and trousers.

As the evening wore on Elizabeth saw her hostess glance now and then at the clock, her brows tucked together disapprovingly. There was still no sign of Adam.

She was in the kitchen, refilling the punch jug, when knuckles beat at the front door.

'I'll see to it,' she said hurriedly, and the maid settled back in her seat with a sigh of relief.

Elizabeth put the heavy jug down carefully on a small table and, candle in hand, opened the door.

'It's yourself, Elizabeth.' He stepped inside, closed the door quietly, and put a delaying hand on her arm as she was about to lead him to the drawing-room.

'Is there a crowd in there?'

'Aye – and all waiting for you. Your cousin's getting more long-faced by the minute. You promised, Adam!'

He screwed up his nose. 'I know I did, but – ach, I was never one for reunions. All those folk peering at me and asking questions and treating me as though I was in a side-show.'

'They mean it kindly.'

He began to take off his coat. 'It's their very kindness that sticks in my throat.' As he turned to slip the coat off a draught from the sleeve blew out the candle, leaving them in darkness. The coat dropped to the floor with a rustle, and Adam cursed.

'I'm feared to move in case I knock over one of those daft ornaments Christian sets such store by! Elizabeth—'

'Here—' She captured his flailing hand in hers. Her eyes were becoming used to the dark quickly, and she had located the thin line of light beneath the drawing-room door. '—Just come with me, I know where to go.'

Their fingers entwined, then his tightened and drew her back towards him.

'Ach, I'm in two minds about this. It's all a palaver! Could we no' skip out quiet-like, you and me, Elizabeth—' His free hand found her shoulder, drew her closer, a fellow conspirator. She could feel his breath warm on her cheek, feel herself being drawn into the spell of the words murmured into her hair. 'We'll go off back to the High Street and sit by the kitchen fire, and I'll tell you about India, and the sun, and the strange animals, and the fine clothes—'

It sounded so tempting. She had to bite back words of swift acceptance and make herself say sternly 'We'll do nothing of the sort, for your cousin's waiting for you to attend her party!'

'Women were always nags!' he grumbled, then tried wheedling again, 'I thought you were different, Elizabeth.' His lips were brushing her ear now, setting up shivers throughout her body. She felt the breath flutter in her throat like a trapped butterfly, and knew, as his fingers tightened on her shoulder, that he knew very well what was happening to her. 'Lass – come away with me—'

The drawing-room door was thrown wide and Elizabeth swung away from him, suddenly aware that in the light from the door they might be mistaken for an embracing couple. She had forgotten in her confusion that anyone coming from a lighted room would be unable to see the hall clearly. Beside her, Adam swore softly beneath his breath.

A slender, graceful figure hesitated in the lit doorway and one slim arm reached back for a lamp on a nearby table.

'Is that you, Elizabeth?' a clear voice asked, half nervous, half amused. There was a note or two of soft musical laughter. 'Elizabeth! Don't fright me like this!'

Elizabeth's lips parted immediately to call out but her voice was silenced by the tremor that ran through Adam's body, down his arm to the fingers that clasped hers. His grip tightened sharply then loosened, fell away. She heard him catch his breath, sensed the lift of his head towards the doorway, the way his eyes widened.

The woman silhouetted against the light raised the lamp she held so that its glow travelled from her slim waist to her breasts, her white throat and shoulders, and at last to her face, eyes wide, lips parted, skin like the sheen of a flawless pearl. It was Helen Grant.

'Elizabeth?' she said again, and moved a tentative step or two into the darkened hall. Now the lamp she carried dazzled her own eyes, and if Adam hadn't gone forward swiftly, freed from his trance, and caught her arm, she would have blundered into a small carved chair.

'Be careful—' he said, as though her safety was

the most important thing in the world. The lamp illuminated his face and Helen's mouth curved into a sudden delighted smile.

'Adam? Is it really you, after all this time? Oh – welcome home!' With the unselfconscious grace of an old friend she caught his shoulder, raised herself on tiptoe, and kissed him. 'D'you not know me?' she added with that musical laughter bubbling again in her voice.

'Helen?'

'Of course it's Helen – and not nearly as changed as you are. You're so handsome, and so tall – come and meet everyone!'

Laughing, talking, asking questions and too excited to notice that he was too busy looking at her to answer, she linked her arm through his and pulled him into the room, leaving Elizabeth to follow, alone and forgotten.

Adam's reluctance to become part of the gathering melted away. Helen demanded to hear about his life as a naval surgeon and her word was his command. His unexpectedly poetic tongue brought the heat and dust of India and the roar and crash of a sea-storm into the Scottish drawing-room and captivated his listeners. Only Elizabeth was apart from the crowd, only she was too preoccupied with her own thoughts to pay much attention to what he was saying. Nobody, including Adam, noticed her silence.

'Now you're going to stay with us, in Paisley?' Helen asked. He let his eyes linger on her face for a few seconds.

'I've no plans at the moment.'

'Have you had experience of this cholera?' Alec wanted to know. Adam nodded.

'I've seen it.'

'Is it as bad as they say?'

Adam's dark blue eyes were fathomless. 'From what I hear you'll have the chance to find out for yourselves.'

Helen shivered and reached for Alec's hand. 'It's no subject for a time like this,' she said firmly. 'Anyway – the cholera'll never get as far as Paisley.'

Looking at her, Elizabeth almost believed what she said. It was impossible to think that anything as terrible as a cholera epidemic could touch the world Helen Grant lived in.

'I hope you're right,' was all Adam said.

Even his sharp-eyed cousin seemed to be unaware of the sudden passion he felt for Alec Grant's wife. To Elizabeth, who had been with him when he first saw Helen, it was obvious, as though a finely-spun rope of pure gold stretched between

Adam and Helen. When she was at the other end of the room and Adam, his back towards her, was immersed in conversation with someone else, awareness of her presence radiated from him.

And yet, watching Helen closely, Elizabeth realised that even she was not conscious of Adam's new feelings. She was happily married, she was used to male admiration, and to her Adam was merely a childhood friend who had come home after a long absence.

The intensity in his gaze as he once, thinking himself unobserved, allowed his eyes to rest on Helen for a full thirty seconds, struck a chill in Elizabeth. She knew instinctively that he was not a man to love lightly.

She was afraid of the result of his passion, if he couldn't overcome it by himself. And she found herself wishing with a passion of her own that Adam Montgomery had never decided to return home to Paisley.

IV

Isobel Gibson was pale, red-eyed, but determinedly cheerful as she sat at the kitchen table in the High Street house, Elizabeth by her side.

'I can manage fine on my own,' she insisted tremulously for the third time since Matthew had brought her in. 'Whatever happens I don't want to be the cause of trouble between Matt and his father. I'd never want to come between them.'

Matthew, staring out of the window, seeing nothing of the laundry decorating the bushes in the garden, gave a sardonic bark of laughter.

'You flatter yourself, lass. There's little love lost between me and him. The man's changed out of all recognition since my mother died. He's a stubborn, difficult old—'

'He's lonely, Matt!' Isobel automatically came to the defence of the sour old man who disapproved of his son's love for her.

'So there's all the more reason to believe that he'll welcome a grandchild,' Adam, the fourth member of the group, pointed out. 'It's the best thing that can happen – another Montgomery to carry on the family name. I take it that you intend to marry Isobel?' he asked his brother bluntly, and Matt flushed to the roots of his hair.

'Of course I do – what d'ye take me for?' he asked angrily. At the same moment Isobel said swiftly, 'He doesnae need to marry me!'

'Don't be daft!' her sweetheart told her harshly, and she subsided, her fingers twining nervously together. Elizabeth reached out and put her own hand over her friend's and Adam, leaning back against the dresser, looked with a hint of impatience from his half-brother to Isobel.

'Then the matter's settled, surely. What's all this fuss about?'

'It's no' as easy as that!' Elizabeth said angrily. She wished that he would learn to look at a problem from every angle instead of cutting, with the efficient ruthlessness of the surgeon, through every argument as though it didn't exist.

He stared down at her, contempt in his dark blue eyes. 'A man, a woman, a bairn on the way, a wedding. That's not easy?'

'You're forgetting about your father.'

'He'll be grateful enough that Matt's found himself a good wee wife.'

'Aye, but—' Matt stopped short and darted an embarrassed look at Isobel. She wasn't afraid to say what he and Elizabeth were thinking. Her gaze met Adam's with nothing to hide.

'Your father's a manufacturer with a big house. Mine is a weaver with a rented cottage. And I clip shawls for the Montgomery company. It's no' what anyone could call a fine marriage for the likes of Matt.'

Adam's eyes darkened, his mouth took a downward droop. Elizabeth had come to recognise the signs of anger in the few short weeks he had been in the house.

'If Matt's satisfied with his choice, it has nothing to do with my father,' he said curtly. Matt ran both hands through his thick brown hair. He looked utterly miserable, torn between fear of his father and love for Isobel. Elizabeth's heart went out to him and she felt anger of her own at Adam. Surely he should show sympathy towards the younger man instead of refusing to see Matt's difficulties.

'He pays my wages, that's what's bothering me,' Matt blurted out. 'If he sees fit to put me out then how can I support Isobel, let alone the child?'

'Rubbish!' Adam rang the word out, and

Elizabeth was reminded of the way he had tossed a coin onto the table at the Maxwellton weaver's cottage.

'Look at this—' Isobel indicated the kitchen. 'I know nothing of fine houses like this. One day Matt's going to own the warehouse, and I know as well as Mister Montgomery does that I'd make a poor wife for a manufacturer, me living in a cottage all my days.'

Now Adam's anger was there for them all to see. 'Are you going to stand there like a loon and let the lassie lower herself with talk like this?' he barked at his brother.

Matt shot him a glance of loathing and put his arms awkwardly about Isobel. 'Hush, lass, I'm no' shamed to take you for my wife before the whole town, have I no' told you that time and again?'

Adam moved from the dresser and leaned both fists on the table. Since arriving home he had taken to wearing the plain clothes favoured by the local men – linen shirt, patterned waistcoat, brown trousers, and a cravat tied loosely about his throat. Even so he retained that air of confidence and authority that set him apart. Now, as he looked down at his brother's sweetheart, his anger was tempered with warmth.

'Listen to what I have to tell you, Isobel. Our

great-grandfather, Duncan Montgomery, came from Beith with nothing but his trade and his new wife. His son Robert was a weaver, and proud to be one. And his son, the same Rab Montgomery that owns this house, would have been at the loom all his days if he hadnae damaged his leg and had to give up his chosen trade. You and Matt come from the same stock, and whether he goes back to the loom or takes over the warehouse he'll always be proud to call you his wife. Am I right, Matt?'

'Of course he is,' Matt rushed to assure Isobel. 'He's just got a better way of putting it than I have.'

'Oh – Matt!' Isobel got up and held him close. Over her head he gave Adam and Elizabeth a look that was half-embarrassed, half-belligerent.

'It'll be all right. If my father doesnae take to the idea of a marriage I'll leave the warehouse and go back to my own trade, as Adam says.'

The words were brave, but Elizabeth wished that Matthew himself had been the first to reassure Isobel instead of leaving it to his brother.

'If you ask me,' Adam was saying, 'getting out of that warehouse would be the making of you, Matt. A man sickens when he's doing work he hates. All you have to do is face him with the truth of the matter. He'd never be foolish enough to turn

86

you out. It'll never come to that. He'll admit defeat.'

Matt looked pityingly at him. 'You might have learned a lot while you were away from home, Adam, but it seems to me you've forgotten as much again.'

Elizabeth agreed with him, though she had the sense to keep her thoughts to herself. Adam didn't take kindly to opposition from a woman.

She herself shared all of Matt's misgivings, and added to that, she was worried about Adam's passion for Helen Grant.

Helen had been a favourite of Rachel Montgomery's, and after the older woman's death she had continued to visit the High Street house. She and Elizabeth were firm friends, and on several occasions Helen and Alec had shown her special kindness – a small present, an invitation to join them at the theatre, a sharing of confidences. Elizabeth didn't want to see Adam trampling on all that they had in their marriage, and she had a feeling that he wasn't a man to love silently and selflessly for long.

There was the scandal to consider, too. Rab was an important man in Paisley, Matt and James well thought of. If Adam made a bid for another man's wife in his home town, the place would rock with the result. The world, as she knew it, would come to an end.

While she watched and worried Adam and the Grants walked together, dined together, rode together, attended theatre performances and assemblies together. When Adam was preparing for one of those occasions he was cheerful; when he had to spend a full day without sight of Helen he was morose and silent. Rab, concerned with his own business worries, seemed quite unaware of his son's preoccupation, and James worked at his writing, oblivious to the rest of the uneasy household.

And each day the threat of the cholera epidemic moved a little closer. Walls in the town erupted in a rash of notices giving warnings and advice on how to tackle the disease. Meetings were held, arrangements made to dispense disinfectants and medicines if necessary. Under Adam's direction Elizabeth stocked a cupboard with powdered mustard and castor oil, spirit of turpentine, spirit of hartshorn, tincture of capsicum, laudanum and opium, ether and calomel. She put flannel strips aside, ready to be heated and wrapped about affected limbs.

Each time she looked at the cupboard she shivered at the thought that one of the people within those sturdy walls might need such attention. She agreed with Helen when, on a visit with her mother, that young woman announced that thinking of the cholera must surely be worse than experiencing it.

'Only yesterday Alec made me sit down and read through the latest notice so that I might recognise the illness at once – and I experienced every symptom as I read it!'

She screwed her nose up in a grimace of self-mockery. Her hair was like flames against the black bonnet and black-centred shawl she wore and her gown was a rich blue. She looked radiantly healthy.

'Chills and aches and cramps and other things I wouldn't mention! It isn't possible that one illness could do all that. Adam—' her brown eyes swept up at him from under long gold lashes '—tell me that they're trying to fright us!'

But he refused to be drawn. 'They can't print the truth of it. It's the devil's punishment on earth. You must promise me, Helen—' his voice was intense '—that you'll take great care, and avoid those places where the air might be unclean.'

'Really, Adam!' Helen's mother said sharply, her nostrils quivering with outrage. 'Cholera is known to affect only people of low habits and lack of

Christian feeling. I scarcely think that my daughter could be in any danger!'

A spasm of sheer anger flickered across his face and was gone almost at once. 'That's what they say,' he drawled from where he leaned elegantly against the mantelpiece, 'but I have no reason to believe that it's true. Besides, there's some would say that Christianity and piety might not be the—'

'You'll have some more tea, Helen?' Elizabeth said deliberately, knowing what was coming next. Adam had already scandalised his father with his cynical observations about folk who thought that they could buy their way to Heaven, and Helen's parents were staunch supporters and benefactors of the High Church.

'Elizabeth—' he said, with a coolness in his voice, but she pretended she hadn't heard.

'You must bring wee Catherine to see me soon. Is she on her feet yet?'

Catherine's mother and grandmother, eyes shining, immediately launched into the latest stories of the baby's exploits. Adam was quite forgotten.

'My knuckles were fair stinging with the rap your tongue gave them,' he said dryly when the guests had left. 'I've noticed, Elizabeth, that for all your youth you seem to rule the roost where Matt and James are concerned. I have no memory of telling you that you could do the same with me.'

She coloured, but stood her ground. 'I've heard enough of your views on religion to know that they'd not have been well received – and you'd never want to upset Helen.'

'So you think folk should be sheltered from the truth?'

'Why fright them when they can do nothing about it?'

Irritation sharpened his gaze, honed the edge of his voice. 'Of course they can do something about it! They can realise that folk get diseases because they live in filth and despair. They need help instead of contempt. And if folk like Helen's father and her father-in-law can't aid those wretches, God help humanity!'

'You can't change the world, Adam.'

'You sound like my cousin Christian,' he said in disgust. 'I only seek to change Paisley – let the rest of the world take care of itself.'

She stacked cups and plates on a tray. 'You'd have a better chance if you started with the rest of the world, for this town has a fine conceit of itself, and one man'll no' make it any different.'

'I thought you were more of a fighter than that,' he challenged as he opened the parlour door for her.

'I know my place.'

'That you don't,' said Adam. 'Or you'd never be content to stay in my father's kitchen.'

She waited until she had deposited her burden on the kitchen table then faced him.

'There's nothing wrong with being in the kitchen!'

'There is when you're too intelligent to stay there.' His eyes took in her neat figure and face with a dispassionate sweep. There was a great difference, she realised, in the way he looked at Helen and the way he looked at her.

'My brain's my concern!' she rallied.

'Not when it's wasted on puddings and porridge.'

She rattled dishes angrily. 'I'm proud to be able to earn my keep!'

That maddening grin tickled at the corners of his mouth again. 'Meaning that it's time I started earning mine?'

She didn't dare meet his eyes any more. 'I'm surprised you're no' finding life tedious, with nothing at all to do.'

'There's enough to keep me busy.'

'They do say that Satan finds mischief for idle hands,' she retorted, and could have bitten her silly tongue off.

'Do they, now?' he asked softly. 'And what does Elizabeth say, since she's such a fountain of knowledge all at once?'

'You're talking riddles!' She plunged her hands into the dishwater, head lowered. She had gone too far.

'And so are you,' he told her, his voice cool. 'Look to your own business, Elizabeth, and leave me to worry about mine.'

Matt came in the back way late that night when Jean was out and Elizabeth sat alone in the kitchen. His face was set, his eyes blazing with purpose.

'Is my father alone? Right—' he said, when she nodded. 'See that we're not disturbed, Elizabeth. I have something to discuss with him.'

It took a moment to get up, spilling her sewing from her lap. By the time she caught up with him he was halfway across the hall.

'Matt!' She snatched at his arm, halting him. 'Not tonight – he's in a temper and best left alone!'

'What I have to say cannae wait any longer. Let me be, Elizabeth!' Matt tore her fingers from his sleeve as the parlour door was thrown open and Rab Montgomery's bulk appeared.

'What's that noise?' he barked.

'I want a word with you, father,' Matt said crisply.

'Aye – well – I can do nothing to stop you.' Rab stumped back to his chair and Matt, without another look at Elizabeth, followed him into the room and closed the door, shutting her out.

There was a small carved chair in the hall; she sank onto it, knees weak. She had no plans to eavesdrop but she couldn't go back to the kitchen and leave Matt alone to face his father.

For a moment, there was only the soft murmur of Matt's voice then silence. Rab's reaction came clearly to her ears.

'You senseless, moon-eyed fool! Have you no idea at all of the ways of the world? Am I made of money, that I'm expected to support this lassie and her bairn? That is—' there was a change of tone '— if it's yours. Have you been daft enough to accept responsibility?'

'I'd no' think of denying it!' Matt's voice, too, had risen. 'I'm no' asking any favours of you. I'm just telling you that I'm going to marry Isobel and I'll expect her to be accepted into this family as my wife!'

'You what?' Rab roared. 'Laddie, you might have lost your wits but you can scarce expect me to do the same. I'll have none of this nonsense and you'll get no help from me if you go on with it!'

There was a thud and the rattle of glass and

Elizabeth, now on her feet and clutching at the chair-back, knew that Rab's huge fist had crashed onto the table.

'I'm no' asking for your help,' Matt said angrily. 'I'll support my wife myself!'

There was a derisive laugh from his father. 'What with?'

'We'll manage with my wages from the warehouse and the little she earns.'

This time Rab's voice was a bellow. 'D'ye expect me to keep you on as my foreman when you defy me as my son? I'll be damned first! There's no room in your life for a wife just now – and when there is, you'll make a good marriage with a lassie who can bring a dowry. And that's my last word on it, so you can get to your room and thank the good God that you've been brought to your senses before it was too late!'

'You old devil!' Matt's shaking voice was almost unrecognisable. 'You dare to expect me to turn away from Isobel and my own bairn like that? Is this the thanks I get for giving up the loom and spending day after day in that damned warehouse of yours, putting up with your black moods and your foul temper—'

'You impudent pup—' Rab screamed. A hand touched Elizabeth's arm. James had been drawn from upstairs by the noise. His face was ashen.

'—I'll teach you how to speak to your father!'
Rab shouted, and there was the crash of fire irons.

'Get in and put a stop to it!' Elizabeth pushed
James towards the door, but he hung back.

'They'd never listen to me!'

'Then I will—'

He pulled her back as her fingers touched the
door-handle.

'For God's sake, Elizabeth, he's likely to kill you
if you get in his way now!'

'We can't leave Matt to face this on his own!' She
caught James's hand, reached out to open the door.
'We'll go in together!'

The street door opened and Adam stepped into
the hall. Before Elizabeth could open the parlour
door he had taken in the situation, and swept her
and James aside.

'That daft gowk – I told him to wait for me
before he told the old man,' he said, and threw the
parlour door open. Peeping round his shoulder
Elizabeth saw Rab by the fire, face mottled, eyes
starting from his head. He clutched the heavy
poker. Matt grasped the hand that held the poker
and the two men were locked in a struggle.

'For God's sake!' Adam stormed into the room,
dragged his father and brother apart, and stood

between them, eyes bright with anger. The poker was thrown back on the hearth. 'Have you no thought of the folk living round here? D'you want them to hear your business down at the Cross?'

'They're welcome to hear mine, for I've nothing to hide!' Matthew threw himself towards the door, his face dark and distorted with rage. A livid scarlet welt stood out down one side. Adam caught at his arm and was cast aside with murderous fury.

'Leave me be!' his brother warned him and raged from the house without stopping to take his hat and coat. The front door crashed back on its hinges and was left open to the night until James closed it.

'Let him go – all of you!' Rab ordered thickly, spittle drooling down his chin. His eyes were bloodshot, his face a bluish colour. 'He's no son of mine from this day on!'

'Stop your wild talk and get a grip of yourself, man!' Adam ordered, forcing his father into a fireside chair. At first Rab resisted, then something about the steely fire in his eldest son's blue eyes made him think better of it. With a grunt deep in his throat he subsided.

'Elizabeth? Damn you, girl, stop staring as though I was some curiosity in a side-show—' He peered round Adam at her. 'Fetch the whisky!'

'You'll have a little brandy, just, with water. And you'll sit quietly until I tell you that you can get up.' Adam's voice was crisp. 'James, tend to the fire.'

He put his fingers to the pulse that fluttered at Rab's temple, and the older man beat him away with flailing hands.

'Let me be! I'll tell you when I've need of a physician!'

Elizabeth brought his drink, noting the tremor in the hand that snatched the glass from her. For a long time there was silence in the room apart from the fire's crackle and the noise of Rab sucking brandy and water through loose lips. James fiddled uneasily with the curtains, Elizabeth stood behind Rab's chair, and Adam, seated opposite his father, watched him with narrowed eyes.

'I'd advise you to go to your bed,' he said when the glass was empty.

'I was going!' Rab barked at him. 'Elizabeth, help me to my feet!'

'James, you'll take charge of the warehouse tomorrow,' he said at the door.

'You'd be best to wait until the morning, when your temper's cooled, before you make such decisions,' Adam said levelly, and his father glared at him.

'It'll all be the same in the morning – unless thon fool of a brother of yours does as he's told!'

They were all in bed when Matt came home. In the morning he stayed in his room until his father and James left the house.

Elizabeth set Jean to work in the dining-room, where she was safely out of the way, and returned to the kitchen.

'Should you not go upstairs and talk to Matt?'

Adam, still lounging at the table, shook his dark head.

'Leave him be. If he's no' man enough to handle this business without my help, he's no' worth worrying over. What were you thinking of doing when I came in last night?'

'Putting a stop to the scene before Matt and your father killed each other.'

He gave her a sardonic look from beneath thick dark lashes. 'All on your lone?'

'James was with me.'

'James is a poet, never a warrior. Lord's sakes, Elizabeth, the old man would have split you in two with that poker, the mood he was in. Have you no sense?'

'I could hardly stand by and—' she began hotly, then Adam's eyes suddenly slid to a point beyond and above her, and she turned.

Matt stood in the doorway. His face was grey, apart from the ugly black and blue and yellow bruise that showed where his father had struck him. His eyes were sunk in his head and there were lines that showed how he would look in old age. Elizabeth was shocked to see how like his father he would look in some forty years' time.

She hurried to fill a bowl with food, but he shook his head, coming to sit at the table. 'I'll eat nothing under his roof.'

'Then you'll be away to skin and bone within the week, man,' his brother said sarcastically. 'My, thon's a bonny bruise.'

Matt ducked his head away from the surgeon's probing fingers and looked at Adam and Elizabeth with dead eyes.

'You're wrong. I'm going to stay with Isobel and her father today, and never setting foot in this house again.'

Somehow Elizabeth had never believed that it would come to this. Neither, obviously, had Adam. While she stared in dismay at Matt, his brother said angrily 'Don't be a fool, man – the whole business can be sorted out tonight with a wee bit of sense from the pair of you!'

But Matt's normally cheerful face was set in stubborn lines. 'There's nothing to sort out.

Isobel's father needs her to look after his house. He's fair crippled with the rheumatics, and I'm to take over his loom. I'm finished with the warehouse, and I'm finished with the whole business!'

'Matt – it's no' easy to find work, and your father—' Elizabeth couldn't bring herself to finish the sentence. Matt did it for her.

'—My father might make it difficult for me? Aye, he might well try,' he held up a hand to stop Adam's words. 'You've got a strange faith in folk's duty, Adam,' he told him, and for once their roles were reversed. When it came to Paisley, and to Rab Montgomery, Matt knew more than Adam. 'He'll mebbe try, but I'm going to follow my own plans.' His eyes brightened slightly. 'I talked to Isobel's brother about it last night, then to James when I got home. I'm going to find a manufacturer who'll help me to set up my loom for a new shawl, using John's yarn and a design from James. I'm going to weave the shawl my father refused to consider. And I'm going to show him that it'll work!'

An hour later he paused in the hall, his possessions in one bag, and took a last look round the home he had known for most of his life.

Adam, unable to get him to change his mind, had finally walked out in a temper, so there was only Elizabeth to see Matt leave.

'It's no' too late to change your mind, as Adam says.'

He shook his head and, unexpectedly, bent to kiss her cheek. 'I'll never talk with him again, or set foot in his house, without an invitation. You'll dance at my wedding, Elizabeth?'

She nodded, lips trembling, then he was gone.

The town buzzed for a few days with the news, but Rab Montgomery paid the gossips no heed. Matt's name was never mentioned in his house.

James made some protest about being promoted to the post of foreman in the warehouse, but being of weaker material than either of his brothers, he gave in before his father's mounting anger. His hopes were pinned, now, on the poems that were with the London publisher.

'If they sell,' he told Elizabeth, 'I'm going there whether my father likes it or not. All I need is for one poem to be published, and I'll know where my path leads!'

A day or two after Matt walked out Adam returned home in a black mood. 'Can you read?' he asked Elizabeth abruptly.

'You know fine I can. I told you that your step-mother had sent me to the charity school.'

'Then look at that.' He threw the latest edition of the *Paisley Advertiser* on the carpet before her as she black-leaded the parlour grate. There was an announcement on the page that fell uppermost, to the effect that as Matthew Montgomery no longer was employed as warehouse foreman for the company of Robert Montgomery, Forbes Place, the said Robert Montgomery, shawl manufacturer, was not responsible for any of the said Matthew's debts or liabilities.

Rab was dining out that day. Adam was out for a while after the evening meal, and when he returned the paper was tossed onto a table by Rab's elbow, without comment. Rab glanced at it.

'I've seen it.'

'By God,' said Adam, white-faced, standing over him, 'You're a bitter, twisted old devil!'

James caught his breath with an audible gasp. Elizabeth stabbed her finger with her needle and didn't notice until later that blood stained the shirt she was mending. After a long, angry pause Rab looked up. Small pale blue eyes set in a lattice of red met and locked with furious dark blue eyes.

'And by God—' said Rab at last, picking up the newspaper and ripping it across as though it was a piece of flimsy lace, 'I learned in a harder school than you or your brother'll ever know!'

He tossed the newsprint carelessly onto the fire, and turned away from his son. Adam swung round on his heel and walked out. Sent to fetch him for the Bible reading five minutes later, Elizabeth found him in the hall, gripping the finely carved banisters.

'The wee lassie in Maxwellton died tonight,' he said without looking round when he heard the rustle of her skirts. 'You'd best burn the coat I was wearing. There's – blood on it.'

She put a hand on his arm, but he didn't seem to notice. 'Adam, your father's waiting with the Bible—'

He drew a deep, ragged breath, expelled it slowly. Then his shoulders straightened and he turned, eyes hooded, face carefully expressionless.

'I might as well,' he said bleakly. 'Whatever happens we must never forget to thank the Lord for the day he's given to us.'

Matt wasn't the only young man in the area to be at odds with his father. For some time rumours had been flying about Alec Grant, Helen's husband, and his fondness for the gambling tables. His father, a staunch Presbyterian, was opposed to games of chance, and the gossips who predicted trouble between father and son were proved right.

Helen's growing unhappiness was obvious. She spent a lot of time at her parents' Paisley house, and visited Elizabeth frequently.

'I could never tell my mother the whole truth of it,' she said wretchedly, twining her white fingers together. 'Even when Alec and his father aren't quarrelling about money and Alec's duties, the house rings with the echoes of, it seems to me. Mistress Grant's a poor, purse-mouthed woman, so there's no help for us from her. Alec should never have left the Fusiliers, that's the truth of it. He was happy as a soldier, and he only left for my sake, when we wed. He's so unhappy, working for his father as estate manager. He sees his friends often because he needs to be with folk that take him as he is. But they're never away from the tables or from the bottle—'

Elizabeth felt helpless in the face of such misery. 'Is there no way he can leave Barrhead and make a new life for himself?'

Helen shook her red head. 'What could he do? He was raised to go into the Army and it was always understood that he'd work for his father after that. He's dependent on the old man. Thank God it's a daughter I have, and not a son!' she added bitterly.

One day when she found Adam at home she appealed to him to talk to Alec about his increasing dependence on drink.

'You must have seen his restlessness yourself,

coming about the house so much, and being a close friend of his.'

Elizabeth felt, rather than saw, the way he winced at the words. Obviously Helen saw his presence at Barrhead as friendship for her husband alone and had no idea that she was the reason.

'I know he's unhappy. I've often seen that look on board ship, when a man was raging inside to get away from duty and live his own life.'

Helen's mouth trembled. She looked swiftly down at her own clasped hands, and missed the sudden, brief movement Adam made, as if preventing himself from going to her. 'And he's getting into debt too. I'm that feared his father'll find out! Adam—' she looked up again, pleading with him. 'Could you mebbe talk to him? You know more about the world than any of us, and he'd listen to you.'

'And lose – his friendship?' Adam's voice was thick, strangled deep in his throat. He turned away abruptly and the hand Helen put out to him dropped to her side, rejected. 'Helen, a man who's bent on going his own way doesnae take kindly to advice.'

'You're my only hope, Adam. Please – for his sake, if you'll no' do it for mine!'

It seemed inconceivable to Elizabeth that Helen

didn't know how much she was torturing the man who stood staring out of the window, his back to the room. She began to speak, trying in clumsy fashion to help him out of the agony he must be enduring; but before she had said more than a few words Adam had turned, his face like a carving in stone.

'I'll do my best – since you ask me,' he said, and the smile that illuminated Helen's face made the tears in her eyes sparkle like diamonds.

Surely, Elizabeth thought, watching that radiant smile, Adam must realise that despite everything, Helen loved Alec deeply, and there was no other man for her. If he did, he gave no sign of it.

Matt married Isobel Gibson at the end of October. Their wedding party was held in her father's house, a cottage in Shuttle Street with the living quarters and the four-loom weaving shop separated by a through-passage from back to front of the house.

Elizabeth, Adam and James all attended. Isobel, noticeably stouter, glowed with happiness, but Elizabeth felt there were shadows on the bride-groom's round face, and his smile wasn't as ready or carefree as it had once been.

'He's grown up at last,' Adam dismissed her concern. 'It's past time – he's twenty-three years old.'

The weeks since he left his father's house hadn't been easy for Matt. Rab had used his powers in the town to block several work opportunities for his rebellious son. But Matt proved to have the tenacity of a bulldog. He had found the goodwill of a manufacturer indifferent to Rab's wishes, and the man had agreed to finance the new shawl. Matt's meagre savings had gone into the venture and he had found more work as a weaver to support himself and Isobel and her father, who had given up his loom to Matt, while the shawl was worked on.

Being a plain weaver himself, Matt could only provide the centre of the shawl. His search for a skilled man to weave the more intricate patterned border had brought him to Daniel McGill, a harness loom weaver of considerable talents, but also a notorious character.

Dan, a tall, lanky, shabbily dressed bachelor, was at the wedding celebrations, his fiery red hair like a beacon above every other head.

'I hope you know what you're taking on, with Dan,' James said apprehensively as he watched the man down a tumblerful of whisky as though it was water. Dan was one of the most skilful weavers in the town. He was also the least trustworthy, always ready to forsake his loom for the gaming tables and the tavern. He could have found work with any manufacturer he chose, but because money meant nothing to him he was continually in debt and seldom employed.

'I'll see to it that he works well on this shawl – and I'll see to it that my father's made to acknowledge his mistake,' Matt vowed, and Isobel's hand slid into his as the last words took on a bleak note.

Her smile had faltered, and her clear eyes were worried. Rab Montgomery no longer bought yarn from her brother's small factory, and she herself had found the warehouse door closed to her after Matt left home. Her entire family had been affected by her love for the wrong man.

Matt was quick to sense his young wife's mood. 'Ach, we'll manage just fine, you wait and see,' he said cheerfully, but as he looked round the small room with its low smoky ceiling and the little wall bed where he and Isobel would sleep Elizabeth knew that he was comparing it with the home he had known.

She fretted over Matt as she and Adam walked back to High Street later. There was no doubt that he loved Isobel, but there was a new restlessness in him that reminded her of an animal in a cage. All his hopes and ambitions were centred on the success of the shawl he planned. If that failed, what would become of Matt?

Adam's thoughts were occupied with more pressing matters.

'Did you see the newspaper today?' He put a hand beneath her elbow to guide her round a stagnant puddle. 'The cholera's reached Britain. A man named Sproat died of it in Sunderland.'

'It might not be the blue cholera.' That was the name given to the terrible death that had swept the globe from India.

'It is. The paper listed his symptoms. I'd know them anywhere.'

'It might not reach Paisley.' She was clutching at straws and Adam mercilessly snatched them from her one by one.

'It will. There's no doubt of that.' His voice was harsh. 'They have no real notion of what's coming to them, Elizabeth. They talk about sobriety and a respectable, pious life – they suck at cholera sweeties and call the epidemic God's punishment on the wicked. They've got no notion!' he repeated in frustration as they turned off High Street to go down the dark passageway that led to the back door of the Montgomery house.

She wished that she could change the subject, yet there was a morbid fascination in this disease that had killed thousands, and couldn't be stopped.

'Have you seen it, Adam?'

'Seen it? Aye, I've touched it, I've fought with it, and I've been defeated almost every time. Win or lose, I've never known whether a patient died because of my treatment, or whether a patient who lived would have survived anyway. It's an evil thing, cholera, and I'd no' wish my worst enemy to see it at work.'

She was suddenly racked by a shiver from head to foot; he stopped speaking and turned, as they reached the back door, to put his hands on her shoulders. The long garden was in darkness, bushes and trees black against the dark blue of the sky. Beyond the drystone wall fields stretched to the hills. It was a pleasant garden by day, but at night there was something sinister about it, Elizabeth thought for the first time.

'You're right, Elizabeth – cholera's no' a pleasant subject for young ladies like Helen and you.'

'I didnae say you shouldn't talk to me about it,' she protested, and he laughed.

'D'you no' consider yourself a lady, then?' His hands still held her shoulders. Jean had left a lamp in the kitchen window and its pale glow caught the lines and shadows of his downbent face and made his eyes glitter. 'Mebbe someone should take you in hand – someone like my cousin Christian Selbie.

It's time you began to think of your own future, Elizabeth.'

'It'll be here, in your father's kitchen.'

'Ach, he can employ a fat old wifie any day of the week to run the house and see to his meals. You've more to do with your life. Marriage, for one. Surely there's some young man who calls on you?'

She was glad that he couldn't see the colour rush to her face. 'Don't make a fool of me, Adam!'

'I'm not. Is there nobody? Or have you mebbe got thoughts about James? You're just a year or two younger than he is, when all's said and done.'

'Of course I've no thoughts of James, or him of me!' She tried to pull free, but he held her.

'It's time you considered marriage. There's plenty of good men right here in the town who'd be proud to wed you. You should be mistress of your own home, not keeping a clean hearth and a good table for a cranky old creature and his quarrelsome sons.'

'Who'd take me?' Her hand flew up to touch her scarred cheek, but almost at once it was caught in his fingers and drawn away. Then he cupped her chin, tracing the line of the scar with a gentle thumb.

'You're bonny enough – you've no need to worry about that. A man worth having looks for more than a pretty face, did you never learn that? He wants a woman with a ready smile and a happy nature and a kind heart. And you've got all of those, Elizabeth.'

Unexpectedly, he bent towards her. His lips brushed the line of the scar, then moved to settle for a brief moment on her mouth. Then he straightened up and added crisply, 'But what are we doing standing out here when there's a good warm house waiting for us?'

She was glad when he strode through the kitchen and on into the hall, leaving her alone to take off her cloak and fuss about the kitchen, setting oatmeal to soak for the morning porridge, damping the fire down, cleaning an imaginary speck of dust from the grate.

Her hands trembled slightly and her mind was in confusion. Adam's kiss, if it could be called that, had succeeded in sweeping away the chill fear brought by talk of cholera. Her body tingled, from toes to lips, where his kiss still throbbed and burned. She had never been kissed before, and had never felt the loss of it.

Now she realised what it must be like to be really close to someone, to be loved, to have someone to depend on, someone confident and invincible like Adam Montgomery.

Jealousy had never been part of Elizabeth's nature. But as she put the lamps out and made sure that the front door was locked before going silently to her little attic room, she envied her friend Isobel, who from that day on had a man of her own to call husband.

V

Adam was not one to let a matter alone once his mind had fixed on it, Elizabeth discovered.

A few days after Matt's wedding, he wandered, bored, into the kitchen where she was alone, finishing off the week's ironing. The room was hot and stuffy, a fire burning fiercely in the range to keep the irons hot. Elizabeth's face was crimson and strands of damp hair escaped from beneath her cap as she worked.

'Did James ever tell you of his friend Thomas?' he began. 'Buried his sweetheart on the very day before their wedding. And him with a nice wee house all ready for his bride, and a good job as a cobbler—'

'And a temper that made some folk think that mebbe his sweetheart was as well under the ground as in his kitchen,' Elizabeth cut in. 'If you're thinking of marrying me off to that man, Adam Montgomery, you can think again.'

She glared at him and thumped the flatiron viciously onto the shirt she was ironing. 'I'll find my own husband in my own time. And it seems to me that you should be thinking of your own heart, and the way it's running away with your brains!'

She stopped, horrified. After a brief, terrible pause Adam said softly, 'And what of my heart?'

She swallowed hard. She had gone too far to retreat now. 'Helen Grant's a good friend to me, Adam, and I'd never want her to be unhappy.'

He drew in his breath with a hiss, and caught at a chair, swinging it round so that he could straddle the seat, hands gripping the back. Now he was below her and within her vision. His eyes were blue chips of ice beneath hooded lids.

'Mind your own business!'

She completed a full sweep of the iron. 'It is my business when it concerns folk I know well. What will your father have to say about this pickle you've fallen into?'

'To hell with my father!' he said through tight lips.

'And what about Helen herself, and Alec, and their bairn?'

'That's no concern of yours! Even Helen knows

nothing of – God knows how your sharp wee nose smelled it out!'

'I was there – the night you met her.' She heard an unfamiliar bitterness in her voice. 'I wish you'd never set eyes on her again.' She put the iron back on the range. 'Go away from Paisley now, and leave Helen to her marriage.'

'At your bidding?' he asked mockingly.

'I know you, Adam Montgomery. You're not a man to hold your tongue for ever. You'll only cause trouble and unhappiness. And it'll be wrong, all of it!'

'Helen—'

'Helen loves her husband, do you no' realise that?'

He got to his feet in a clumsy movement that sent the chair crashing to the floor. Adam made no move to pick it up. His face was a mask, lit by glittering narrowed eyes.

'She doesn't know what love is!'

'It means different things to different folk. Let her be, Adam, she's no' meant for you.'

For a moment she shrank back, convinced that he was going to strike her. But he stayed where he was, the impulsive move forward checked.

'Keep your tongue and your thoughts off my concerns, Elizabeth. You're the housekeeper here, no' my conscience. By God, Fate's already done its worst with me – nobody's going to take Helen away from me!'

'Adam, she's no' free to belong to you!'

The intensity in his voice was frightening. 'She could win her freedom. Wait and see, Elizabeth, wait and see. One day Helen's going to be my wife!'

The door crashed shut behind him. Stunned by the force of their quarrel, dazed by angry voices and by Adam's last words, Elizabeth righted the chair, smoothed another garment onto the table, and reached for a fresh iron, only to draw back with a gasp of pain as her bare fingers touched the hot handle.

No more was said about Helen. Adam's behaviour towards her was more guarded, and he stopped strolling into the kitchen to talk to her during the day, to her relief. She buried herself in work and tried not to worry about his plans.

As it happened Alec Grant went off to Edinburgh on business a few days later, depriving Adam of the chance to visit Barrhead. Helen called to see Elizabeth now and then, and Adam usually managed to be at home for these occasions, hungrily watching the young woman when he could.

he lends the money it'll take time. You know Peter – aye wants to think about things.'

'What about Christian?'

'You know fine Matt would never ask her. She's a woman – and besides, it would come between her and my father.'

'If I had it, I'd give it to Matt here and now. I'd like fine to see that old man taught a lesson.'

'Matt never asked this, it's my own idea – would you talk to him, Adam? Ask if he'd advance the money himself, as a loan?'

'I'd no' ask him for help if I was at the gates of Hell!' Adam said viciously.

'It might be the only answer.' Elizabeth's fingers were clasped as though in prayer, her eyes fixed on Adam. 'What could you do to teach him a lesson anyway? He knows more about the shawl business than any of you – give in, Adam, and talk to him, for Matt's sake.'

But his long, capable fingers were rubbing his chin thoughtfully. 'Wait a minute – he might know more than me about business, but there's things I know about—' His voice trailed off, then he sprang into life, blue eyes snapping fire. 'James – get word to Matt that he's got to persuade Peter to make that loan, whatever the terms. We can worry about high interest later. And tell him that the two of us'll visit

Dan tonight. Elizabeth – the key of the cupboard the medication's stored in. Come on, lassie, don't just gape at me, I've work to do!'

James, mystified but unenlightened, galloped back to work. Elizabeth was whisked into the kitchen, fumbling in the bunch of keys about her slim waist. Adam opened the cupboard and let his fingers dance along the collection of bottles and packets. A small package was slipped into his pocket.

'What are you doing?'

'This town's jumpy over the cholera,' he made for the hall, caught up his hat and coat. 'If the jailer thought that Dan was sickening for something like that, he'd no' be keen to keep him, would he?'

'Adam, you'd no'—' She caught at his arm as he opened the door. 'Adam! It's criminal!'

The grin on his face slipped and his eyes hardened as he looked down at her. 'So's trying to destroy your own son when he's struggling to prove that he's a man,' he said, and the door closed behind him.

The ground floor of the new prison by the river was given over to a howff where debtors and their visitors could talk over a glass of porter or ale, sold by Mr Hart, the jailer. The Paisley people always felt that this was a civilised Scottish custom, and at the moment it suited Adam's purpose very well.

Dan's long face brightened when he saw his visitor waiting with two generous tumblers of porter.

'You don't look well, man,' Adam told him cheerfully.

Dan took a large mouthful of drink, wiped his mouth on his sleeve, and said that he was fine.

'But I'm vexed for Matt. This has never happened to me before.' He gazed about the place, his brow wrinkled. The debtor's prison had always been a threat over his red head, but he had never expected anything to come of it. Usually, he paid his debts at the last minute, then set about making new ones. 'That flower-lasher knew fine he'd get his money – he always has!'

'Mebbe he's been talking to the wrong folk. You're sure you're well?' Adam peered at the other man. 'What did you have for your dinner?'

'Tripe.'

Adam tutted. 'I'd never touch the stuff, myself. Matt's trying to raise the money to pay off your debt. But it might take time. And in the meantime, what about this web on your loom? Matt's fair anxious to see it finished.'

Dan took another long drink. 'As God's my witness, Adam, I've been working hard at that web. But what can I do now? They'll never let me bring it into the jail to work on.'

'So we'll have to get you out.' Adam leaned across the table and refilled Dan's glass. 'Tell me – d'you ever have a ringing sound in your ears?'

'Like a bell?' Dan was perplexed.

'Just so. And then there's a feeling of giddiness, and a bad stomach. They'd no' want to keep you in here for another minute if they ever thought you'd caught something dangerous, like the cholera—'

'What?' Dan's voice rose sharply and a few heads were lifted. His eyes rolled in a suddenly white face. 'God sakes, man, don't joke about a thing like that! I never felt—'

'Shut your mouth and listen to me!' Adam hissed at him, and he subsided. 'Now – if you were to be a wee thing unsteady on your feet when you leave here, and for the rest of the day too, and if you complained tonight about a ringing noise in your ears—'

Understanding was beginning to dawn in the green eyes opposite. 'They'd think I was – oh, but it'd take worse than that to make them put me out.'

'I can see to that for you.' A small packet found its way beneath the table into Dan's hand. 'Put that in your pocket. When dusk comes, swallow it down and throw the paper away. It'll make you awful sick, but it'll no' kill you.'

'Aye, but—' Dan swallowed nervously, '— they'll send for the physician, and he'll know it's nothing bad.'

'I'm a physician myself, man – and I've seen the cholera. If I'm visiting you at the time they'll be happy enough to take my word for it that you should be kept away from folk. Me and Matt'll take you home and keep you alone for two days. That'll be long enough for Matt to find the money.'

'Are you sure I'll get better?' Dan eyed him suspiciously.

'There'd be no point in getting you out of here if I couldnae get you back at your loom within a few hours. All you'll need to see you right's a tot or two of whisky – and I'll have that waiting for you,' Adam added swiftly, and the weaver's eyes brightened.

'Wait a minute, though – if I'm as sick as all that my drawboy'll no' come near me. I cannae work without someone to operate the harness.'

Adam wasn't in the mood to suffer obstacles. 'Matt trained as a drawboy, didn't he? He'll work with you, and I'll see to the money. Will you do it, Dan?'

It took a little persuasion, but Adam could be

very persuasive when he put his mind to it. When he left thirty minutes later, he was gratified to see Dan stagger on his way back to the cells, knocking over a respectable town councillor who was visiting another prisoner.

Dan was spectacularly ill when Matt and Adam called on him that evening. The anxious jailer was only too pleased to see him carried into a carriage under the supervision of a medical man. Dan was then whisked off to his house, where he was put to bed, moaning and convinced that he had been poisoned.

A few generous doses of whisky revived him enough to work up a rage as he watched Adam and Matt fumigating his house, scrubbing walls and floors with disinfectant, and washing his clothes.

'There's nothing wrong with me, you know that yourself – and will you put my best coat down!' he bawled from the wall-bed.

Adam, bent over a tub of water and strong lye soap, straightened his back and winced. 'We've to be seen to be taking all the proper precautions, you daft loon,' he said, and plunged the coat into the water. 'Think yourself lucky we're no' scrubbing you too.'

'First he tries to kill me, then he ruins my best

coat,' Dan mourned, clutching the whisky bottle for comfort.

'Kill you? You'll be better than you've ever been by the morning. A good purging never did anyone any harm,' Adam told him callously. 'Jings, Matt, I had no notion that washing was so hard. I'd rather have a full day walking the wards in some hospital than a morning as a laundrywoman!'

Elizabeth, anxious to hear what happened, sat up late into the night waiting for Adam to come home, then went to bed, her curiosity unsatisfied. The next morning she found him sprawled across his bed, fully-clothed and fast asleep, reeking of disinfectant. She closed the door, and told Jean to keep away from the upper floor in case he was disturbed.

He arrived in the kitchen at noon, demanding food and looking fresh and rested. He was like a schoolboy, she thought with a mixture of exasperation and affection, as she set a place at the kitchen table for him. The escapade with Matt had put new life into him, and in his eagerness to tell the story he swept aside the coolness that had lain between them.

'You're nothing but a pair of silly bairns, you and your brother!' She felt years older than him when she looked at the sheer mischief in his eyes.

'How long d'you think a daft ploy like that's going to fool folk?'

He grinned and bit into a thick slice of bread with white teeth. 'Long enough.'

'If you find yourselves in the jail along with Dan tomorrow don't look to me for sympathy,' she scolded.

His hand caught at her wrist, turning her to look down at him as he sat at the kitchen table.

'Who else would I look to? You're a sharp wee thing, Elizabeth – too sharp for your age. But for some reason beyond my understanding,' his eyes held hers in a level look, 'you'd never want me to fall into bad ways.'

It was the nearest he had come to referring to the quarrel they had had over Helen.

Elizabeth, embarrassed, jerked her hand away. His look, his touch, set up a confusion in her that was hard to understand.

'You'll always worry about me and watch over me,' he finished smugly, going back to the bread.

'I hope you never have cause to find out if that's so,' she snapped, to cover the turmoil within.

'Anyway, who can blame me for being cautious about Dan's health, with the cholera on its way? I'll discover tomorrow that it must have been bad tripe he ate yesterday. And who'll be any the wiser? In the meantime, folks are scared to go near him and prove me a liar.'

He laughed, reaching for a scone. 'There's a corporal posted outside his door to see that nobody but me goes in or out, so Dan and Matt are free to get on with their work in peace.'

The smile faded slightly as he inspected his hands, reddened by scrubbing. 'And on top of that, Dan's house has never been cleaner!'

'And what if one of the other physicians wants to see Dan?'

Adam winked. 'I've already had a word with them. Those that couldn't be told the truth were happy enough to agree that I should deal with this case myself, and call them in if the patient got worse.'

When he had eaten he hurried to the weaver's cottage where a police officer stood on duty, seemingly unconcerned by the steady thump and clack of the loom within. Obviously he believed in doing as he was told, and he hadn't been ordered to see that the possible cholera victim didn't work.

Matt and Dan were both drawn after hours of toil. The cloth, face down on the rollers, was a misty confusion of coloured threads to Adam's unpractised eye, but the other two men knew exactly what the pattern on the other side looked like, and they kept their gaze fixed on the work as they talked, each of them automatically registering the tension of the material and the number of lines still to be 'shot'.

'I'm no' sure how you'll get on with Peter Todd, Adam. He's an honest soul, but awful careful when it comes to parting with money. He always wants time to sleep on it.'

'He's had that – which is more than I can say for you two,' Adam eyed them with swift sympathy. 'I'll sweeten my tongue when I talk to the old miser,' he promised blithely, and departed with a suitably grave expression, having left a fresh bottle of whisky and some food with the prisoners. He knew, as he looked at the little knot of people hurrying by on the far side of the road, that he was playing a cruel trick on Paisley; but loyalty to Matt came first.

Like Rab Montgomery, Peter Todd had given up weaving and had become an employer. Peter had made a comfortable fortune in Paisley's flourishing thread industry, enough to ensure a pleasant retiral. He was a bachelor, and he and Matt had always been friendly. Peter's grandfather had employed Adam's great-grandfather when he first came to Paisley, and Matt had been Peter's drawboy many years before. There was a family link that Peter cherished.

Even so, Adam tapped the brass door-knocker meekly, quite sure that he'd have to curb his usual brusque tongue if he wanted to win the old man over. But he was pleasantly surprised. Peter greeted him with a smile, and poured out glasses of claret before saying, 'You'll have come about that wee matter for Matthew.'

'That's right.' Adam took a sip of claret. It was excellent.

'Well, I've been thinking about it—' Peter tucked his hands beneath his tails of his coat. 'For old time's sake, and because I know he's a hard-working man, and honest, I'm prepared to give him a loan – but mind you—' he swung round, finger raised, '—I'm just covering six months, and I'd be looking for a good return on the money.'

'You'll be repaid – every penny of it, within the time,' Adam promised recklessly, elation bubbling up in him as he watched the old man writing out his personal note for the Provident Bank.

'There you are, then—' The slip of paper that meant so much to Matt was put into his brother's hand. 'You'll have another wee glass,' Peter added and Adam, longing to get to the bank and pay in the note, hesitated, smiled, and said that he'd be happy to drink another wee glass. It was, after all, the least he could do under the circumstances.

'Emmmm—' Peter delayed him again on the doorstep. 'You're a man that's travelled a lot, and seen a lot, they tell me. What's your opinion of this venture your brother's embarked on? D'ye think he's going to get this fine shawl, when all's said and done?'

Adam looked down on the grey head and lined face of the man. 'I think, Mister Todd, that I'd have to travel a sight further and see a lot more, before I'd meet a man as honest as my brother. Your money's safe with him – and a good return you'll get, that's a promise.'

Then, at last, he was free to go plunging down the street, and just managed to get to the bank, housed in the Chamberlain's office, before it closed for the day. Dan was freed from the threat of cholera and Matt's brave new future was secured again.

Rab Montgomery made no sign that he knew anything of Adam's part in the whole business. He had remained carefully aloof from Dan's arrest, and he could not show any reaction to his release.

'But I'll wager he's eating his heart out over it right now,' said James the next night when Rab had limped up to bed. 'D'you think he'll try anything else?'

Adam, in his father's favourite chair, put one

heel on the footstool Rab scorned, and swung the other foot on top of it with the air of a man who had done a fine day's work.

'He's no' a complete fool. He'll leave it at that. But man, it was one of the finest operations I've carried out since I don't know when!'

'And you didn't lose a patient!' James gave him a mock salute.

A grin cracked his brother's face wide and his blue eyes danced. 'No – but for all that I managed to amputate my father's intentions skilfully,' he said, and he and James laughed until the tears ran down their faces.

Watching them, trying without success to look disapproving, Elizabeth realised that Adam's laugh was a natural, free sound that must have been heard often at one time. She wondered how many times he had permitted himself to laugh since his fiancée's death.

'We've shocked poor Elizabeth,' he warned his brother.

'I'm no' shocked, I just—' she began, then Adam started laughing again, James was set off once more, and she was laughing with them and wishing that the fine house could ring to the sound of young happy people more often.

As though echoing her thoughts Adam said,

when the hysteria had died down, 'You don't laugh often enough, Elizabeth.'

'It's this house.' James mopped his face. 'The folk in it never have anything to feel joyous about.'

Adam was still looking at Elizabeth, his eyes brilliant, taking on an intent look. 'You're young and bonny – I wish I could tell you, as a physician, to make sure that you laugh at least once a day.'

She flushed. 'That would be daft. Most folk never have occasion to laugh every day!'

He stood up, stretched, yawned. 'I'm off to my bed. But I think you're wrong – most folk just never think of looking for cheeriness. Mind what I said.'

She wondered, as she got ready for bed in her attic room, if Adam had ever considered taking his own advice. It would do him good too, she thought, remembering the pleasure of hearing his laugh. But all thought of that was swept aside the next day when Helen Grant arrived at the High Street house, white-faced and with tears in her brown eyes.

'It's Alec – he's ill—' she burst out as soon as Elizabeth opened the door. 'I had to bring Catherine over to my mother's, for there's nobody in Barrhead can care for her day and night. I came to tell you—'

'Is it bad?' Elizabeth tried to lead her friend into the parlour but Helen stayed where she was, just inside the door, shaking her head when Elizabeth held out a hand for her cloak.

'I can't stay – I've to get the next stage-coach. It's smallpox. Oh, Elizabeth, I'm so frightened for him! I'm going to try to get the Edinburgh coach when it comes through at two o'clock, else I'll have to go to Glasgow first—'

'You can't go!'

Elizabeth and Helen swung round and looked up at Adam, who was standing at the bend in the stairs. He came swiftly down, his eyes fixed on Helen, his face set. 'You can't go!' he repeated.

'Adam—' she caught at his sleeve. 'Did you hear what I said? Alec's ill in Edinburgh. I must get there!'

He ignored the fingers on his arm and gripped her shoulders. 'Don't you understand? Were you ever inoculated against smallpox?'

'Adam—' she began, then as he shook her slightly she submitted. 'No, I wasn't – there was a lass near us went weak in the head after she was done and my mother would never let them touch me.'

'Then you could catch it!' He shook her again. 'You could die of it, Helen! You could – be blinded, or go mad, or—'

Elizabeth's hand flew to her face to touch the mark there. She could see the horror in Adam's eyes as he looked down on Helen's beauty and imagined it scarred as she, Elizabeth, was scarred.

'What does that matter to me?' Helen was demanding fretfully. She pulled away from him.

'It matters! Stay here, where you're safe—'

She was angry now. 'You think that my safety matters more to me than my husband's life? He's sick, alone – he needs me. We belong together, me and Alec – I'm his wife!'

The last three words were low-voiced, intense, and Elizabeth saw them strike Adam with the force of a thonged whip.

Helplessly she watched him flinch, saw his hands drop, empty, to his sides. Helen added gently, 'It's kind of you to be concerned, Adam, but you must see that if I could save him by taking the sickness on myself, I'd do it gladly. Elizabeth, you'll visit Catherine while I'm away? And if I should—' She stopped herself, then went on, 'I'll be home as soon as I can bring Alec with me.'

'Of course I'll visit Catherine, and your mother. I'll walk part of the way with you.' Elizabeth turned to fetch her shawl as Adam went back upstairs without another word.

He scarcely ate a mouthful that night at dinner. The following morning he announced that the time had come for him to go to England.

Elizabeth stirred automatically at the food she was simmering over the range. Adam had admitted defeat. He was going away, leaving Helen and Alec to their marriage.

The second thought came hard on the heels of the first. Adam was going, and a cold hand touched her heart. Life would be less perilous without him – but very bleak.

'Why not?' Rab grunted dourly. 'My sons never seem to realise when they're well off. I'm thankful for James here – at least he's got the sense to be content with what he's got.'

James, who was waiting impatiently every day for good news from the London publisher, flushed scarlet and attacked his porridge with great concentration.

His father didn't notice. 'And when do you plan to go?' He scowled at his eldest, and most exasperating, son.

'As soon as I can make arrangements.'

'It's a pity you had to decide to leave now,'

Christian said later when she called in to talk about Alec Grant's illness, 'You could have set up an office. We could always do with another good medical man.'

Adam stared moodily out of the window. 'I couldnae do anything for you – nobody can if the cholera comes.'

Christian tutted and smoothed the fringe of her shawl, a striped pattern known as Zebra. 'And they say women are fickle. All this fuss about whether you should stay or whether you should go – you belong here, when all's said and done.'

'I don't!' he said curtly, and stamped out.

'Tuts! There's something amiss, but nobody could ever get a secret from Adam,' was all Christian said.

Daniel McKinlay, a surgeon with a practice in New Street, gave Adam a letter of introduction to a former colleague who worked in St Thomas's teaching hospital in London, and he began to make plans for his departure.

There was a cloud over the house. Rab was in a bad temper over Adam's desertion, and Adam himself, deprived of Helen's company and wounded by her devotion to Alec, scarcely had a word to say to anyone.

The days leading to his departure seemed to

whirl by. While he made his farewells and began to collect his belongings together Elizabeth shut herself in the kitchen, baking and cooking and washing and ironing until she fell into bed exhausted each night.

She didn't want to have time to think, and she didn't know why. She told herself that all the changes – Adam's arrival, his imminent departure, James's plans to go to London if his poems were accepted, Matt's marriage – had unsettled her. She needed to find a routine again.

She visited Helen's mother's house and played with little Catherine, and she spent as much free time as possible with Isobel, who was lonely.

Since the time when he had had to borrow money from Peter Todd Matt had become obsessed by the desire to defeat his father. He worked at his loom late at night, lamplight turning the other, silent looms into grotesque creatures watching over his efforts. When he wasn't working, he was with Dan, watching the shawl grow, or with Cassidy, the manufacturer.

'He comes home at night so tired he can scarcely get into his bed, and in the morning he goes back to the loom half-asleep,' Isobel said wistfully. 'I never see him to talk to.'

Elizabeth took the other girl's hand in hers.

'Wait until that shawl's finished. Matt'll make you so proud of him one day.'

'I'm proud of him now,' Isobel hurried to say. 'I always was. But it would be nice to walk up the street with him, the way it used to be.'

Adam's departure rushed closer. He was looking through a pile of books in the dining-room one day, ignoring Elizabeth, who was waxing the big table, when Jean erupted from the kitchen, still wrapped in the shawl she had put on to do the shopping.

'Mind your dirty feet!' Down on her knees by the table-legs, Elizabeth saw with horror that Jean's feet were still in her outdoor, muddy boots. They advanced, and their owner, cheeks red with cold and excitement, pushed the dining room door further open. From where Jean stood Adam, in a corner by the window, wasn't noticed.

'Did you hear the news? I was in the cheese market a few minutes ago and a woman told me that Lieutenant Grant of Barrhead died of the smallpox in Edinburgh! That poor young wi—!'

She stopped short as she saw Adam. A rough, chilblained hand fled to her mouth.

'Get out of here with your boots on, you stupid gowk!' Elizabeth knew that she was shrill, screeching like a fish-wife, but she had to get the girl away

140

from the sight of Adam, ashen faced ınd motionless. 'And stop tattling – have you no' been told that before?'

Jean whirled and ran, but not before protesting. 'It's the truth! I met someone else on the way home and she says it's right enough!'

As the kitchen door banged Adam, a book still in his hand, turned to look out of the window, his broad back to Elizabeth.

'If – if it's the truth, Helen's going to be in a fair taking, poor lass—' she said at last.

'Aye.' It was like a long-released sigh. 'Poor lass. Poor Alec.'

'Adam—?' A strange unease was stiffening Elizabeth's throat. He turned very slowly to face her, and as he spoke she knew what he was thinking; knew, too, why she was uneasy.

'Would you say,' asked Adam very quietly, 'that it would be reasonable enough to leave a young widow such as Helen for a full year to mourn, before making her a proposal of marriage?'

Elizabeth moistened her lips, the polishing cloth dropping from her fingers.

'I'd say that it's a terrible thing to think of a wedding when you're in the presence of death. I'd say you should think shame of yourself for talking like that!'

His eyes glittered at her. 'It's well seen, Elizabeth, that you have no notion of the grip love can have on a man.'

'Promise me you'll say nothing to Helen!'

'I promise you this – I'll say nothing of it to her for a year and a day. And you'll say nothing to anyone about what you know.'

He smiled at her faintly, and his face was like a weird mask, with its bright, narrowed eyes and its thin-lipped, humourless smile.

'I never wished ill on Alec – but I did tell you, did I not, that one day Helen would be my own wife?' said Adam, and began to put the books back on the shelves, one by one.

VI

It was considered seemly for a widow to wear black from head to toe and shut herself away in mourning for a year. But within a few weeks of Alec's death, Helen Grant moved to her parents' home with her baby daughter and, chin high, set about taking up the reins of her life again.

'My mother's fair shocked at me, but sitting in that big house with only Alec's family for company would have driven me to the grave myself!' she declared stubbornly, arriving at the Montgomery house one day with the baby.

'Tell me you're no' shocked, Elizabeth,' she begged. Elizabeth was shocked, but a look at Helen's lovely face, thinner and sharper since she returned from Edinburgh after burying her young husband, told her that the widow was fighting grief in her own way, the tears not far behind those wide, luminous eyes.

'Of course not!'

Catherine, angelic in a blue woollen dress and pantalettes, snarled balls of wool contentedly on the hearth between them, quite unaware of the tragedy that had hit her life. She picked up a ball, toddled to her mother with it. Helen received it with a brilliant smile.

'You see, Elizabeth, Alec was so full of – of life. I could never betray him by sitting in that dark house, letting Catherine here feel the misery of it all around her. I'm not going back. I'll stay here, in Paisley.'

'What about Alec's inheritance?'

Helen blinked rapidly. 'I'll not buy it with my baby's happiness. It was the finish of her father, and Alec's brothers can take it for all I care. I'll support my bairn and myself in my own way. It's a ploy I was thinking of before – before Alec went to Edinburgh. A way of getting the three of us back to Paisley. A sweetie shop.'

As Elizabeth stared at her, stunned, she burst into shaky laughter.

'You should see the look on your face! I'm serious, Elizabeth. I was always good at making confectioneries. It's the only thing I'm good at. There's a wee shop for rent in George Street, and if my father'll lend me the money to start, I might be able to pay my way.'

Her brown eyes, darker than Elizabeth's, were fixed imploringly on her friend. 'I need to keep myself busy,' she sounded almost desperate. 'I know fine that my mother thinks I should have hopes of finding some other man to support me and Catherine after a suitable time. But how could there ever be anyone else for me but Alec?'

Her voice broke on his name, and she fought to control her trembling mouth. At that moment Adam, who had come in unnoticed, said from the doorway, 'Helen!'

Helen's face blurred, dissolved. Tears filled her eyes and she stood up, said, 'Oh – Adam!' and went to him. His arms were waiting for her.

Catherine's rosebud mouth drooped uncertainly, she gave a little whimper. Elizabeth scooped her up, holding the warm solid little body close as she watched Adam and Helen over the baby's fair curls.

Adam held Helen tightly as she wept into his shoulder. He murmured soothingly to her, with that rare tenderness he had shown in the Maxwellton house, when he was reassuring the consumptive child.

But now there was a hunger, a male longing that fluttered Elizabeth's heart and dried her throat.

Catherine's whimper broke into a wail, and she struggled to reach her mother. Helen drew away from Adam and his arms released her with great reluctance. Smiling through her tears, she took the baby and sat down, searching in her reticule for a handkerchief.

Adam seated himself close to her, his face taut with concern.

'I promised myself I'd not cry like that.' Helen mopped her eyes vigorously. 'It was seeing you, Adam, and minding the times the three of us had those past few weeks. Well, mebbe it did me good, just this once, but no more!'

She put the handkerchief away and pinned the bright smile on her face once more. Weeping didn't redden her eyes or blotch her skin. Her dark eyes were dewy and her mouth soft.

'Adam, I'm glad you arrived, for I'd like your opinion of my plans as well.'

Elizabeth watched him closely as Helen spoke about the shop and her determination to support herself and her daughter. Shock and anger raced across his face, and when Helen had finished he said explosively, 'A shop? You? For any favour, Helen, you're far too – fragile – to take on such a responsibility. If it's money you need—'

His reaction swept away the last trace of tears.

Helen's red hair seemed to take on a fiery look, her mouth firmed.

'Adam Montgomery, you're as bad as the rest of them. There's no reason why I shouldn't work for my money, like Elizabeth.'

'Elizabeth,' said Adam icily, without looking at her, 'is used to it. It's different for her.'

'And why?' Helen asked before Elizabeth could start to defend herself indignantly. 'The only difference between us is that she's got more courage and sense than I have. Whether you like it or not, Adam, I'm going to have my wee shop. And you needn't feel obliged to patronise it!'

'Wait a minute!' he said swiftly as she put Catherine on the floor and started to rise. 'If your heart's set on this ploy then I'd never want to stop you. It's just—' He put his hand over hers. 'Will you promise me one thing? If it's too much for you, will you tell me and let me help you?'

Helen paused, the anger dying out of her face. She removed her fingers from beneath his and patted his hand lightly.

'Of course I will. But I'm determined that it'll work. I hear that you're planning to stay on here after all?' she added as she scooped her daughter up and prepared to go.

'You're not the only one to make a fresh start.

I'm looking for an office in the town – for a while, anyway.'

'I'm glad,' Helen said sincerely. 'It'll be good to have friends near me at a time like this.'

The door had scarcely closed behind her when Adam said savagely, 'How much of this stupid idea came from you?'

Elizabeth stared at him, anger bubbling up in her.

'If you mean the shop it was Helen's idea, not mine. She's well able to think for herself!'

'But not able to take on work like that!'

'I don't see why not!'

They were still in the hall, glaring at each other.

'Just because you're too independent to contemplate marriage with a mere male it doesnae mean that Helen has to be encouraged to think the same way!'

'Helen has a mind of her own. It's time you realised, Adam Montgomery,' Elizabeth told him tartly, 'that some women do, in Scotland!' And she flounced off to the kitchen, leaving him to his own thoughts.

There was little reason for Paisley people to celebrate the start of 1832. There were still too many skilled men out of work, and each day, it seemed, a cholera cloud was rolling across the grey skies towards the town.

Edinburgh's first case was reported in January. The capital was a considerable distance away but it was said that the disease travelled through the air, which meant that it could travel faster than a horse or a boat.

Adam, still searching for a suitable office, put his name onto the town's medical register. Subscriptions were being raised so that those who couldn't afford to pay for disinfectants, medicines, and medical treatment could get help. Adam, working in the hospital, would receive some form of payment from these subscriptions and the poor-rates, though it would be little.

The only cheerful, optimistic member of the household was James, who had been invited to send more work to the London publisher. He was waiting for a letter from the man, and as the only person he could confide in was Elizabeth a lot of his spare time was spent in the kitchen, where he talked and she patiently listened.

'It's the waiting that's bad. I'd leave for London tomorrow if I got just one poem accepted.'

'And what would you live on?' She chopped vegetables with practised speed.

'I'd live on crusts and water, and sleep on the

pavements if need be,' the young poet said dramatically.

'You're daft!'

He laughed. 'Just ambitious. Writers have to suffer a bit to make them better at their craft. A wee bit starving would do me no harm. I've never suffered in my life, now that I think of it. Look at poor Rob Tannahill.'

Tannahill, a weaver and the most famous of the town's many poets, had drowned on the town's outskirts some twenty years before.

'From what I heard, he was a lonely soul, and crossed in love.' Elizabeth sniffed as the onion she was slicing stung her eyes.

'I've never even been in love – not really.' James sounded gloomy. 'I'll have to break my heart – and suffer a bit into the bargain. Then I'll write my best stuff, or mebbe even paint a fine picture.'

'Your father would just think it a waste of time – and leave that bread alone!' She slapped his fingers from the warm loaves from the oven.

'My father'll be proud of me once I'm a well-known literary figure. And you can be my house-keeper, if you like.'

He went off to his duties in the warehouse, whistling cheerfully. Elizabeth finished the vegetables and began to roll out pastry, her mind on

James. She had no doubt that he would succeed as a poet. He was the gentlest of the family, but he had the Montgomery determination that dominated his father and brothers.

'What a place!' Adam threw the inner door open and erupted into the kitchen, scowling. 'I was just in the Coffee Rooms at the Cross, and one idiot with all his brains in his paunch had the impertinence to tell me that Paisley could never be affected by the cholera. An industrious, pious town, he called it. A God-fearing community protected from harm by Divine right!'

He hurled his big frame into a chair, and Elizabeth sighed inwardly as she realised that her peaceful afternoon was to be interrupted again.

'They only need to open their eyes and look around—' he ran his fingers through his hair. 'The streets are filthy, half the folk not fed properly, a fair number of them in rags – and the river's a sewer. D'you know what I heard of yesterday? Nine folk living in one room in George Street. No furniture, no blanket – scarcely any rags between them. How can they miss any disease that arrives, poor devils!'

Adam had a way of making Elizabeth feel that she should be able to improve the town single-handed. Scattering flour on the table, thumping the dough into a ball, she said defensively, 'But you've got to remember that to the Council and the gentry, there's no place in the world but Paisley. They'd never acknowledge its faults. I sometimes think that the Bailies believe that when the Lord himself dies he'll come to Paisley—'

She stopped, her own words ringing in her ears, and dropped the bowl of flour, clasping her hands to her scarlet face, horrified by her own blasphemy.

After an astonished look at her, as though he hadn't been able to believe his ears, Adam howled with mirth, deep genuine peals that rolled about her shamed head as she stood rooted to the spot, flour all down her apron and the bowl, still intact, rolling by her small feet. He laughed until he had to mop the tears from his cheeks, while Elizabeth scrabbled for the bowl and keened over the mess on the floor, half-convinced that she was going to be struck down by a bolt of lightning for her impudence.

'There's still hope for you, lassie – for all that you live in a mausoleum like this.' He wiped his eyes and took the bowl from her. 'God, Elizabeth, you're a certain cure for a sore heart!'

'Look at the floor!' Her voice shook and she turned away hastily, fumbling for the broom in the corner. Adam took it from her.

'You'll just make flour fly all over the place. Here – I'll see to it.'

She stood looking down on his dark head as he knelt and deftly blotted up the flour with a damp cloth. Then he straightened and began, gently, to brush the clinging powder from her clothes. His touch was light and efficient, but suddenly she realised that her skin was burning beneath the sturdy, plain material that separated it from Adam's fingers. Warmth rose to her face and she tried to pull away, confused and embarrassed. He caught her shoulders and made her stand still, his eyes intent as he worked. Then he looked at her face, and his own features crinkled into laughter again.

'Lassie, you're like a barber's pole with half your face white from flour and the other half red. Stand still, now—'

She closed her eyes as his finger-tips moved over her mouth. Then to her horror she felt two tears ease their way beneath her lowered lashes.

'Elizabeth?' His voice was warm, concerned. 'There's no need to take on like that over some spilled flour. The bowl's no' even broken.'

'It's not – it's—' How could she tell him what was wrong, when she didn't know herself? How could she explain that since he had arrived in the house she was no longer sure of herself or anyone else?

Adam, typical man, misunderstood. 'It's about what you said?' He folded her into his arms and for a precious moment she leaned against his shoulder, savouring the wonder of close contact with another human being, the hardness of his chest beneath her cheek, the strength of him, the rumble of his voice just above her head.

'Elizabeth, the words weren't spoken in malice. You'll have to learn that a quick wit's a blessing, no' a sin!'

Then, too soon, he was holding her at arm's length and laughing again, this time at the white smear her cheek had left on his green jacket.

The comfort of that embrace was stored away in her memory, together with the light kiss he had given her on the night of Matt's wedding. Adam, that abrasive, impatient, quick-tempered man, had somehow managed to show her that close contact with another person was sweet. He had set up a restlessness in her, a yearning that could bring her nothing but dissatisfaction; she had the sense to realise that. Perhaps one day she would find someone to fulfil the new need in her – in the meantime, she tried hard not to think of it.

Soup kitchens were set up, and she volunteered

her help in the kitchen near the Montgomery home, at Town-head. She was shocked to find how much need there was for charity in Paisley. Each day there was a long line of men, women and children waiting patiently, and Elizabeth grew to be ashamed of her own rounded face and clear, healthy skin as she served bowls of broth to people with grey faces and helpless, hopeless eyes. She began to realise why Adam was so bitter in his attacks on well-fleshed citizens.

In the second week of February a hawker living near the river fell ill and died of cholera the following day. A woman living nearby was next to know the dreaded symptoms. Then a warper fell sick – a carter – a flesher's assistant – another carter. All at once Paisley was under attack and panic raced through the streets.

Flaming tar barrels flickered eerily on house walls at night as they were carried through the streets to cleanse the air. The street cleaners fought to keep the gutters clear, but the familiar stench of rotting waste remained, now mingled with burning pitch. Suspect houses were white-washed, clothes fumigated, the bodies of cholera victims sprinkled with vinegar before burial. The Council decided that a large open stretch of land at the Moss, on the outskirts of Paisley, should be used for cholera burials.

Almost at the moment the disease struck Paisley the House of Commons was deliberating an Anatomy Bill which would, if carried, permit anatomists to use dead bodies. Reports of the Bill fuelled rumours that local doctors were allowing poor people to die of the disease so that they could dig the bodies up from the Moss and dissect them. Now and then mobs of terrified people prevented physicians from reaching patients, or stopped the funeral van on its way to the Moss. One woman was said to have paid some boys to dig up her sister's body as proof that the physicians hadn't substituted a coffin weighted with stones. Some three years earlier the notorious Burke and Hare case had electrified Edinburgh, and in Paisley suspicion and terror prowled the streets hand in hand.

'Fear gives folk strange notions,' Adam said wearily as he dragged himself from his bed after a few hours' sleep. 'They'd be better advised to think on what causes the sickness and how they can stop it.'

His face, in those terrible, hurried first days, was bleak and furrowed with new lines carved into the flesh. Elizabeth, scarred by her work in the soup-kitchen, could understand why he felt increasing bitterness towards those who had more than they needed and ignored the fact that others not a stone's throw away were in desperate straits.

'You're all lucky that they're too ignorant or too defeated to think of doing something about it,' he said one night when he and his father had been arguing over the supper table. 'Want can make a man dangerous. Look at France.'

Rab's mouth twisted. 'The time for that's long by. I should know – I was one of those who thought that if most of the people wanted reform, they'd get it. I was a hot-headed fool. What have I to show for it? A crippled leg, and the country no' much better, for all the fine talk in London.'

'It'll happen again. And the next time mebbe the workers'll be better led and more able.'

'You're havering!' Rab snapped, and Adam subsided, though there was a cynical look in his blue eyes.

Frost whitened the ground and set Jean crying over the pain of chilblains on her toes and fingers. Elizabeth was busy rubbing them with chalk dipped in vinegar one grey afternoon when Rab, who had come home early and settled himself in the parlour, crashed without warning into the kitchen and out again, on his way to the outside privy.

Jean screamed, startled, and knocked the bowl

of vinegar over. Mopping up the mess and scold-ing the girl, Elizabeth was aware of a trickle of ice down her spine. It wasn't like her employer to sit at home during daylight hours. He had refused food, and had chosen to huddle by the parlour fire, which was lit for him, with a bottle of brandy by his side.

He was gone for so long that she was almost out of her mind with worry by the time he came back into the house, his big red face now greyish and fallen in.

'Are you all right, Mister Montgomery?'

He glanced at her with bloodshot eyes. 'You mean, have I got the cholera?'

Jean whimpered, and he rounded on her. 'Hold your noise, girl! And you too—' he whirled back at Elizabeth, breathing hard. 'You know fine that the sickness wouldnae come to a house like this! It's only in the old part of the town they're visited by it!'

That wasn't true, and they all knew it. Cholera had already begun to poke an inquisitive finger into areas where cleanliness and comfort reigned. But neither Jean nor Elizabeth had the courage to say so.

Rab swung his lowered head from one girl to the other and Elizabeth was reminded of an old bull at bay. 'I've got a chilled stomach from standing talking too long in the street,' he said ponderously, then added, 'I'll away to my bed. You can bring a hot bottle and a basin – and more brandy!'

The door slammed behind him.

An hour later Elizabeth was really frightened. Rab was undeniably worse, though when she tried to question him about his symptoms he roared at her to get out of the room.

'No wonder I'm ill with the likes of you pestering me!' He clutched at the blankets and looked alarmingly small and insignificant in the big marriage bed. 'Out – and dinnae come back! I'll cure myself!'

She fled to the kitchen and drew a shawl about her shoulders.

'Jean, I'll have to go to the hospital to fetch Adam.'

The girl's normally blank face was ashen and filled with fear. 'Is it—?'

'Of course not!' Elizabeth managed to put conviction into her voice. 'It's a chill, as he says. But he's getting old, and it's best to let Adam deal with him. Now – keep an eye on that soup pot and see to the potatoes. I'll be back soon.'

Cold air stung her face as she ran, slipping on frosty stones, to the cholera hospital at Oakshaw. It was an uphill journey and her breathing tore at her throat by the time she got there. The ambulance wagon was rattling and bumping away from the door when she arrived, and there was a constant stream of people passing in and out of the hospital.

She had never been inside before. There was a chilly ante-room, where a few people stood talking softly, some weeping. The place smelled of vinegar and turpentine and spirits of camphor, all used to fumigate the town. There was nobody who could direct her, so Elizabeth went on through the double doors and found herself in a huge room packed with beds.

The smell of death and disease was new to her. So was the noise – a continual chorus, strangely muted, of moans and harsh breathing and sobs, with now and then a voice suddenly lifted in delirium or anguish. A group of men stood talking near the door, and she saw to her relief that one of them was Adam.

As though her look had disturbed him he glanced at her absently and turned away. Then his head was raised sharply and he looked at her again. With a swift word to the others he made his way among the beds to get to her.

'What do you think you're doing here!' Without waiting for an answer he seized her arm and ran her from the ward into the ante-chamber. She had only time to glimpse one blue, skeletal face on a grey pillow as she was hurried past. A brief glimpse, but one that she would never forget. The eyes were sunken and the mouth hung open. She had heard Asiatic cholera described as the blue cholera. Now she knew why.

Mercifully, she wasn't given time to dwell on what she had seen. Adam stopped, swung her to face him, his eyes blazing down at her.

'You've got no right to be here! You could catch the sickness just by being in here, d'you no' realise that?'

'It's your father!' she almost shouted at him, and the blood drained from his tired face.

'God help us! Wait here, I'll be back.'

She waited, watching the flow of relatives, physicians, ministers and priests. She turned away when a patient was brought in, arms and legs lolling. A young woman, screaming and cursing, her face wet with tears, clutched at the sick man and had to be pulled away. Elizabeth swallowed hard as the ward doors closed behind the small party. She hadn't realised that people like Adam spent hour after hour in such a place. Even her vivid imagination hadn't prepared her for this brief sight of reality.

He re-appeared and hurried her out of the hospital into fresh air, dragging her after him so fast that her feet stumbled over the rough footpath and she had to clutch at him to remain upright. As they went he shot out questions and she managed to find the breath to answer.

'And did you manage to give him anything?' he asked as they finally reached the house.

'Thirty drops of laudanum in brandy and water, as you told me.'

'That's good.' They went into the hall and his hand rested briefly on her shoulder before he raced upstairs. She leaned on the newel post at the foot of the stairs to regain her breath and calm the trembling in her knees. It was a full minute before she realised that the house smelled of burning food.

The soup pot was still on the fire, black and sticky. Jean had disappeared. Almost in tears, Elizabeth peeled the potatoes and began to clean the burned pot.

She was still working at it, attacking it viciously and wishing that it was Jean she had between her hands, when James arrived home.

His cheerful smile died when she told him about his father and he was on his way upstairs before she had finished speaking. He came back a few minutes later and dropped into a chair at the kitchen table, staring at the scrubbed, grained surface intently.

'Adam says there's nothing I can do. I felt so useless and helpless, standing there. The old man looks – he looks as if he's dying—' His voice trembled.

'He probably looks a lot worse than he is,' she said, as much for herself as for him. 'James, the dinner's wasted, but if you wait a half hour I'll have something ready for you.'

He shook his head. 'I couldnae eat a thing.' One finger went out to trace a crack in the table. His head was still lowered. 'It's funny – I've miscalled him so often, and now I wish I'd cut my tongue out instead. Ever since Adam came back I've been thinking and talking of moving to London. I've never given my father a thought. I never realised that with Matt away, he needs me.' He attempted a shaky laugh, and failed. 'This is a fine time to start feeling guilty – when the man might be at death's door—'

The words shot up a few notes and he stopped abruptly, covering his eyes with his hand.

'James—' She went over to him and he rested his head on her shoulder with a natural movement, his arms going about her.

'I've been selfish. I'll promise you this, Elizabeth

– if he gets better, if he escapes the cholera, I'll stay and I'll work in the warehouse for as long as he needs me! And I'll never complain about my life again!'

'You're over quick to go promising your youth away for his sake,' Adam said dryly from the door, where he stood surveying them.

They jumped apart like guilty lovers. 'Is he—?' There were tears in James's eyes, and he made no effort to hide them.

'He's ill – but I've no way of knowing yet just what's wrong with him.'

'What about Matt?' Elizabeth suddenly remembered. Adam gave her a swift glance.

'If the man upstairs has the cholera, then for Isobel's sake as well as his own Matt should stay away. If he hasnae got the cholera, there's no sense in frightening Matt. We can fetch him later, if we need him. James, I thought you were going off to some literary meeting?'

'I'll stay here, just in case he wants me.'

Adam lifted an eyebrow. 'He's never wanted any of us much in the past, and he's no' likely to begin now, for all that he thinks he's on his death bed. You're too soft with him, waiting about here for news.'

James looked at his brother challengingly

through a curtain of tears. 'Haven't you got a theatre appointment yourself?'

Adam's brows came down and his gaze, for once, faltered before his brother's. 'Aye – well, I'm a physician. We're noted for our stupidity,' he said gruffly. 'Elizabeth, do you think you could have some food on that table within the hour? I'm starved.'

When he re-appeared he threw the meal down his throat without seeming to notice what he was eating, then disappeared upstairs again. Elizabeth and James kept each other company, scarcely speaking, and listening intently for sound from above, until late at night Adam reappeared, looking exhausted.

'I think the old fool's right – it's a chill and mebbe something he ate as well,' he announced. A radiant smile broke over James's face.

'By God – we might have known that the cholera wouldn't dare to set foot in Rab Montgomery's house!' he whooped, and threw his arms around Elizabeth, lifting her off her feet and whirling her round. Adam watched unsmilingly.

'I'll sit with him for a wee while—' Elizabeth offered hurriedly when James released her.

'No, I'll do it, Adam.'

'I'll do it myself, just to make sure that he's all

right. I'll call the two of you if I need you. Where's the lassie?'

'She's gone, and I've no notion where.'

'She's probably taken to her heels at the first thought of the cholera in the house.' He locked the back door. 'She'll no' be back tonight. Get to bed, the pair of you.'

They went, obedient as two well-behaved children. As she went upstairs Elizabeth heard the bolts being shot on the front door. Brushing out her hair, staring solemnly into her own mirrored eyes, she felt a sense of security. Adam was under the same roof, and nothing could go wrong. She yawned, and the glass reflected a pink tongue, small white teeth, a face pretty in its contentment, framed by thick brown curls of shining hair.

Adam was eating bread and butter in the kitchen when she went downstairs in the morning. He had changed his clothes, and looked rested. He had lit the fire and the kettle was steaming softly.

'He's well,' he assured her before she could speak. 'He had a chill that might have carried off a weaker man, but he'll be fine after a day in bed. You're going to have trouble getting him to keep off the drink and eat the right food.' He grinned. 'I don't envy you. Make me a decent meal before I get back to the hospital.'

He sat down to breakfast with enthusiasm, after making sure that his father was still sleeping.

'I chapped James's door on my way down. He'll have to get to the warehouse soon if he's going to take over from the old man.' He attacked a huge bowl of porridge, well salted and awash with milk. 'It's all right for laddies like him, lying abed till all hours. Away and tell him I'll be up with a stoup of cold water if he's no' down by the time I finish this.'

Smiling, Elizabeth went upstairs. James was well known for his dislike of early rising. She tapped on the door, then opened it slightly and put her head round it.

'If you don't get up now Adam's going to—' The words died on her lips. In the glow of the lamp she carried James looked ghastly as he struggled to sit up in bed. The sheets were tangled about him, the pillow on the floor, and his eyes were large and bright in a waxen face that was only a poor copy of the James that she knew.

'Elizabeth—' his voice was a harsh whisper. 'I'm – I'm feared I'm no' very well this morning—' said James, and fell back, his body suddenly convulsed in a spasm that made the whole bed rattle on the floor.

Clutching the lamp in numbed fingers and

remembering, even in her panic, that she mustn't waken her employer, Elizabeth flew downstairs, her feet skimming the treads. She didn't have to speak when she opened the kitchen door. Adam looked up, smiling – then the spoonful of porridge on its way to his mouth dropped back onto the plate and he pushed past her, out of the room while his chair was still rolling about the floor.

There was no doubt at all about what was wrong with James. Elizabeth, back in the bedroom and holding the lamp for Adam, could tell by the flat hardness of his eyes that he held out little hope for his young brother.

He worked swiftly, efficiently, giving crisp orders to Elizabeth, who followed them without stopping to think. She brought cans of hot water, emptied pails, soaked strips of flannel in warm water and helped to wrap them about James's limbs, now racked by cramps.

'You shouldnae be here,' Adam said once, suddenly noticing her as their hands met across the bed. 'You could catch it yourself.'

'I'll be fine,' she rapped back, then straightening to push a lock of hair from her damp forehead with the back of her wrist she remembered the other invalid. 'What about your father?'

'I forgot about him.' Adam massaged his

brother's hands, his gaze fixed on the sick man's face. 'You'll have to see to him – get word to Christian to come and look after him. And let Mister Stewart know about this. James is his patient when all's said and done.'

'Will I tell your father about James?'

'Tell him the truth – there's no sense in molly-coddling the man!' he suddenly flared irritably, and she fled.

Rab was still asleep, and looking a little better. Elizabeth found a passing youngster willing to carry messages, and Christian and the doctor were there before Rab woke.

Christian demanded to see James, but Adam refused to let her go upstairs.

'There's enough of us in danger,' he said from the top landing, his shirt rumpled and his big hands hanging helplessly by his sides for the moment. 'You'd be of more use if you'd take my father off to your own house and leave us in peace.'

'What about Matt? Have you thought to tell him?'

Adam rubbed a hand over his face. 'Mebbe you could see to that too, Christian. But tell him to keep away – he's got enough to worry him without taking sick and passing it to Isobel.'

'He'll want to see his brother!' she objected, and his eyes sparked blue fire at her.

'Damn it, woman, James isn't wasting away prettily of some easy condition! I doubt if Matt would want to see what the cholera's made of the laddie. And you can tell him that if he sets foot over this front door before I send for him I'll throw him back out myself!'

'Well!' squawked Christian in outrage, and flounced into the parlour.

'You'd no cause to speak to her like that!' Elizabeth said hotly, halfway up the stairs. He rounded on her and she stood her ground. 'She's only trying to think of the right thing to do.'

The heat went out of his eyes. 'Mebbe. But she has no idea what's happening up there.' He jerked his head in the direction of his brother's room. 'You should go off to Christian's house too. You'd be safe there.'

His shoulders lifted in a slight shrug when she shook her head. 'It's your own choice. Best see to the old man, then,' he said, and went back into the room where Allan Stewart, the family physician, watched over James.

Elizabeth thought at first that Rab was going to collapse when he heard the news. He stared at her, his face reverting back to the grey sheen it had had the day before. Then he swore and tried to push past her to the door, still in nightshirt and bare feet.

'Adam says you cannae go in, Mister Montgomery—' She caught at his arm and he threw her off, roaring:

'You'll no' tell me what to do in my own house, you slut! You'll take orders from me alone, or you'll go back to the poors' house you came from!'

'Hold your tongue!' an icy voice interrupted him. Adam, eyes wild in a stony face, filled the doorway. 'D'you no' think the lad's got enough trouble without you screaming all over the house?'

Rab's grey hair was standing up in stiff peaks and his cheek-bones burned like red lamps, incongruous against the pallor about them. 'Take James to the hospital – now!'

Adam's chin came up and he spread his arms, putting a hand on each side of the door-frame and physically blocking his father's way. 'He'll stay here. I'll no' allow anyone to take him to that place if I can help it. I can tend him myself.'

'Damn you for a wooden-headed idiot – will you do as I tell you!' Rab roared, trying to force his son aside. But he was weak from his own illness, and Adam was determined. He stayed where he was and Rab, after a futile, humiliating struggle to move him, had to fall back, coughing and gasping with weakness and rage.

'You're a manufacturer, father, no' a medical man. You didnae like it when I tried to tell you who you should employ.' There was open contempt in Adam's eyes. 'Now you can keep your nose out of my business.'

'You—' Rab's voice broke. To her horror Elizabeth saw tears glisten on his cheeks. Adam was unmoved.

'Get dressed, and get yourself out of here. Christian's waiting for you, and you're only a hindrance to me,' he said curtly. 'You're sick and you're raving, and you're too damned old and pig-headed to be of use at a time like this.'

A finger jabbed him in the back, and he jumped, startled, and stepped aside. Christian Selbie swept into the room and went to Rab, her arms going around him much as Elizabeth's had gone around James a few hours earlier.

'Rab – you're no' well, and you're upset.' Her voice was surprisingly gentle. 'Put some warm clothes on, and you and me'll drive up to Oakshawhill – leave the physicians to see to James.'

He turned away, head down, and fumbled for the clothes over the back of a chair. His shoulders shook, and he moved like a very old man. Christian pushed Adam and Elizabeth out of the room and closed the door. Her faded blue eyes were sharp and hard as she looked up at her young cousin.

'If you're going to tell me I should have stayed down below, save your breath,' she snapped. 'Rab needs someone of his own generation with him now. I'll wait here until he comes out, then I'll take him away. And I'll tell you this, Adam Montgomery,' she added, the ribbons on her bonnet trembling with anger. 'You're a hard-tongued, merciless man. May God forgive you for talking like that to your own father!'

A curious blankness came over his eyes. The anger disappeared, and all at once looking at him was like looking into windows made of dark blue glass that reflected what they saw, and showed nothing of what was on the other side.

'If you saw James now, you'd know that God's forgiveness doesn't exist,' he said, his voice flat, and turned away.

Christian sighed as the door of James's room opened just wide enough to admit Adam, then closed.

'What's happening to this family?' She looked years older now that the anger was gone. 'Is James bad, Elizabeth?'

'Aye.'

Christian blinked fast. 'Adam's wrong – there is a God, but at times I find him a difficult sort of creature to follow. You'll send word if anything—'

Her voice faltered. 'Aye, I will. You'll mind that Mister Montgomery should just eat mild foods today, and keep away from spirits?'

'I'll take good care of him. You've got a generous heart, lassie.' Her hand patted Elizabeth's cheek. 'You'd need it – to take on James and Adam at the moment. I'm glad Adam's got you by his side. He mebbe seems strong, but the strongest men are the very ones who need someone when the bad times arrive.'

Mister Stewart agreed with Adam. James was as well in his own home, and there was nothing more to be done apart from the treatment Adam was giving. Adam steadfastly refused to try cold baths, blistering, or bleeding.

'He's suffering enough, and I know they do little to help. I'd as soon try to keep him comfortable, if I can.' He looked down at the figure on the bed, and the older man picked up his bag.

'I've got my own doubts about those fancy cures. You'll call me if I'm needed?'

After that they were alone, the three of them – and the cholera. Elizabeth found herself thinking of the disease as a being, an entity that occupied its own space as surely as she occupied hers. It was a personal enemy, and it had chosen James as its battlefield.

They watched over him throughout the day. Life was an island, with only the three of them on it; but James scarcely counted as a person now. He had gone, leaving a small, shrunken, old effigy of himself in his narrow bed.

Going into the parlour to get more brandy at some time in the day Elizabeth glanced from the window at the unreal life outside the house, and saw Matt. He stood huddled against a doorway opposite, trying to keep out of the wind, waiting.

She went to the front door, moving quietly so that Adam didn't hear her. Matt hurried across the street, skipping in front of a cart-horse. His face was blue-red with cold, his teeth chattering: he could hardly speak.

'Is it bad?'

'Adam says it is.'

'Can I no' see him?' he begged.

'You could catch it yourself, or infect Isobel. Adam's right, you have to keep away.'

For a moment she thought he was going to push her aside and force his way into the house.

'Think about Isobel, and the bairn, Matt. Think what you might take home to them!'

He stopped with one hand on the door, then nodded and turned away. At the last moment she saw the tears welling into his eyes. He went back across the road, moving slowly and stiffly, and she closed the door.

As the afternoon drew on James quietened and seemed to become easier. Adam had at last agreed to snatch a few hours' rest, and Elizabeth watched alone over the invalid, noting that the cramps had gone, and his moaning breath was calmer.

She began to hope for a recovery, but when Adam came back into the room he took one look at his brother and shook his head.

'It's just the next stage. His body's collapsed. At least he doesnae feel anything now.'

'He can still get better?'

He gave her the ghost of a smile. 'Poor Elizabeth. He's as good as dead now.'

She got up, fists clenched, ready to fight tooth and nail for James's life.

'How can you know?' she hissed at him, and he lifted his shoulders again in that faint, tired shrug.

'I've seen it more than once. D'you think I haven't hoped for a miracle, just like you? But I've learned that it won't happen.' He stood by the bed, looking down at his brother's still figure. 'My own fiancée died just like this. That's when I learned that hoping's for fools.'

'Adam—' Her immediate reaction was one of sympathy. She reached out a hand towards him, then drew it back as his face hardened and his eyes narrowed.

'I've no time for sympathy! Folk die, and that's all there is to it!' His voice was a barrier, shutting her out. 'Go to your bed, Elizabeth, it's late, and there's no sense in us both being tired. I'll give you a shout if I need you.'

Rejected, she went to the door. Working together, fighting for his brother's life, they had been drawn together. Now, they were strangers again.

'You'd best sleep in my room—' he ordered as she was going out. 'Then you'll be close at hand.'

She fetched her night clothes, and lay awake in the strange room before sleep rolled in like a black cloud and enveloped her.

She awoke in a fright. The room was lit by a lamp and someone was standing by the bed, looking down at her. With a whimper of fear she sat up, and a hand touched her shoulder.

'It's all right, Elizabeth – it's me.'

She remembered, and pushed the bedclothes

aside, sweeping her long silky hair free of her face, ignoring the fact that she wore only her night-shift. 'Is he worse—?'

He sat on the bed. 'It's all right, lass, there's no more you can do for him.'

She sat still, one hand still smoothing a curl, unable to understand him. Realisation came slowly, probably because she didn't want it to be true. James was a poet, an artist. He deserved something better than an early, terrible ending.

'Can – can I see him?'

Adam's mouth twisted briefly. 'He's gone. I had to send for the funeral cart at once. The rest of them can be told in the morning. I—' He hesitated, then went on, 'I don't want anyone to know just yet.'

'But you cannae just let him—'

'Do you not understand, woman? Folk who die of the cholera have to be buried as soon as possible. There's no time for moping over a bonny-looking corpse!'

He was right, and she was being stupid, she realised that as the last traces of sleep left her mind. She must be practical.

'I'll get his room scrubbed out—' The floor was cold beneath her bare feet.

'In the morning.' His voice was drained of emotion. 'I cannae face any more – I'll have to sleep.'

She could see that he was almost at the end of his strength, emotionally and physically. 'I'll go to my room, and waken you in the morning.'

'Aye.'

At the door she paused. He was still sitting on the bed, his head sunk between his shoulders. His hands, she realised, trembled slightly. She spoke his name softly, afraid to leave him like that, but afraid, too, of provoking one of his outbursts.

He looked up at her, his eyes dark and blank again. His lips parted, just enough to let the words squeeze out, as though against his own inclination.

'Don't – don't leave me on my lone.'

She put the lamp down and went to him, smoothing the tangled black hair back from his brow. His face was cold and clammy with sweat as it was lifted to her. He closed his eyes, put his arms about her, and held her as though afraid that he would be lost forever if he let go.

The early morning street sounds, louder on this floor than they were in the attic, woke her before dawn. She and Adam were clasped closely together on his narrow bed, and her limbs were stiff and cramped.

He was still deeply asleep, and didn't waken when she eased herself slowly and gently from his grip. She rubbed her sore shoulders as she stood looking down on him.

He stirred, mumbled something, threw an arm out so that his fingers touched the floor, but didn't wake. He was still fully dressed. They hadn't spoken after she went into his arms. They hadn't even kissed, she remembered with vague surprise. They had lain on the bed together, Adam's embrace painfully tight, his face pressed into her hair, and they had stayed like that while the trembling in his hands transmitted itself to his whole body, shaking as though he was in the grip of a fever.

Then, slowly, it had eased, his body had relaxed, though his arms retained their hold, and she had been able to tell by his regular breathing that he was asleep.

Soon she would have to waken him. But not just yet. For one thing, she wanted to be respectably dressed, her loose hair brushed and tucked beneath her cap, before she faced him again.

Elizabeth went noiselessly from the room towards her attic, passing the closed door of the room where James Montgomery had once dreamed of a future in London.

VII

Elizabeth could find no tears for James. The horror of his final hours seemed to dry her eyes and polish them into hot stones in her head.

She drew down the blinds in every window but Adam's, muffled the door knocker with black cloth, and went back indoors, ignoring the inquisitive stares and whispers of the few early passers-by.

It was only after she had set the table for the morning meal that she realised that there were four places, one for Rab, one for each of his sons.

She was staring stupidly at the cutlery when someone began to pound on the front door. Shocked at such an intrusion on a house of death she hurried to answer.

Matt crashed into the hall, white-faced. 'Is it true what they say? Let me by, Elizabeth, let me see him—'

He pushed her aside and was halfway up the stairs when Adam appeared on the landing. He had brushed his hair and changed into a black coat and dark red trousers.

'There's nothing to see. He's gone to the Moss.'

The cool, clipped tones stopped Matt's headlong rush. He stared up at his brother, then began to retreat down the stairs, step by step, as Adam advanced.

'You should have sent for me! You should have let me be there at the last!'

'For what?' Adam asked with frightening control. He didn't glance at Elizabeth. 'So that you could have talked with him? He wouldnae have heard you. So that you could have seen him? Best remember the way he was. As for self-pity – I'd enough to do caring for James without having a handful of mourners weeping over the living corpse.'

'Where are you going?' Elizabeth asked sharply. He turned, one hand on the door. His eyes were withdrawn, surveying her as they would a stranger.

'To the hospital. There are living folk still waiting for help. You'd best get back to your wife, Matt, instead of grieving round here.'

'Damn you for a cold-blooded—'

'Matt – no—!' Elizabeth tried to catch his arm as he moved swiftly past her, murder in his eyes. He brushed her off, and made for his brother.

Adam side-stepped, ducked, and suddenly Matt was held in an iron grip, cursing furiously as he struggled to free himself.

'You learn all sorts of things on board one of His Majesty's ships,' Adam said breathlessly. He let his brother go, stepped back. Matt stood where he was for a moment, then his hands came up to cover his face.

Elizabeth moved towards him, but Adam stopped her.

'Come on, Matt,' he said, putting one hand on his brother's shoulder and opening the front door with the other. 'We'll walk to Shuttle Street and see Isobel. There are a lot of ways to mourn, you'll learn that in time.'

The door closed behind them, and Elizabeth was glad to be alone as her tears at last began to flow.

With three and four deaths in the town each day from cholera alone, grief was a luxury few families could afford. James had gone, Elizabeth still had to run a house, Adam was busy in the hospital; Rab, grey and sullen when he came back from Christian's, had even more to occupy him at the warehouse, now that he had no sons to share the burden. Routine claimed them all with shocking speed.

Nobody else in the household came down with cholera, but even so Jean refused to return to the Montgomery kitchen. Tibby, the shrew who had assisted Elizabeth on the night of Adam's return, was taken on in her place.

Her triumph was short-lived. Her habit of always being underfoot when she wasn't wanted infuriated Rab.

'I'd like to walk out of a room in my own house without falling over that besom,' he snarled at Elizabeth. 'Mebbe we've got the best polished keyholes in the town since she came here, but keyholes are meant for keys, no' for eyes!'

Elizabeth was glad to oust Tibby. The woman was meddlesome and sour-tongued, and the kitchen buzzed like a bee-hive when she was in it.

It was decided that Elizabeth should choose a girl from the Town Hospital to be trained into the ways of the household. To her relief, Christian agreed to go with her on her errand.

'See and pick a lassie who'll handle the work and keep her opinions to herself,' the older woman advised as the carriage rolled to a halt before the building.

As she stepped into the gloomy entrance hall,

onto the floor she had scrubbed many a time, Elizabeth felt the years falling away. It was a surprise to be greeted with a smile by Mistress Jamieson, instead of being scolded for some misdemeanour. Her past crimes were apparently quite forgotten and she was treated with almost as much deference as Christian, who took charge of the situation.

'An able-bodied lassie, one who knows her Catechism and can keep a still tongue in her head,' she said briskly, as though buying sausages in a butcher's shop.

Her brows rose when Elizabeth opted for a thin, shy girl called Mary.

'There's no' a pick on the lassie!' She eyed the girl's skinny arms.

'She'll manage. And she doesnae need to know her Catechism to know how to bake a good pie,' Elizabeth said firmly, and saw Mistress Jamieson's nostrils flare slightly at her impudence. Christian laughed.

'Well – if you're certain, that's all there is to say. It's your kitchen.'

Elizabeth was certain. There was something about Mary that reminded her of herself on that day Rachel Montgomery had rescued her. Now it was her turn to rescue Mary. She owed somebody something for her good fortune, she thought in a confused way, aware of the envious glances the inmates gave her good blue gown and red-bordered shawl.

Mary arrived the following day, complete with Bible and change of clothing, and Elizabeth set about training her, glad to have a companion now that Rab and Adam were rarely at home.

Cholera still held the town in its grip, and seemed likely to stay for many months. The smell of burning tar barrels was everywhere and not a day went by without the cholera bier being trundled at least once to the Moss for a hurried burial.

Rab, bereft of his two sons, was in sole charge of the warehouse, and had to work long hours. He took to eating his meals in the Coffee House near the river, and when he was in the house every room seemed to be filled with shadows.

Hutcheson's Charity School, where Elizabeth had received her education, had been turned into a cholera hospital, and work was underway on a new hospital in Bridge Street, near to the Dispensary and House of Recovery. Adam was out almost all the time too, and he became obsessed by the need to find out what caused cholera, and how to cure and prevent it.

His training as a physician and as a naval surgeon gave him the right to make up prescriptions, and he began to set up a small laboratory in his bedroom where he could work. He had no time for the pious belief that cholera was sent from Heaven to chastise those who had fallen from grace.

'Nobody's going to tell me that folk like James deserved a punishment like that,' he said, and filled his small rooms with bottles and flasks, jars and packets. Elizabeth and Mary were forbidden access to the room, and they were happy to obey orders. Elizabeth was convinced that he would either burn down the house or poison them all with the strange-smelling, bubbling liquids she sometimes glimpsed over his shoulder if she took food to him. He worked most of the day and then came home and worked far into the night.

He had nothing but mocking scorn for the fast days held throughout the country because of the cholera.

'It would make more sense to give the folk bread, not hunger. It's all very well for the King and those with fat bellies to make a display of fasting to appease the Almighty. They want to think of those who have to do that day in and day out. And what reward do those poor devils get? They die of the cholera,' he said sourly, and was accused by his father of forgetting his Christian upbringing.

James's death seemed to have forced Adam and Rab apart, instead of drawing them together. Elizabeth, a silent, concerned observer, knew that there were times when Adam, exhausted and embittered as he was by the sights he had to endure each day, made an attempt to behave well towards his father; but each time, he was rebuffed.

'Confound the old fool!' he exploded to Elizabeth after Rab had stormed out of the room on one occasion. 'If he wants my civility from now on, let him crawl for it – I've more to do than wonder what's up with him!'

Two weeks after James was laid beneath the cold earth at the Moss Elizabeth was shocked to see his name on a small bundle delivered by the letter-carrier. She stood in the hall staring at the familiar words written in flowing black letters. Tears suddenly stung at the back of her eyes.

Rab was eating his breakfast in the kitchen. She knew that the parcel should be given to him along with his own letters. But as she crossed the hall she thrust it into the pocket of her apron. All morning it lay heavily against her thigh, then Adam came home at noon to write some letters, and she handed it to him.

His mouth tightened as he stared down at his

dead brother's name. 'Should you no' have given this to my father?'

'I couldnae bring myself to do it.'

He shot a swift glance at her. 'You're over thoughtful about hurting his feelings,' he said dryly. 'Wait—' as she turned to the door. She watched as he slit the packet open. It contained a bundle of papers tied with tape, and a letter, which Adam scanned hurriedly.

'It's from that London man. He's returned James's poems. He says they're well written, pleasing, but not quite what's needed.' His mouth grimaced into a mirthless smile as he balanced the bundle of poems on the palm of one large hand. 'The man says he hopes James'll continue to write, and send some of his more mature work one day.'

'He'd have been awful disappointed,' she said without thinking. 'Are you going to give them to your father?'

In answer he bent suddenly and picked up the poker. Before she could stop him he had thrown the bundle into the parlour fire and was holding it down firmly. Even as Elizabeth caught his arm and was shrugged off the paper burst into flames.

'Adam – no!' It was a cry from the heart, unheeded. She watched, horrified, as the sheets curled and peeled away from each other, the tape burned through, and the poems that had taken hours to write disappeared in seconds, turned to ash.

'They belonged to James – you should have kept them!' She could have flown at Adam in her anger.

He dropped the poker and kicked the coals with the toe of his sturdy leather boot. They collapsed inward, covering the last fragments of his brother's work.

'Kept them? For what? Until they turned yellow and old? Who would read them? He had to keep them secret from my father, and poems are wasted on the likes of Matt and me,' he said savagely, his face turned away from her as he stared down at the fire. 'I'll remember James in my own way. I'd as soon destroy the sickness that killed him as sit in comfort and read pretty words!'

On the following day she got back from the market to find him at home, in the room James and Matthew had shared. She stood in the hall, gaping through the door that had not been opened since James's death. 'Adam Montgomery, what do you think you're doing?'

He straightened from the task of pulling the two cots to the back of the room and grinned at her, brushing dust from his hands.

'I'm clearing the place. Fetch a pail and brush, the floor needs scrubbing.'

'But—' She went into the room and watched, open-mouthed, as he began to clear the top of the chest of drawers, stacking books onto the beds.

'I need more room for my laboratory work,' he explained patiently, as though speaking to a child. 'And I need a clean room. There's too much stour in here. Get me some hot water.'

'Did your father say you could do this?'

He gave her a look of sheer exasperation. 'Elizabeth, this room isnae used, so why should he object? And I'll see to him,' he added as she opened her mouth to protest. 'Go and get that pail and brush when you're told, woman!'

It was the voice that reminded her that she was, after all, a servant, and he was her employer's son. Humiliated, frustrated, she did as she was told. For the rest of the afternoon the two of them scrubbed and cleaned until he was satisfied the room was fit to use. Then she began to help him to bring in his glass tubes and bottles, gingerly handling the scientific equipment.

Intent on their work, neither of them even knew Rab had arrived home until he spoke from the doorway.

'What the blazes do you two think you're up to?'

Elizabeth jumped, almost dropping the flask in her hands. Adam took it from her, unmoved by his father's sudden appearance.

'I need more room to set up my laboratory.'

Rab's face set in mulish lines. 'You've already got a room in this house. Be content with that.'

'It's more like a cupboard.'

'If you're no' taken with the accommodation I give you—' Rab began ominously. Elizabeth edged towards the door, but he stood there, unmoving, blocking her way.

Adam's voice was quite easy. 'My own room's fine – for sleeping in. But I need more space for the work I'm doing, and this place is empty. It might as well be put to good use.'

Rab's eyes moved about the room. 'This is my sons' bedroom, no' a laboratory.'

Adam's face flamed, then paled. 'Neither Matt nor James has use for it as a bedroom now.'

Rab's nostrils flared and his cheeks took on a deeper shade of red. 'Well now, Elizabeth—' His eyes fixed on her. 'And you agree with my son here?'

She stared at him, unable to speak. Adam said swiftly, 'I ordered Elizabeth to help me, this has nothing to do with her. You've surely got no objection to me using the place?'

To Elizabeth's relief, her employer's gaze slid from her, back to the surgeon. 'Why not? When the fox digs himself a lair he should be allowed to lie in it, eh?' His voice, soft to start with, ended on a snarl.

'You're speaking in riddles.'

'So – the clever surgeon cannae figure out what I mean? I mean, sir, that you're the one that cleared this room. Matt was contented enough here until you came back with your high ideas. You're the one that encouraged him to go off and marry that lassie. You're the one – and you neednae deny it, for I've got informers all over this town – that got Dan McGill out of the jail and back at his loom. And you're the one—' his voice suddenly shot up, out of control, '—that let my son James die!'

Elizabeth heard herself cry out, but neither of the men looked in her direction. Adam's eyes, sapphires set in white marble, flared wide then narrowed to become blue slits. He spoke through tight, colourless lips.

'You old fool – you're insane!'

'Am I, by God!' Rab lashed out. His stubby fingers closed round the neck of a flask, and he threw it at Adam, swinging blindly so that the missile went nowhere near its target. Instead it hit the wall near Elizabeth, exploding into greenish fragments with a noise that tore through her head. As it struck, Adam's arm flew out, caught her, and swept her across the front of his body to safety, away from the tinkling shards of glass. She was tossed onto one of the beds where she stayed, watching as Rab advanced on his son, one forefinger stabbing the air before him.

'I told you, did I no'? I told you to take that laddie to the hospital when he fell sick. But you saw fit to defy me, the way you've always defied me!'

There was anger, now, in Adam's voice. 'He would have died just the same! And he would have died in the noise and the misery of the place instead of in his own home. You'd have done that to him? You'd have condemned him to a place you've never seen? You don't know what you're talking about!'

Foam flecked the corners of Rab's mouth. His rage filled the room, threatened to burst the walls. Elizabeth, huddled on the bed, could scarcely breathe because the very air was charged with fury.

'Some recovered after they were taken to the hospital. James could have been one of them, if you'd given him the chance!'

'Aye, some recover – but most die, and we've no

way of knowing why. That's why I want to get on with my work!'

Rab's laugh was a weird cackle. 'It's a bit late for that, is it no'? Your brother died of your so-called healing. And now you want to use his room, to try to save the rag-tag out in the streets? D'ye think I give a damn what becomes of them? It's James you should have saved – James! No' these swilling, carousing scum from the gutters!'

There was a moment's silence before Adam spoke. 'So – that's the truth of it, out at last.' He sat down on the other bed, ran his hands over his face. 'That's why you've never been able to look me in the eyes those past two weeks. You thought I'd let my own brother die. All this time, you've let your suspicions fester in you, poison you. Man, you're in sore need of healing yourself.'

Rab's eyes bulged. 'Aye, it's out. You killed him as sure as Cain killed Abel, and I curse you for it, Adam Montgomery. I curse the day you first drew breath!'

'But nobody could have saved James!' Adam said in a sing-song voice, as though to din the fact into a child. 'He had the worst form of the sickness. Nobody's survived it.'

'What gave you the right to decide that while there was still breath in his body?'

Elizabeth saw that there were tears in the old man's eyes. Rab, who had never shown any warmth towards his youngest son in the time she had spent in the house, was totally bereft by his death. If only, she thought drearily, James had been given an indication of that love when he was alive.

'I know fine what I'm talking about.' There was fire in Adam's voice. 'I've seen other people taking the path James took. That's what happened to Caroline.'

If he had hoped for pity, he was disappointed. Rab fixed on the name, used it to punish his son further.

'My, my, Adam, mebbe you're in the wrong profession after all. First your bride, then your brother – you've been letting the folk you love die like fleas, while you—'

The words became a gurgle. Adam surged up from the bed to grip his father by the lapels and lift him, heavy as he was, onto his toes. He shook Rab like a rat, then released him with a contemptuous push. Rab, choking, reeled back as Elizabeth scrambled to her feet.

'Damn you—' said Adam thickly, and swept a box of glass bottles off a nearby table with a wide swing of one arm. The crash echoed through the room and left behind it a tense silence, broken only by Rab's efforts to catch his breath again.

When he did, he ordered, 'Elizabeth – clear up this mess and lock this door!'

'Father—' Adam's clear voice halted him on his way out. 'You think James could have been saved? You didnae see him, towards the end. Tell him, Elizabeth, what it was like.'

'Adam – let it be!' She caught at his sleeve, shaking his arm, but his blue gaze raked her mercilessly before returning to his father.

'Since he's got his own opinions he should know more about it. You'd as soon hide away from the truth about sickness, wouldn't you, father? You know nothing of the cramps, and the convulsions, and the pain that's like a sword being drawn through the body – handle and all—'

Rab's turkey-red face took on a grey tinge. He went into the hall, and Adam, ignoring Elizabeth's tugging at his sleeve, followed him. The surgeon's voice went on mercilessly describing the illness in detail, as Rab went down the stairs to the hall clumsily, catching at the banisters and tripping over the bottom step. Adam stayed at the top of the steps, raising his voice to make sure that his father heard every word. He didn't stop until the front door slammed shut behind Rab.

Then, with the bang of the door, the clear voice was cut short and he stood still, knuckles clenching the wooden rail, head lowered as though his strength had suddenly given out.

Below, Elizabeth heard the kitchen door open and Mary's frightened voice calling her name. She ran down to reassure the child and set her to work on the evening meal that would probably not be required.

Adam wasn't on the stairs when she ventured out of the kitchen. She went into the parlour to make up the fire before tackling the mess in the upstairs room, and found him slumped in Rab's favourite chair, his eyes fixed on the cold, empty grate.

She began to retreat, then made herself stop, twisting her fingers in her apron. 'That was a wicked thing to do to an old man.'

His mouth twisted. 'So you're going to take his side, are you? And what d'you think he did to me?'

'He's grieving. He's no' able to show his sorrow like other folk. He should be pitied.'

'Sometimes, Elizabeth, I think you're wise, and sometimes I think you're a fool. I've never in my life met a mystery like you.' He stood up slowly, stiffly, in a way quite unlike his usual supple movement. 'So you agree with him.'

'I said nothing of the sort! I know fine what you did for James. I was there.'

He considered her for a moment, then the ghost of a crooked smile touched one corner of his wide, well-shaped mouth. 'Aye, you were there.'

Neither of them had ever referred to that night spent in Adam's room. Now, recalling it, she flushed. If Adam thought of it, or saw the sudden colour in her face, he gave no sign.

'That man drives us all away one way or another. I'm leaving, Elizabeth.'

A chill gripped her. 'Where are you going?'

'There's places – I can get a bed at the hospital for the night, or mebbe Christian would take me in.'

His eyes had taken on a curiously smoky grey-blue colour. 'I'm getting out, Elizabeth, and so should you. You'll grow old here, you'll die long before your heart stops beating. You'll be forgotten and you'll become as soured as he is, if you stay with him.'

Her lips were stiff. 'I have no place else to go.'

For all his caring about those less fortunate than he was, Adam knew little about them, she thought. Domestic servants were no longer bound by law to their employers, but they were expected to stay where they found work, unless they were put out. Rab Montgomery was well known in Paisley – his housekeeper would find it hard to get a good place in any other house in the area if she deserted him.

'Poor lassie,' Adam said with sudden gentleness, as though reading her mind. His hand caressed her scarred cheek gently, the palm warm and strong against her skin. 'I'll take you to Christian. Come with me now if you value your happiness.'

She wanted to lean her cheek against the comfort of that warm hand, wanted to walk out of the house with him. But she drew back, shaking her head.

'I made a promise to your step-mother in her last illness. I told her I'd not leave the house. And your father kept me on after she died. I couldnae walk away from him.'

The smoky haze in his eyes hardened to flint.

'My step-mother had no right to make a young girl like you promise her life away!'

'She asked for my word and I gave it to her!'

'He'll never thank you for it!'

'I'm no' looking for thanks. I couldnae live with myself if I broke a promise.'

He laughed shortly. 'So – you'd as soon martyr yourself as break a promise? You know fine the woman was dying. Probably not in her right mind!'

The torment was more than she could bear.

'I've had little kindness in my life—' she rounded on him and saw his eyes widen with surprise. 'So I cannae afford to forget it! Mistress Montgomery was good to me, and I gave her my word knowing what it meant. Mebbe the likes of you can forget a promise, but I never will! And that's an end to it!'

There was a long pause before he spoke again. When he did, his voice was remote.

'Well – you've made your bed. Let you lie on it. Or mebbe that's what's in your mind already?'

She stared at him, puzzled.

His gaze was cold, angry. His voice hardened, ripping and slashing at her. 'Is it the promise you're thinking of, or your own future? A wealthy, lonely man – one son dead, the other two driven away. You could do worse than become a third wife.'

The colour rose slowly, burningly, to her face. She could have struck him down in her rage. Instead she moved back, opened the parlour door.

'You have a foul tongue, Adam Montgomery. Get out of this house – now!'

For the moment his anger matched hers.

'You're a thrawn, stubborn fool of a lassie!' he said, and walked past her. She stood very still until she heard the front door slam behind him, then she wrapped her arms tightly about herself, trying in vain to stop the trembling, and the chill that his going had brought.

Rab made no reference to Adam's departure. On the following morning Elizabeth set the breakfast table for one, and he fed himself silently, as though used to being alone.

She discovered later that Adam had taken himself off to Christian's house on Oakshawhill. Later that morning when she was on her knees busily polishing the hall woodwork he came back for his belongings.

After one quick, impersonal glance at her he led two labourers up the stairs, telling them over his shoulder 'Mind how you step in this house – the mistress is particular.'

Almost spluttering with frustrated rage, she whisked into the kitchen and stayed there with the door shut, listening to the tramp of feet on the stairs as Adam's possessions were taken out. Only when the front door closed with a definite sound did she venture to investigate.

His books had gone from the shelves in the dining-room and all his medical apparatus was cleared from his small room and from the room he had planned to use.

It was as though Adam had never lived under his father's roof.

'What made Adam move into Mistress Selbie's house?' Helen Grant asked with mild curiosity a few days later. She and Elizabeth were hard at work, cleaning up the tiny shop that Helen had found.

She was on her knees, sleeves rolled up, scrubbing a floor for the first time in her life, and enjoying it. Elizabeth was working on the small, dirt-encrusted window panes.

'He needed more room for his work.' Nothing would make her tell the truth.

'He's a strange man, Adam. He comes in here if he's passing, and has a word with me.' She sat back on her heels and scrubbed a dirty hand across her face. 'We might have got wed once, did you know that? But all he could think of was medicine.'

Elizabeth saw Matt hurry past, head down and eyes unfocused as he occupied himself with his thoughts. He was gone before she could tap on the glass.

'I wonder what would have happened if he'd stayed in Paisley?' Helen was musing. 'He was a fine looking lad – not as hard as he is now. But he's had sorrow in his life since then. We all do, sooner or later—'

Her voice trailed away, her head drooped on its long slender neck; then she looked up again, and went back to her work.

'I'm going to have shelves put up over there, and a table about here for serving customers. And my mother's agreed to let me make the sweets in her kitchen just now – uugghhh, beasties!' She snatched up a broom and used it to crush a nest of spiders that she had disturbed in a corner. Watching her, Elizabeth decided that Helen was a more capable and independent young woman than Adam realised.

She didn't see him in the first three weeks after he left his father's house, and as the days went by her anger ebbed away. To see his fiancée and then his brother die so horribly, to be unable to save them, and then to be accused by his father, must have driven him wild with helpless rage.

But his final words on that day echoed again and again in her mind. He was right – she could grow old and soured in the Montgomery house, now a silent and dismal place. Everyone had a future – Helen with her shop, Isobel with her baby, Matt with his work. Only she, Elizabeth, saw her days stretch ahead to the grave without change.

She and Adam finally came face to face in Matt's home just after his son was born. When Elizabeth went to see Isobel on the day after the baby's birth Matt was there, taking time from his loom to gloat over his child. Isobel lay in the wall-bed, the shawled bundle in her arms.

'Be careful—' she admonished anxiously as her husband took the baby. He grinned confidently.

'D'you think I'd ever let anything happen to this wee lad? See, Elizabeth – look at his fingers—' he marvelled over the baby, a doting father.

Elizabeth took the warm solid bundle into her own arms, cradling the sweetness of him against her breast. 'What name do you have for him?'

'I thought it should be Robert,' Isobel began at once, but Matt interrupted.

'And I said I'd never have that man's name in my house! He's to be known as Duncan,' he said firmly. 'It's Isobel's father's name, and it was my great-grandfather's given name too.'

The passage door opened and a familiar voice called.

'We're here, Adam—' Matt shouted back and the baby jumped in Elizabeth's arms at the sudden noise, his alarm masking hers.

Adam's eyes met hers briefly as he appeared in the doorway. 'You're here, Elizabeth,' he said easily, and dropped an unexpected kiss on his sister-in-law's cheek before slapping Matt on the back.

'He's a Montgomery – poor bairn.' He poked a finger at the baby's cheek, his breath stirring Elizabeth's hair as he stood close by her. 'Well, Matt – that's one of your ploys safely seen to; how's the shawl?'

Matt beamed. 'Another two weeks and it'll be ready. Mister Cassidy wants me to take it down to London with him.' He glowed with happiness on that day. There was no more restlessness, no bitterness. Matt had found his place in life.

'You could warm your hands at him,' Adam said as he and Elizabeth left the young family. 'I knew that getting out of the warehouse and marrying Isobel would be the making of him.'

'Do you think Isobel looks too pale?'

'We didnae deal much with childbirth in the navy,' he said dryly. 'She seems fine to me.'

He himself looked well, she thought, darting sidelong glances at him as they walked. Despite his hard work his eyes were clear, his shoulders straight, now that he was away from his father's house. He wore a claret-coloured coat with ruffled shirt and blue striped waistcoat. There were good Hessian knee-length boots of soft black leather on his feet and a smart beaver hat rode his dark head.

He was less discreet in his study of her.

Elizabeth flushed and stared down at the path as he turned and looked her over.

'You're pale yourself. You don't get out enough.'

'I'm out every day.'

'But never for pleasure. I told you, did I not, what would become of you if you stayed in that house?'

She stopped, glared up at him. 'You told me – and I'll hear no more of it!' she said, and walked on, quickly.

He laughed, his long easy strides keeping up with her. 'You're as nebby as ever, anyway. You looked bonny back there, with the bairn in your arms. Have you no notion of children, Elizabeth?'

When she didn't answer, he laughed again. They were passing the little sweet shop Helen had bought, and he automatically stooped and peered through the window. The shop was deserted.

'Are you still angry with me?' he teased, catching up with her again.

'Why should I be?'

'Did you know that when you're in a rage that wee nose of yours quivers?'

She clapped a hand to her face, and he laughed.

'Just a wee bit. It suits you, but when you're trying to be high and mighty it spoils the effect.'

To her relief, they reached the corner of the

street, and their ways divided. Adam put a hand
on her arm as she was turning away.

'Remember – I'll always find somewhere for you
if you decide to leave that old devil.'

She pulled back from his touch. 'I'm no' a piece of
furniture to be shifted from one house to the other
by the likes of you – and I'm no' interested in your
opinions of a possible marriage for me either!'

Surprise widened his blue eyes.

'Aye – well – I deserve that, for the things I said
that night. My apologies, Elizabeth. I was angry
with the old man, and angry with you for your
loyalty to him when I thought you should have
come away with me. But I worry about you.'

'I'm no concern of yours!' she almost shrieked at
him. 'I'm a person, can you not understand that?
And I'd as soon be a dry old maid in a garret as live
with the sort of man you'd choose for me. I have
no faith in your tastes!'

She turned to stamp back to his father's house,
then whirled back.

'And you can just keep my nose out of your
conversation!' she said in a final, confused burst of
rage, and saw his astonishment begin to dissolve
into amusement before she rushed off, furious
with herself, and with him for putting her into
such a state.

Christian was delighted to have Adam as a lodger.

'It gives the house a bit of life, having a man about the place,' she crowed to Elizabeth. 'His glass stuff does well enough in the wee conservatory, where my own father kept his tubes and bottles, God rest his soul. Men aye need something to keep them occupied, or they get into mischief.'

She sighed, and scratched her head with one of her knitting wires. 'Whiles I take a wee peek at the stuff, when he's out. I'd have been interested in work like that if I'd just been born a man.'

James used to say that if all Christian's ambitions had been realised she would have been the most experienced and talented Jack of all trades in history.

Matt and Dan finished the new shawl in the middle of March. The new design and new thread excited a lot of interest in the town, but Rab Montgomery remained aloof.

Elizabeth had never seen such a beautiful shawl. The borders were stitched on in reverse, so that when the cloth was folded its jewel-like colouring could be seen to best advantage. The thread was fine, silky, and yet strong and warm. The centre, woven by Matt, was black, and Dan's skilled hands had created deep borders of rich red exotic design, shot through with deeper red, black, green, and tiny flowers of vivid blue.

'It's beautiful, Matt!' Standing in the loom shop she let him drape the shawl about her shoulders. It lay there, wrapping her in luxurious folds, making her feel more elegant and beautiful than ever before.

'And to think that my father could have been the man to have this, if he'd only listened to me,' Matt exulted, then his smile faded, and he said what had been in Elizabeth's mind. 'I just wish James could have seen it – he'd have been proud.'

Isobel came through from the living-room where she had been settling little Duncan in his crib. Matt's sunny smile broke through again at the sight of her.

'But we should only look forward, eh, lass? Did I tell you, Elizabeth, that old Cassidy asked me to come into his warehouse as foreman?'

Reluctantly, she took the shawl off. 'Are you going?'

'He wants to stay at the loom,' Isobel said, her eyes fixed on Matt, her voice soft.

'That's right. We're weaving folk, and that's the way we'll stay. Now that I've proved myself and paid my debts and got a son to follow – I've no need of anything more.'

Laughing, he hugged Isobel then draped the shawl about her and stepped back to admire the way its soft folds covered her shoulders.

But it seemed to Elizabeth that the rich colours only served to make Isobel's skin look paler, her eyes more sunken in her face, and her once rounded, sturdy body thinner.

VIII

Isobel's health continued to deteriorate, and Matt's trip to London was cancelled.

It was as though the baby, large and rosy and healthy, was sucking the life from his young mother along with her milk. Isobel was always tired, she lapsed into long silences, and soon a wet nurse had to be found for Duncan because she couldn't give him enough nourishment.

Matt, desperately worried over her, and behind with his work, had to look after Isobel and the baby as well as his father-in-law, now badly crippled by rheumatism and becoming vague. Elizabeth spent every spare moment at Shuttle Street, caring for Matt's family so that he could snatch some hours at his loom.

Rab Montgomery was as bad-tempered and cantankerous as ever. The only person who could do anything with him was Christian. She, as she told him outright, persevered when any other woman would have given up.

'You've no need to call on me if you've better things to do,' he growled at her.

'Someone has to keep an eye on you. You've made your wealth and your name – be content with that, and sell the business.'

'Sell it – after all the work I've put into it? Woman, you're a fool!'

'And you're a heathen if all you can do is worship money and the making of it. You've years of pleasure ahead of you. A fine wee grandson for a start, and you never clapped eyes on him yet!'

He glared. 'If that's all you've come to say – you can get out!'

She bristled. 'I'll go when I'm good and ready! I swear, Rab, you'd try the patience of a saint.'

'I wouldnae ken about that,' Rab said pointedly, 'since I've never met one.'

'Mebbe you have, but you're too coarse to recognise her,' his cousin rapped back tartly. It was a conversation they had every week; usually Elizabeth and Mary heard most of it in the kitchen, for both Rab and Christian tended to get louder as they grew more exasperated with each other.

Adam took to calling at Matt's home often, and no longer brushed Elizabeth's anxiety aside.

'I'm hoping it's no' childbed fever,' he said gravely as they left the cottage together one afternoon. Her heart turned over.

'It could just be the worry they've had, and her father's health, and the cholera here—' she said swiftly.

He shrugged. 'We'll hope so. When she can get out into the sunshine again it could make a difference.'

Though his mouth smiled at her, his eyes were serious.

To Matt's surprise old Peter Todd refused to take repayment of the loan he had made when Dan was put into prison.

'They say Tom Cassidy's invited you to go into his warehouse.' He looked at the young man shrewdly.

'He did. But I'm just weaving for him.'

'Still – he's no fool, is Tom. I'm thinking that there's a good future for you with him, if ever you decide to leave the loom again. I'll tell you what I'll do – I'll take the interest on my loan, and I'll leave the original amount in your hands. You can give me your signature on a promise of another six months' interest.'

Matt was astounded. Peter wasn't known for his willingness to trust others with his money. The renewed loan gave him the opportunity to employ another plain silk weaver, and as Dan agreed to stay with him, Matt was able to guarantee plain work for the Cassidy house as well as another elaborate shawl to follow the first, which had been snapped up by a London dealer.

The only cloud on his horizon was his wife's health, and that cloud grew until it began to darken his life. Daily he prayed for an improvement, and daily the laughing, plump girl he had married became more of a stranger to him. At times she seemed to be better, but those days grew scarce, and most of the time Isobel barely acknowledged him or her father and baby.

Her first spate of violence took him completely by surprise. Elizabeth and Adam, summoned on a rainy morning, found Matt pale and drawn, and Isobel sleeping peacefully in the wall-bed.

'Mister Falconer's bled her and given her some opium. I was frightened out of my wits during the night.' He rolled up the sleeves of his linen shirt to show them the angry scratches and purpling bruises on his muscular forearms. 'I had to cover her mouth in case her father heard the noise – I damned near smothered her.'

It was hard to believe the story, looking at his wife's calm, pale face on the pillow.

'I got John's wife to take Duncan and the old man in case Isobel woke up in the same mood. I just said that she'd had a restless night and needed to sleep. I couldnae tell the truth—' Matt's mouth softened, trembled, and he rubbed a hand fiercely over his face. 'Adam, if she goes on like that—'

They all knew what it would mean. A room in the Town Hospital, and a strait-jacket. Matt's eyes were filled with nameless horrors as he contemplated such a future.

'I'm at my wit's end – Adam, what am I to do?'

Adam's face was grim, but he tried to sound reassuring. 'There might be a good hospital in Glasgow where they'd help her.'

Matt set his lips stubbornly. 'I'll no' let her be taken from me. It would kill her for sure. D'ye think I could take her and the bairn away to some quiet place? She's aye been fond of the braes, has Isobel. If I could find work on one of the bleach-fields, or a farm—'

'And give up everything you've worked for? Man, you'd never be content!'

'What would that matter?' Matt asked his brother fretfully. 'As long as it cured Isobel – we could come back, later.'

Adam took his shoulders and turned him away

from the bed. 'Listen to me. She's quiet enough for the moment, so mebbe it's all by and she's going to get better. You go off and work your loom. Elizabeth'll stay with Isobel for a while.'

Reluctantly, stopping to touch Isobel's fingers gently, Matt went. Adam's hand brushed the sick woman's wrist, lingered.

'Somewhere in there's the answer. But we have no way of knowing what it is!'

'You're doing your best, Matt knows that.'

Adam scowled at the patient. 'It's no' enough, though, is it? Mebbe this sickness lies in a woman all her life. Mebbe it's in the blood, waiting to be roused. I don't know.' His blue gaze sharpened, studied Isobel as though trying to see beyond the skin to the mysteries beneath. 'All I know is that some can have bairns without any bother, and others take the fever. Fine lady or weaver's wife, it makes no difference. If we only knew why!'

When Matt came back Isobel was awake and perfectly calm. Clearly, she had no memory of what had happened during the night. Elizabeth left husband and wife together and hurried back to the High Street, noticing as she went that more doors were adorned with papers on which the word 'Sick' was printed to warn callers. The cholera showed no sign, six weeks after it had arrived, of leaving them in peace.

A noisy crowd pushed past her as she went towards the Montgomery house and she was hustled into the roadway. In the late afternoon light their eyes were like slits, their mouths gaping as they shouted a meaningless jumble of words. There was a menacing air about them. She had no sooner stepped back onto the footpath again than Tibby, the local gossipmonger, grabbed at her arm.

'Have you heard? They're going to the Moss to dig up the graves!' Her nose was bright red with excitement and her bonnet, thrown on in her haste to get into the street, was squint.

'To dig them up?' Elizabeth echoed the words stupidly.

Tibby's thin-lipped grin was that of a hunter after a fine specimen. 'Someone found shovels and a rope with a hook. They've been put on show in a shop window for all to see. It's grave-robbers at work! It proves what they've been saying—' her voice rattled on, scarcely stopping for breath, '—the physicians are taking the poor dead corpses and cutting them up. Denying them decent Christian rest. The folk are going to look into every coffin buried out there, to make sure—'

Bile stung the back of Elizabeth's throat. She

wrenched herself away from Tibby violently and ran the rest of the way home, trying to close her mind to the picture the woman's words had printed in her mind. The thought of James disturbed from his final sleep by rough hands shot her night's sleep through with bad dreams.

The mob appeared in the streets on the following day. Elizabeth was choosing trimming for a new dress in Peter Brough's shop in Moss Street when they passed.

This time there was a lot more of them, jostling their way along the street, pushing under the very noses of the cart horses and causing chaos.

The angry shouting took Elizabeth and the shop assistant to the window. Men carrying shovels led the way, with a gaggle of women and children following.

'It's a disgrace!' muttered the assistant. 'A rabble – where's the magistrates? I've heard that they're going to lay hands on the physicians if they find any coffins empty.'

Elizabeth had only a moment to feel concern for Adam's safety when her eyes were caught and held by a face in the crowd. She stared, then ran to the door, ignoring the assistant's warning to stay where she was until danger was past.

Outside, she picked up her skirts and scurried

through the scatter of children following the crowd until she managed to catch at the arm of one of the women.

'Isobel!'

A familiar and yet strange face turned and smiled uncertainly at her. 'I have to hurry—' Isobel slid from her grasp.

'Come back – you have no business here!'

Isobel eluded her grasping hand. 'I have to go to the braes—' Her light voice floated back to Elizabeth as she hurried on, to be lost in the gathering crowd.

Elizabeth started to run after her, but just then a huge man burst from a close-mouth and sent her spinning.

'We'll learn those Burking spalpeens!' he bellowed, and sped off towards the Moss. Someone caught Elizabeth up out of the path of a carriage and pulled her to the wall of a house. By the time she had gathered her wits the mob had gone, taking Isobel with them.

Muddy, bruised on the stones of the road, Elizabeth fought her way back up Moss Street against the flow of people hurrying towards the Moss. She wove in and out like an eel, using her elbows and her well-shod feet when she had to.

Matt's loom shop was tranquil. Linnets chirruped

in wicker cages and the men's voices murmured beneath the steady clack of the looms. When Elizabeth broke in on the scene five faces gaped up at her – Matt, the other three weavers, and old Mr Gibson, sitting by the fire enjoying his pipe.

'It's Isobel—' She leaned against Matt's loom, dragging breath into her lungs. The skirt of her gown was torn and muddy, her bonnet hanging down her back by its ribbons.

'She's in by,' Matt was perplexed. 'The bairn's with John's wife, and Isobel's sleeping, so I thought I'd just—'

She all but tore him from the loom in her urgency. 'Matt – she's up and dressed and away to the Moss with the crowd! I couldn't stop her, she's deranged—'

His face changed colour. 'Dear God!' he said, and pushed past her. She heard him throwing open the house door at the other side of the passage, calling Isobel's name, then he was back, gathering his fellow weavers, shouting to her over his shoulder to take the old man to a neighbour's and fetch Adam.

Adam was at the hospital. For the second time she ran through its doors, and this time he was in the ante-room on his way out, so that she was spared the sights of the ward beyond.

'Go home or go to Christian's house,' he ordered when she had gasped out her story.

'I'll stay with you.'

'I've no time to argue – though you're mebbe taking your life in your hands, being seen with a surgeon this day,' he threw the words at her as he strode through the hospital gates and down the narrow road. She had to run to keep up with him.

He led her without hesitation through a maze of narrow alleys and backlands that she had never seen before, then lifted her bodily over a tumble-down brick wall, across a greasy, slippery yard, and into a foul-smelling dark close.

'We're in Moss Street—' he began, then stopped and pressed her against the wall behind him as a dull murmur in the street beyond began to swell to a roar.

'I doubt we're too late. They're coming back into the town. If you value your skin stay still and keep your mouth shut!'

Huddled close to him in the damp, narrow passageway, she peered from beneath his shelter-ing arm at the grey oblong of the close-mouth. It darkened and flickered in a series of erratic pictures as the mob began to surge past on their way back up Moss Street.

The ground shook to the tramping of hundreds

of feet. She heard, for the first time, the voice of a mob, high and shrill, filled with hate and hysteria. Faces blurred into a collection of mouths, fists stabbed into the air, some carrying ropes or shovels. Mercifully, nobody turned to look in the dark close as they passed, and she and Adam, motionless, weren't seen.

Elizabeth had never thought that she could be so frightened in her home town. Many of the people going by only a few yards away, screaming hate, might have brushed past her in the street again and again. Today, each person was part of one frightening animal, a dragon that shouted and stormed up the street, accompanied now and then by the brittle sound of a window smashing or a door being kicked in.

Something flashed past the oblong of light, long and dark, carried high. She thought that she could make out a chant in the midst of the noise.

Then the people were gone and Adam was hurrying her back the way they had come.

'They've brought an empty coffin into the town,' he said breathlessly as they ran. 'That means they'll be looking for the physicians. I'll have to get back to the hospital before they get there.'

As they gained Oakshawhill again the sound of the approaching mob rolled up towards them. The district had once been a Roman camp, and it rose above the rest of Paisley. The crowd would just be starting the uphill climb to the hospital, as Adam had predicted.

'Listen to me, Elizabeth—' He stopped, whirled her about to face him. 'Get to Christian's house and stay there, no matter how long you have to wait, do you hear me? Stay safe until I come to take you home.'

'I won't!' She tried to hold onto his coat. She didn't want to be separated from him while he was in danger. He shook her hard, tearing her fingers from his lapels. Her hair, released from the lace cap, flew about her face and whipped against his shoulder.

'Listen to me!' he shouted into her upraised face. 'Get to that house and wait for me or by God I'll strangle you where you stand and save the mob the trouble. Go on!'

He released her with a violent push that sent her headlong to the ground. She scrambled to her feet, sobs choking her throat, to see him striding away without a backward glance.

At first she didn't think she was going to get into Christian's house. That lady had gone off in the morning to visit friends outside Paisley, and the cook and Effie only opened the door after

Elizabeth had convinced them, through its sturdy panels, of her identity.

The two of them wrung their hands and exclaimed over her wild appearance and torn clothing.

'I kenned these wild rag-tags from the gutters would get up to something wicked!' wailed the cook, an elderly lady who was as thin as a stick, but had a superb talent for preparing food.

They brought hot water and towels for Elizabeth, then settled her in the parlour and gave her tea, properly served in one of their mistress's best tea services.

Distracted with worry over Adam and Isobel, she couldn't even sip the hot liquid, but left it to cool in the cup while she paced about the room, longing to go outside but afraid to disobey Adam.

An hour after he had left her a fringe of the mob came straggling along the road. Cold fear struck into Elizabeth as she peered from behind the curtains and saw a dozen or so men stop and eye the house.

'There's one of the thieving spalpeens lives here—' she heard a voice say, then a man stooped, an arm went back, and a large stone crashed through the drawing-room window, landing almost at her feet.

Splinters of glass dropped from her skirt as she ran through the hall to the kitchen, meeting the two women on their way out and bundling them back.

'They're here – they might try to get in—' In a frenzy she slammed the door to the hall, threw herself at the heavy dresser beside it. 'Help me to pull this over. And make sure that the back door's locked!'

Breathless, terrified, they turned the kitchen into a fortress and huddled together, waiting. There were shouts from the front of the house and glass crashed twice more, but nobody tried to force the front door, or came in through the walled back garden.

After a long silence, they decided that it was safe to venture out, and had just begun to draw the dresser clear of the hall door when fists began pounding on the front door.

Effie screamed and threw herself into a corner. The cook pulled her out and slapped her face, and a familiar voice roared, 'For the love of God, Christian, will you let me in!'

Elizabeth's feet couldn't carry her across the hall fast enough. Adam stormed in as soon as the handle turned and made straight for the side room where he had his laboratory. He emerged almost at once, nearly knocking her down on his way across to the drawing-room.

'If they thought to do damage they failed. A broken window or two, but the apparatus isn't broken. Is my cousin at home?'

'She's in Elderslie—'

He stopped short in the drawing-room, looking at the smashed window and the glass lying on the rich carpet and over the furniture. 'She'll be in a fine taking about this when she sets eyes on it.'

'Adam, are you all right?' Elizabeth was surprised by the steadiness of her own voice.

'Me?' He frowned at her, puzzled, then glanced into a mirror. 'Oh – they broke down the hospital gates and made off with the cholera bier, the daft loons. It's just a wee disagreement I had with a man who was all for taking the patients as well.'

His clothes were as torn and muddy as hers. There was bruising round his left eye, which was half-closed, and dried blood, apparently from a shallow cut on one cheekbone, crusted part of his face. Looking at him reminded her of the picture she must make herself. She pushed her long, tangled hair back, tried without success to pull together a tear in her sleeve.

Then she remembered. 'Have you heard anything of Isobel?'

'I've been no further than the hospital. I'll get

down to Shuttle Street now. Likely Matt found her and took her home safely.'

Effie, red-eyed but obviously fighting to restore normality, appeared with a tea-tray set, again, with attractive china and a silver teapot.

'You'll take some tea, Mister Montgomery?'

'Tea?' Adam asked as though he couldn't believe his ears. 'Tea?' His voice rose to a bellow. 'Brandy, woman – for any favour, brandy!'

She put the tray down carefully, with a slight crunch of broken glass underfoot, clasped both hands to her mouth, and fled. Adam marched to the corner cupboard, snatched out a large glass and a bottle, and filled the glass to the brim. Then he swallowed half of it in one movement of his strong throat.

'What's up with the old besom?'

'I think—' Elizabeth said carefully '—that she's a wee thing upset, Adam. She's no' used to riots and folk breaking windows. And to tell you the truth—' All at once her composure had begun to slide away, like a wayward coverlet on a bed. It was a strange feeling. '—To tell you the truth, I—'

He shot her a short, puzzled look over the rim of the glass. Then it was put down and Adam was across the room, gathering her into his arms, holding her close, and she was clutching him tightly because she didn't ever want him to move away again.

'Elizabeth—' he said softly into the brown hair spilled over his shoulder, '—lass, was there ever a more thoughtless fool than I am?'

It was then, despite the fear and misery, that Elizabeth realised that she had come home. She knew, with a clarity that almost stopped her heart dead then set it pounding faster, that she didn't care how thoughtless or bad-tempered or intolerant he was, there would never be anyone in the world for her but Adam Montgomery.

She couldn't tell him about it. She could only cling to him and be grateful to him for holding her until the trembling stopped and the dry-eyed sobbing was over. Then he smoothed her hair back, made her sit down, and gave her some brandy, which tasted terrible.

'You're no judge of spirits,' he teased, the ghost of a smile lighting his blue eyes, when she pushed the glass away with a grimace. 'Thon's Cousin Christian's best liquor you're turning your neb up at. Now – I'm going to take you to the High Street, for it's time you were safe home.'

'I'm coming with you to Shuttle Street. I have to know that Isobel's all right,' she insisted as he began to shake his head.

'My father'll no' be pleased at you being out when he gets back.'

She folded her hands in her lap. 'Isobel's my friend,' she said, and he gave in.

The town was in an uproar and it wasn't easy getting to Matt's house. The militia were on their way, they were told as they came down from Oakshawhill to find a trail of broken fencing and smashed windows. The cholera bier had been wrecked then carried through the town. Doctors' homes had been attacked. Now the mob, its first thirst for vengeance dulled, had broken into sullen groups, muttering in corners.

Tibby pounced on them as they made for Shuttle Street. Her mouth was working and her eyes glistened.

'There you are, Elizabeth – and Mister Montgomery too. My, what a state you're in!' She drank in the sight with a blink of her eyes. 'Is it no' terrible what's happened?'

'It's a bad day for Paisley,' he agreed shortly, his arm about Elizabeth's shoulders as he tried to hurry her past the woman. But Tibby was determined to have her say.

'Paisley? Oh, aye – but I was talking of the accident.'

'What accident?' Adam snapped at her, and she

flinched back, then rallied.

'Down at the Moss – poor Isobel—'

Adam released Elizabeth and almost snapped Tibby's thin arm off at the shoulder in his impatience to find out what she was talking about.

'I'm trying to tell you!' She snatched the crushed limb back, rubbed it, glaring at him. But bad news was of more importance to her than a bruised arm. 'She got caught up in the rabble at the Moss and got hit on the head with one of the shovels, poor bairn. They took her to the Town Hospital—'

A carriage belonging to one of the town's bailies was standing nearby, out of the way of the rioters but near enough to make out what was happening. Adam whirled Elizabeth up into it and followed her without a pause. Fortunately, the occupant knew who he was, and was willing to drive them to the hospital.

They had to take a roundabout route to keep clear of trouble. Adam was on the ground before the wheels had stopped turning and Elizabeth was almost pulled headlong from the door. With a swift word of thanks for their benefactor, Adam ran into the building.

Matt was closeted in a small ground floor room with the hospital master, Mister Crichton. On a table lay a shrouded figure. Adam lifted the edge of the sheet, looked, dropped the cloth.

'Who did this?' he asked, low voiced, murder in the tones.

Matt shook his head. He was dazed, his voice a dull monotone. 'Nobody knows. It was an accident, just. I met them when they were bringing her back. She was – it all happened at once, they say. Just an accident. She was there, the place was crowded, she got in the way of a shovel—' His voice dropped, rose again. 'If there's anyone to blame, it was me. I thought she'd be all right on her own, for a minute. I just wanted to finish a wee bit of work—'

Tears rolled down his waxen face, one after another, and Adam took him in his arms as though he was a child.

As he was being led out to the carriage that was to take him home Matt raised his head and gazed round the high-ceilinged hall.

'I mind I said I'd no' let her come in here.' He tried to smile. 'Poor lass – it's as well we never know what's ahead.'

It was dark when Adam and Elizabeth made their way to High Street. John Gibson was with Matt and Adam planned to go back and stay the night at the cottage. There was an uneasy, brooding air about the streets. The mob had returned to the cholera hospital and had forced the doctors to flee for their lives. The magistrates had appeased them by promising to investigate the coffins in the Moss, and the rabble had retired for the night, hungry beasts waiting for the dawn.

Adam insisted on going into the house with her, but she refused to use the front door while his father was home, and he had to follow her down the side passage.

Mary almost hugged Elizabeth in her relief at seeing her but hung back shyly when Adam, still ragged and bloody, stepped into the kitchen.

'Is Mister Montgomery home?' Elizabeth marvelled over how normal the kitchen seemed after the events of the day.

'These two hours past.' Mary's eyes were like saucers. 'And he was awful angry when I said you hadnae come home. I was frighted, Elizabeth—'

'There's no need,' Elizabeth said automatically. 'Away to your bed now and I'll talk to you in the morning.'

The hall door flew back on its hinges.

'So you've decided to come back, have you?' Rab asked belligerently, then his eyes narrowed as Adam stepped into the centre of the room. 'Keeping strange company, too.' He ground the words out.

'I have to speak with you, father.'

For a moment Elizabeth thought that the older man was going to ignore his son's presence, then curiosity won the day.

'You know where to find me,' he said curtly and turned into the hall.

'Elizabeth—' Adam made it an order, waiting at the door as though she was a lady, his blue eyes weary but compelling as they held hers. She walked before him to the parlour where Rab waited, legs straddled before the fireplace, hands behind his back and chin up in his most arrogant stance.

'Well?'

'Sit down, Elizabeth,' Adam commanded, then deigned to look at his father at last.

'Elizabeth's been in Christian's house, hiding from the mob. And then she was with me, at Shuttle Street. It's through no fault of hers that she wasnae here earlier.'

Rab's eyes flickered over them both. 'You look as though the mob got you.'

'I'm a physician, father. Today this whole town shares your feelings about us. We kill folk, it seems. You'll no doubt be pleased to see that somebody tried to do something about it.' He indicated his bruised and swollen face.

A muscle jumped in Rab's cheek, but he said nothing.

'I brought Elizabeth home, for it's no' safe for a lassie to be in the streets on a night like this. And I came to tell you that Matt's wife died today.'

There was a slight pause, then, 'Aye?' Rab asked enigmatically.

'I thought you might feel it your duty to go and see the man.'

The muscle jumped again. 'If Matt has anything to say to me, he can come here, as you've done,' Rab said harshly. 'I'll no' seek him out.'

Adam drew a deep, ragged breath, and Elizabeth could see that it was costing him a lot to keep his temper in check. She willed him to remain calm. An outburst now would only be turned to his father's advantage.

'Am I to go back and tell him that?'

'You can tell him what you damned well please! And you can leave my house!'

Their eyes locked, and Rab's shifted almost at once. Adam walked to the door. Elizabeth rose to show him out and he said swiftly, 'I'll manage fine.'

Rab, who had opened his mouth to bellow an order at her, closed it again with an audible click of teeth.

'To think—' Adam said very softly, but with a chill in his voice that almost froze Elizabeth's blood '—that I ever wanted to come back to this town, and this house.'

'To think—' his father's guttural voice followed him as he walked out '—that I ever thought to welcome you back! I rue the day you set your accursed foot in this place!'

The front door closed quietly, and he dropped into his chair, watching Elizabeth from beneath lowered lids, daring her silently to utter a word.

She stood before him, head high, hands folded before her, and in her heart she hated him with all the force she could muster.

'Go to your bed,' he said at last, and she went, leaving him alone with his thoughts.

IX

Just after he buried his wife in the churchyard near her home Matt Montgomery began working in the Cassidy warehouse, as foreman. Without Isobel he lost his ambition to stay at the loom, and turned a new corner in his life.

'If my father had acknowledged her as my wife I could have cared for her better,' he said savagely to Elizabeth. 'She might be with me today.'

She settled a large shawl about her shoulders and scooped the baby expertly into its folds. His warm little body nestling against her breast seemed natural.

'Matt, Adam says the sickness that took Isobel could have been with her no matter how she lived.'

'Mebbe so, but I could have given her more – we could have spent more time together. I'll never forgive that old devil in his fine house!' His face hardened, grew older. Then he touched the baby's cheek gently with the back of one finger. 'You'll fetch him to see me tomorrow, Elizabeth?'

'Aye, as soon as I can get away.' Isobel's father had moved in with John Gibson and his wife; the baby had been farmed out to neighbours. Every day Elizabeth carried him to the weaving shop so that Matt could spend some time with him.

'I'll need to find someone to look after the two of us so that I can bring him here, where he belongs.' He looked about the cottage. 'Or find somewhere else to stay.'

'That takes money.'

His jaw set. 'Then I'll find the money. I've nothing else to do with my time. I tell you this, Elizabeth – if it's anything to do with me, that wee lad's going to have all the comforts his mother never lived to see!'

It was as though the bitter blow he had suffered had cracked the old shell open and released a new man, forged of stronger material than ever. Within weeks of Isobel's death he had started on the road to success. He won the right to have more say in the Cassidy house than he had ever known in his father's employment. He managed to secure a loan from the Union Bank, and took on a new harness loom weaver to increase the shawl output.

The man and his family moved into the Shuttle

Street cottage and Matt rented a new house for himself, in St George's Place. It was near the warehouse and separated from the weaving shop by a communal drying green at the back, enabling him to keep close contact, day and night, with the work under his supervision.

He found a capable widow to act as housekeeper and summoned Elizabeth to inspect the house. It consisted of a downstairs kitchen, and a small room where the baby and the housekeeper could sleep. Upstairs there was a bedroom for Matt and a small, but perfect, high-ceilinged parlour, a room designed on airy, graceful lines, with two large windows, one looking out onto the cobbled Place and the majesty of St George's Church, the other overlooking a lane, with a glimpse of walled gardens opposite.

'It's so – elegant,' she said in wonder, gazing at the carved fireplace.

'It'll do. The devil of it is, what do I put into it? I'll have to buy chairs and tables and suchlike.'

'Not a great deal. Curtains, and a desk there, and mebbe a sofa, but nothing big or dark for this room,' she began, and was interrupted.

'Just as I thought – you've got the right idea, Elizabeth. How would it be if I was to leave it to you to choose the right pieces?'

She realised too late that she had fallen into a trap. 'But, Matt—!'

He looked as though a load had been taken off his shoulders. 'Anything'll do, just so long as I can get the place fit for Duncan and Mistress Mackay. Wallpaper – something on the floor – whatever you think best, lass.'

She left the house in a daze, her mind so full of chairs and tables and sofas that she didn't look where she was going, and cannoned into someone as she turned a corner.

Elizabeth, the smaller and lighter of the two, staggered across the path, bounced off the wall of a house, and landed in the arms of her assailant.

'You daft gowk,' she lashed out, 'you nearly had me in the dirt!' She twisted in his grip to examine the skirt of her good mulberry-coloured gown. The wall had been soft with age and damp, and as she had feared there was a stain on the cloth.

'Look—' She caught a handful of the material and dragged it round to study it. 'Look what you've done to my best gown!'

'Forgive me, ma'am – it was my fault entirely, I confess it!'

She looked up swiftly as she heard the clipped English voice, then reddened. The man before her was immaculately dressed, stylish in a dove-grey coat over black trousers, white shirt, blue satin waistcoat and blue cravat. He was half a head taller than herself, his hair was the colour of corn in sunlight, and his eyes, wide with horror as he looked at the stained dress, were dark brown. He looked, her numbed senses told her, like one of the noble heroes in the romantic novels she was fond of reading.

'Your pardon – it was clumsy of me— ' His voice was deep, beautiful. She realised that she was gaping, and blinked rapidly.

'It's nothing, sir.'

'But your gown—' He stepped to one side to examine the damage and Elizabeth, scarlet with embarrassment, whisked round like an animal at bay, one hand smoothing the marked skirt behind her, out of sight.

'Ach, it's fine. I'll put it to soak in a tub of water when I get home, and it'll be as good as new.'

'You're not hurt, ma'am?'

Nobody had ever called her 'ma'am' before. The splendour of it almost took her breath away.

'Ma'am?' he prompted, anxiety entering his voice, and she realised that she was too caught up in admiring him to listen properly.

'Oh – I'm fit as a – quite hearty, thank you, sir.'

'I'm glad.' She felt his gaze like a touch, travelling

over her, and was pleased to recall that she had put on her new bonnet, the one that framed her neat face and brown hair to advantage. If she could have thought of something else to say, to prolong the meeting, she would have said it gladly. But her stupid tongue couldn't utter the words that would keep him there. He bowed, she sketched a clumsy curtsey, and they turned to go their separate ways.

'Ma'am—'

She spun round. 'Aye, sir?'

The dark brown eyes were like treacle. She was lost in them. 'Could you perhaps direct me to the Montgomery warehouse in Forbes Place?'

She beamed at him. 'It's just across the street and down a bit towards the Cross. I'm—' the lie tripped off her tongue easily 'I'm going past that way myself.'

She saw him raise one eyebrow slightly and glance in the direction she had been walking, away from the Cross. But he had the grace to say nothing, except, 'Then I'm delighted to accept your assistance, ma'am,' as he offered her his arm.

She skimmed across the street as though walking on a cloud. 'I look after Mister Montgomery's house. My name is Elizabeth Cunningham.'

He stopped on the opposite footpath, sketched a

bow. 'Jeremy Forrest. Your servant, ma'am.' Then he tucked her hand back into the crook of his arm and they walked on.

'You're new to Paisley, Mister Forrest?'

'This is my first visit. My father has a business in London. I've been sent up to buy merchandise and to meet the people.'

They reached the warehouse all too soon, making their way through the usual cluster of people about the doors; weavers carrying away new webs in clean white linen bags, women bringing back finished shawls or collecting yarn to be wound, carters delivering new materials. Rab was inside, haggling with a weaver over the price of a shawl.

'Well, girl?' he asked shortly when he glanced up and saw her. His manner changed when Jeremy Forrest introduced himself. He shook hands, beaming, ushering the young man towards his tiny office.

'You can go off home,' he said curtly to Elizabeth, and his eyebrows shot up in astonishment as Jeremy Forrest took time to bow over her work-roughened hand and say, 'Your servant, ma'am. I hope we may meet again.'

Elizabeth's ears were still singing with the excitement of it all when she presented herself at

Christian's house twenty minutes later for advice about Matt's house.

The older woman eyed her closely. 'You're in a right state about a few sticks of furniture,' she commented dryly. 'Roses in your cheeks, and a shine to your eyes that I've never seen before.'

Elizabeth opened her mouth to tell Mistress Selbie about her meeting with the young Englishman, then thought better of it. 'I'm just worried I'll choose the wrong things,' she said lamely.

'He'd no' notice if you filled the place with boxes. And I'm quite sure you'll do a grand job. It'll be practice for you, for when the time comes for you to furnish your own wee house.' She looked up, her eyes sliding beyond Elizabeth. 'It's yourself, Adam. Will you have some tea?'

'I will not,' he said, 'I'll have what I need.'

Christian tutted, but did nothing to stop him as he took a generous ration of whisky from the bottle in the cupboard.

Elizabeth hadn't seen much of him since Isobel's funeral. The cuts and bruising he had received on the day of the riots had gone, but he looked thinner, paler. As though reading her mind, Christian said, 'D'you not think he looks awful tired, Elizabeth?'

He emptied the glass. 'I've told you, cousin – I can take care of myself.'

'Is it bad at the hospital, Adam?'

He looked at Elizabeth, his eyes dark and smoky, as though he didn't really see her. 'Bad enough, for the five poor souls that died in the past week. There's some recovered, mind.'

The smokiness cleared. 'But you're looking well, Elizabeth. Have you found a secret of health that poor physicians like me would like to learn?'

'She's just keeping herself busy. Matt's asked her to furnish his new house.' Christian's knitting wires clicked busily.

'There's an honour for you. See to it well, now – my brother's going to be a man of importance in this town before he's done. Did you know—' he took his eyes from Elizabeth and turned to Christian '—that old Peter Todd's added to the amount he's loaned Matt?'

She raised her eyebrows. 'Has he now? Well, well, the laddie must be giving a good account of himself. I told Peter he was worth trusting when he first asked me if he should lend Matt money.'

Adam, about to pour another drink, put the bottle down. 'You told him?'

Christian took advantage of his surprise to take the bottle from his unresisting hand and put it back

245

into the cupboard. 'Peter always asks my advice.'

'And what would you know of money matters?' her kinsman asked with ungracious bluntness. She looked smug.

'More than you ever will. Did I no' marry a banker? And did my own brother, poor skelf of a man that he was, no' take up law? I've got a good tongue in my head, and a good mind as well. It was a simple enough matter to pick their brains.'

Adam shook his head. 'You're full of surprises, Christian. Tell me this – do you charge poor old Peter for all this advice you give him?'

She picked up her knitting again, gave him a withering look. 'As if I would! Wasn't his father Jamie fair dying to marry my mother at one time? As Peter sees it, we're nearly brother and sister, him and me.'

'I have it in mind to have a wee bit of a gathering,' Rab Montgomery told Elizabeth on the following day as she waited by the front door with his coat and stick. He shrugged into the coat, a lightweight garment now that June had arrived. 'A few folk, just. On Friday.'

She felt her knees tremble beneath her dark gown. 'For their dinner, Mister Montgomery?'

'Aye, for their dinner.' He snatched the silver-knobbed cane from her fingers. 'You ken what dinner is, don't you? It's when folk sit down and stuff their bellies with someone else's hard-earned silver, that's what it is. You'd best find something to please them, even if it bankrupts me. And you'll sit at the table yourself,' he finished crustily, and opened the door to an early morning filled with the promise of a hot day.

'How – how many would there be?' she quavered, dry-mouthed.

'About half a dozen, I suppose. I've not got it in mind to feed the entire town.' The door swung to leaving her trembling in the hall.

It was the first social event to be held in the house since Adam's homecoming. Elizabeth sank down onto the bottom step of the staircase, terrified at the thought of catering for a dinner party. She immediately thought of running to Christian Selbie for help, then thought better of it and went to the kitchen to break the news to Mary.

'We'll manage fine, you and me, will we no'?' she finished, with more confidence than she felt.

'D – d'ye no' think it would be a good idea to ask Mistress Selbie—?' the little maid said doubtfully.

'Shame on you! D'you think I cannae do anything for myself? And isn't it my place to teach you what to do?' Elizabeth's mind was beginning to function again. 'Listen – we'll have beef, and mebbe a goose, and I'll teach you how to make a fine pie.'

The thought of baking and cooking again, after weeks of supplying sketchy meals for Rab, began to appeal to her. As the day wore on she worked out a menu, and her confidence grew.

Christian Selbie appeared at the door the next day.

'I'm told that I'm expected to attend a dinner party here on Friday,' she announced almost accusingly, flouncing into the parlour. 'No' as much as a please or thank you, mind you. Anyone would think a body had nothing else to do but run after Lord Rab Montgomery!'

Elizabeth, who had now set her heart on taking responsibility for the dinner, grew pink with agitation.

'We can manage fine, Mary and me. I'm just away to the butcher's, then the bakery, and I thought Helen might—'

'Tuts, lassie, no need to go on like a burn rushing to the sea!' Christian flapped a hand at her. 'I know you're taking to do with it yourself and I've no mind to stick my nose in unless it's asked for. It's another matter I'm here about – something I'm sure you've never thought of.' She tilted her head to look Elizabeth over. 'What are you going to wear for this grand occasion of Rab's?'

Elizabeth gaped, then rallied. 'My pink muslin.'

'Just as I thought. It's pretty enough in its own way, but never the thing for Friday. You'll have to get a new gown.'

'There's no need.'

'Get your bonnet and shawl and come with me now to a wee seamstress I know,' Christian swept on. 'You can bring your basket and go to the shops after I've done with you.'

Meekly Elizabeth obeyed. It was easier than arguing.

'I'd have liked to take you to a woman in Glasgow, but Rab's not left us much time,' Christian said as they drove to the old bridge, where the seamstress had her little shop. 'I'd enjoy to see you dressed like a lady, Elizabeth, for I think you'd carry the clothes well.'

The dim room, its window overlooking the river below, glowed with colour from materials carelessly tossed over the wooden table. Christian and the seamstress scooped their hands into the cloth, arguing, agreeing, rejecting, selecting. Elizabeth submitted to being measured and pulled about, her mind on the food she must prepare for Friday. When Christian finally led her from the shop she had only a vague idea of the dress that was to be made for her.

'She's a good wee soul,' Christian said as they separated on the footpath. 'She'll have that gown ready on time, even if she has to work late at night to do it. See and be ready at four on Friday.'

True to her word, she was on the doorstep as the parlour clock chimed four on Friday afternoon. Elizabeth was bundled into her shawl and whisked back to the old bridge, calling last minute instructions from the carriage window to Mary. The little maid, running a few steps from the front door to catch her orders, nodded vigorously. Then she was out of sight and Christian was saying, 'Ach, she'll manage fine, don't fret about things.'

Elizabeth couldn't help fretting. The dinner party was the greatest challenge she had faced so far. In the little shop she let the two older women strip her brown dress off and put her in the new gown, while she went over lists and plans in her head.

She paid no attention to the new dress until she was pushed before a long mirror and ordered to look into it.

All thought of the dinner went out of her head at once.

'But – you've made a mistake!' She gaped at the

woman reflected in the glass, her voice rising to a shocked wail. 'My shoulders! I can see my shoulders, Mistress Selbie!'

Christian nodded smugly, as though she had made them herself. 'And very pretty they are, too.'

On anyone else, such as Helen Grant, Elizabeth would have agreed that those smooth rounded shoulders were fine, and worthy of the froth of pale blue lace that cupped them. But shoulders like those, the soft full breasts and elegant throat – they couldn't belong to her, Elizabeth, the charity school girl, the little housekeeper. They couldn't!

'Mistress Selbie—' she quavered.

'Take a good look at yourself, and not a word until you've done it!' the older woman commanded. Elizabeth swallowed her protests and turned back to the mirror obediently.

She was wearing the most beautiful dress she had ever seen. It was of periwinkle blue satin with a pale blue lace frill around the low bodice and pale blue ribbons across the front of the full, graceful skirt. Her arms were left bare and the snug-fitting bodice emphasised her ripe breasts even while it gave them a demure mystery with its drift of lace.

Elizabeth's wide eyes moved down to the skirt then up again, past the slender waist, the pale shoulders, the white column of the neck, surprisingly long and slim – then they met their own stunned reflection in a pink-cheeked face.

'It's bonny,' Christian said with satisfaction, and the seamstress chirruped agreement.

'It's bonny, but—' Elizabeth threw out her red hands with their short, sensible nails. 'It's no' for the likes of me!'

'Of course it is! We'll buy slippers – you've got neat wee feet, always a sign of a lady—' Christian whisked the skirt up, revealing the feet in question, and slender ankles. '—And you'll have long gloves, and since my Effie's to help serve the meal, I'll bring her early and she can help to dress you. Effie's good with hair. I've got a necklace that would go with that dress—' Then she stopped herself. 'No, it'd be a crime to put anything round that bonny white young throat. You'll stay unadorned, and all the prettier for it.'

A few hours later Elizabeth was again studying her own reflection, this time in the long mirror in the upstairs hall of the Montgomery house. Effie's nimble fingers had pinned her hair up in an elegant sweep of shining gold-brown with three ringlets nestling in the curve of her neck on the left. Pale blue gloves to the elbow made the most of her small-boned hands and hid the red, rough skin.

Soft slippers caressed her feet and made her feel as though she was walking on a cloud. Her cheeks were bright with excitement and her blue eyes sparkled.

Her throat had been left unadorned, as Christian had decided, but tiny blue pendant earrings swung from her lobes when she moved her head.

'If they hurt, it makes no difference,' the older woman had said as she clipped them on. 'A bit of pain's nothing if a lady looks right. You carry yourself well enough, and if you're no' sure of anything, watch me.'

She herself was magnificent in deep red with gold lace trimming. Rab, standing before the parlour fire, almost choked on his glass of whisky when they entered.

'You're no' bad – both of you,' he said grudgingly when Christian had thumped him on the back.

'The lassie's a picture, and you know it!' said his cousin tartly, then added, 'And I'm bonny, myself.'

Elizabeth had hoped, when she saw how lovely she looked, that Adam might be among the guests. Rab hadn't troubled to tell her who had been invited, and she hadn't liked to ask. As it turned out Christian was the only blood relation at the dinner. A prominent local manufacturer and town bailie appeared, together with his wife, and shortly after that the last guest arrived. Elizabeth felt her heart stop, then flip over and beat hurriedly as Jeremy Forrest, handsome in a claret-coloured coat with dark green facing, high white collar, green cravat and pale grey trousers, came into the parlour.

He came into the room quickly, bringing with him the fresh vitality of youth, and looked swiftly round the people already there. His eyes lit up when they reached Elizabeth, and he made his way over to her as soon as the introductions were over and he was free.

'Mistress Cunningham – I hoped to meet you again.' He raised her gloved hand to his lips, and she prayed that he wouldn't sense the thrill that ran through her.

She had dreaded the meal, but with Jeremy at her side everything became an adventure, a challenge she met with skill. Now and then she glanced across the snowy tablecloth at Christian, and each time met with a small approving nod.

With Effie's practised guidance Mary served the meal correctly, and Elizabeth was able to relax and even permit herself the luxury of laughter now and then.

When the men joined the ladies in the parlour after port, Jeremy sat by her on the sofa.

'I hope you don't feel that I'm stealing too much of your company, Miss Cunningham?'

'Oh no, I—' She stopped short, remembering just in time that the ladies in the romantic novels were never too enthusiastic. 'I enjoy talking with you.'

He leaned closer, lowered his voice. 'The other ladies are charming, but not as enchanting or as beautiful as you are. That dress—' his warm brown gaze moved slowly over her throat and shoulders and breasts before settling on the satin skirt '—is quite the most perfect I've seen in years. The material is very fine.'

She glowed. 'Isn't it? And the ribbons are – oh!'

She sat upright, eyes wide with horror. Jeremy, fingers daringly within inches of the skirt folds, snatched his hand back as though she had just bitten it.

'I do beg your pardon, Mistress Cunningham, I had no intention of—'

'It's no' you – it's me!' She had forgotten to watch her tongue in this moment of terrible realisation. 'I never even asked how much the gown would cost – I havenae paid for it, and here I am sitting in it like a lady!'

Bewilderment crinkled his face, and was swiftly followed by blazing amusement. 'You—' he began, then went into a fit of coughing, jumping to his feet.

'Did a crumb go down the wrong way, Mister Forrest?' Christian enquired politely from the far side of the room, and he shook his head.

'Thank you – I'm quite all right,' he said at last, voice shaking. 'Mistress Cunningham has a very dry sense of humour.'

Then he caught Elizabeth's hand and drew her up to stand beside him. 'Come and look out of the window.'

She was still absorbed in the horror of her situation. She worked for little more than her keep in the Montgomery house. It would take years to pay for such a fine dress. 'There's nothing to see but the houses across the street,' she said fretfully as she was drawn across the room.

'I don't care what I see. I find that looking out of a window is a very good way of recovering one's composure,' the English voice drawled, his breath tickling her ear.

Side by side, in silence, they stared from the window for a while, Elizabeth frantically going over sums of money in her head.

She was scarcely aware of the sidelong glances her companion gave her now and then.

'I don't care whether you've paid for the gown

or not, Mistress Cunningham,' he murmured at last, 'It becomes you very well.'

'But—'

His voice became firmer. 'Besides, a great many young ladies in London never pay for their gowns until long after they've worn them and thrown them away.'

'That's stealing!'

'Not—' he turned her to face him, and she saw laughter in his eyes, tugging at the corners of his mouth. '—Not if they're ladies of fashion. And you, Mistress Cunningham, were born to be a lady of fashion. I think—' there was faint regret in the words '—that we have neglected the others for long enough. Shall we join them?'

Christian's sharp eyes were on them as Jeremy led Elizabeth to a seat near the fire. 'I was just saying, Mister Forrest, you'll no' have travelled on our fine canal yet? I'm taking a journey to Johnstone on Monday, and I could go by water if you'd care to travel with me?'

He bowed. 'I'd be honoured, ma'am. Perhaps Mistress Cunningham would join us?'

Monday was laundry day. Elizabeth began to shake her head, the little pendant earrings dancing in the light. To her surprise Rab said, 'Havers, lassie, you can manage to take a day from your duties, can you no'? You'll go with my cousin and Mister Forrest.'

He made it plain that he had given an order. Elizabeth bit her lip and saw Jeremy's eyes darken, his brows tuck down as he shot a sidelong look at his host.

'The choice lies with Mistress Cunningham, of course,' he said coolly. 'I would not wish her to take part in this outing if it's going to bore her.'

'Of course it won't.' Rab snapped. 'But by all means, Elizabeth – tell us what you think of my cousin's invitation?' There was mockery in his imitation of the Englishman's courtesy, and the frown deepened on Jeremy's forehead.

'I'll be happy to go,' Elizabeth said quickly, embarrassed by the sudden attention from her employer's guests.

When they had all left, Jeremy with a soft, 'Until Monday, Mistress Cunningham—' Rab stopped at the foot of the stairs on his way up to bed.

'Thon Londoner seems to like your company, Elizabeth. His father's a good man to do business with. Mind that when you're on the canal with him.'

'Mister Montgomery!' She stopped him as he continued on up to the landing. The newel post was hard and smooth beneath her fingers; she gripped it tight for comfort as she glared up at the insensitive man above her.

'Mister Montgomery – I'm your housekeeper. I was never employed to attract men to your ware-house doors!'

He came down two steps, but she held her ground, anchored to the newel post. Rab stabbed a finger at her.

'You—' he said, with level emphasis on each and every word 'are my employee. My servant. The cloth on your back and the food in your belly and the cot you sleep on are all thanks to me. I have the power, if you displease me, to send you back to the paupers' house you came from and make sure no decent folk ever give you work in this town again. Just think about that before you decide whether or not you'll do my bidding, my girl!'

He stumped back upstairs and disappeared into the shadows of the upper floor. Alone, Elizabeth uncurled her fingers with difficulty from the polished wooden post and went back to the kitchen, clashing pots about in her rage.

He was right, she knew that. The doors open to her were of little comfort – she could defy him and return to the Town Hospital in shame, she could leave the town and go elsewhere, alone; she could accept Adam's offer of help and be beholden to him for the rest of her life.

'I'll not dance to that old man's tune!' she vowed to herself as she brushed out her hair before going to bed later. 'I won't!'

She set off for Oakshawhill as soon as she was free on the following morning. First, she had to talk to Christian about the cost of the new gown; then she would turn down the invitation to join Christian and Jeremy on the canal. After that – she shelved the terrible thought for the moment, refusing to start worrying until she had to – she would decide what to do if Rab kept his threat and put her out.

Christian, in a voluminous dressing-gown and big cap, was still having breakfast.

'What a fuss to make over a bit of cloth and a few ribbons!' she said scathingly when her visitor started to explain why she had arrived. 'I know fine Rab doesnae give you enough money to buy decent clothes for yourself. By rights he should pay for the gown, for weren't you playing hostess at his table? But I decided from the start that it would be my own gift to you, so that's an end to the whole matter. It was worth the money just to see you enjoying yourself for once. Now – about the canal—'

Elizabeth opened her mouth to speak, but wasn't given the chance.

'—I've made up my mind that we'll make an outing of it altogether. I'm going to see if Helen'll come – she needs a rest from that shop of hers – and I have it in mind to ask Matt as well. Adam's already said he'll honour us with his company.'

Elizabeth shut her mouth again. She hadn't seen Adam for several days. Although she would scarcely admit it, even to herself, she missed him.

She would go on the canal trip after all – but not to please Rab Montgomery. She had her own reasons now.

X

Rab Montgomery was away from home for the entire day, so after leaving Christian Elizabeth was free to visit a cabinet-maker's shop in Orchard Street. She would have liked to have plenty of time to select furniture for Matt's new home, but he was impatient to move his son and the housekeeper in.

She wasn't entirely displeased with the pieces that the man had to show her. There were some graceful chairs, delicate and yet sturdy, and an elegant wall cupboard.

She was reluctant to make the final decision on her own. She found Matt in the loom-shop and dragged him, protesting, back to Orchard Street.

'I'll no' have you saying something displeased you once it was in the house.'

'I told you – anything'll do!' He was like a peevish child lagging half a step behind its mother. The thought made her smile as she looked up at his powerful body, looming over her, then the smile died on her lips as a familiar voice said, 'Mistress Cunningham!' and she and Matt came to a standstill before Jeremy Forrest.

She was instantly reminded, as she looked at his beaming face, of Rab's plan to use her to gain orders for his warehouse. With this in mind her nod was cool, and Jeremy's eyes clouded over.

It wasn't his fault any more than it was hers, she reminded herself, and immediately regretted her coldness. Jeremy's look of relief as she smiled was quite radiant.

'I dined at your father's house last night,' he shook hands with Matt when Elizabeth had introduced them. 'I'm sorry you weren't with us.'

'My father would as soon break bread with a mad dog as sit at the same table as me,' the weaver said bluntly.

'Matt!' She tugged at his arm, shocked and embarrassed. 'That's no way to speak of your own father!'

'I was never one for pretty words, Elizabeth.' He looked levelly at the Englishman. 'I'm sure Mister Forrest knows that shared blood doesn't always mean shared affections.'

'Indeed,' Jeremy grinned. 'My own father and I

have our quarrels. I think I was sent to Paisley because he was tired of the sight of me.'

'You're on business?'

'I'm buying shawls.'

Matt's eyes narrowed but he only said, mildly, 'You've come to the right town for that. You'll be staying long?'

'Another ten days, perhaps. I'm lodging in the Abbey Close with Mistress Mackay. If it was left to my own discretion—' for a warm moment his eyes rested on Elizabeth, '—I would stay longer. But my father says that time means money.'

'God, he's right about that,' Matt was suddenly reminded of his own work. 'Come on, Elizabeth, I've got to get back to the weaving shop. Good day to you, Mister Forrest, we'll mebbe find our paths crossing again.'

He bustled her off to the cabinet-maker's, approved of all she had selected with one impatient glance, and was off to the loom shop before she could catch her breath. Time did indeed mean money to Matt Montgomery these days.

He was certainly far too busy to spare time for Christian's outing on Monday. Helen, fresh and pretty despite her hard work in her new shop, was there with Adam in close attendance.

To Elizabeth's astonishment, the sight of Helen

didn't draw Jeremy from her side. He made certain, as they were handed aboard the gig-boat in the canal basin, that he obtained a seat beside her. Helen seated herself with Christian and began to chatter about her new business, and Adam was left to his own devices. He chose to sit alone, astern.

It was a warm, still day, and the boat, built to seat about one hundred passengers, was more than half filled. The helmsman aft and the lookout in the bows loftily ignored the bustle of humanity embarking on the trip. Christian scorned the covered cabin, and made sure that her charges got good seats at the side, where they could look down on the water, but where the awning would protect them from the sun. She cast a glance at Adam, apart from the rest of them, but left him to his own devices.

Two patient horses drew the boat from the basin and out onto the canal proper. A small boy, filled with self-importance and brandishing a whip made from a branch, sat astride the hind animal, but the horses knew their way along the tow-path well enough. Wallowing slightly in the shallow, calm water, the boat obediently answered the tug of the tow-rope.

The first part of the four-mile journey took them

past private property on the fringe of the town, then they moved at a stately pace into the surrounding countryside. At intervals they passed close to the road to Johnstone and were stared at enviously by pedestrians and carters. For most of the journey they sailed between fields where their only audience was cows, placidly chewing and unimpressed by the familiar gig.

Grassy banks vividly patterned with wild flowers framed the canal. White yarrow, red and purple knapweed, neat yellow meadow buttercups and marsh marigolds, white and red clovers, dandelions and deep pink ragged robins flourished. White and pink convolvulus twined through the hedges, their bell-like flowers at odds with their groping, choking stems.

Foxgloves rose behind the smaller flowers in stately ranks and delicate shell-pink wild roses massed the hedgerows. Elizabeth felt her anger with Rab melt away.

On a day like this she could forgive anyone.

They arrived all too soon, slipping into the basin at Johnstone half an hour after leaving Paisley. The gig bumped gently against the quay and the travellers were helped out onto dry land.

'Now, Mister Forrest, you must come with me and meet my friends,' Christian ordered. 'They're quiet folk and an Englishman'll be a novelty for them. You too, Elizabeth. And of course, Adam and Helen—' She looked about for the rest of her party as Jeremy's amused eyes caught and held Elizabeth's in shared, secret mirth.

'Tuts, they're off on some ploy of their own,' Christian said irritably, and Elizabeth turned in time to see the two of them, Adam's hand beneath Helen's elbow, disappearing along the path that led away from the small community.

'Well, we'll manage without them,' the older woman said. 'Adam gets fidgety if he's asked to sit still for long anyway. Now, follow me—' And she bustled off in the opposite direction while Jeremy offered Elizabeth his arm.

During the visit Elizabeth's thoughts kept straying to the missing couple. The year that Adam had spoken of wasn't yet over but there had been a growing tension about him, as though his patience was running out. As yet Helen had shown no interest in him other than as a friend, in Elizabeth's opinion. She was enraptured with her shop, and close friends like Elizabeth herself well knew that under her cheerful exterior Helen still grieved deeply for Alec. It was unlikely that any proposal of marriage, even the suggestion of one, would be well received.

To her surprise, the two of them were already waiting at the basin when Christian, Jeremy and herself arrived there.

Adam was swishing at grass heads with a stick, and Helen was staring down into the water, her face still.

She greeted them with a relieved smile. The gig was ready to leave, but as they were going aboard Adam said abruptly, 'I want to stretch my legs – I'll walk back.'

'But—' Christian gaped after him as he strode off with only a slight nod to them all. 'Now what's got into the man this time?' his cousin said in exasperation. 'Helen, do you know?'

'I havenae the faintest idea,' that young lady said shortly, and almost flounced into the boat.

'I trust young Mister Forrest had an enjoyable day,' Rab said heavily that evening.

Elizabeth ladled broth carefully into his bowl. 'He seemed to get on well with Mistress Selbie's friends.'

'Be damned to Christian's friends – did the man get on well with you, is what I'm asking?'

She gave the pot to Mary and nodded to the girl to take it back to the kitchen. 'As to that, I couldn't say. I've no way of knowing how to tempt a young man. I wasn't brought up to it!'

'Eh?' He lifted his head from his food and glowered at her. 'Don't be a fool with me, lassie! Did you smile at him and invite him to sit by you?'

She could feel her face burning. 'I was polite to him, as I was polite to Adam and to—'

'Adam?' Rab barked. 'Was he there? You've no need to waste your time being pleasant to that one, for he'd no' recognise good manners if he supped them from his porridge plate with his own spoon. Ach – away and leave me in peace!'

She went, thankfully, telling herself that she was as bad as he was. While he wanted to know what had transpired between her and Jeremy Forrest, she was longing to find out what had been said between Adam and Helen.

Helen herself brought up the subject when Elizabeth had an excuse to call in at the shop a day or two later. Wiping her hands on her apron, frowning thoughtfully after her last customer, she said abruptly, 'Elizabeth, what do you make of Adam?'

Startled, Elizabeth almost dropped the scale weights she had been fiddling with. 'What do you mean?'

'He's changed in the time he's been home.' Helen's lovely face was perplexed. 'He's become so serious – and downright domineering. He was on at me, that day in Johnstone, to give up the shop and stay home where my father could look after me. You'd think I was Catherine's age instead of a grown woman! Look after me, indeed!'

'He – worries about you. He cares – about your well-being.' Elizabeth had to choose her words as though they were sweets from the colourful jars on the shelves.

Helen's brown eyes were cool. 'He has no need. I know what I'm about and I made that quite clear to him. I'm tired,' she added with a firmness that would have worried Adam if he had heard it, 'of folk who try to make me behave like some soft-handed female with no notion of how to do anything for herself!'

Her chin jutted out and she thumped on the counter with a determined fist. At that moment she looked very capable indeed.

Matt's furniture was moved in, and at last the baby and the housekeeper took up residence. Matt decided to mark the occasion with a small dinner party, and informed Elizabeth bluntly that he must have her help.

'Mistress Crombie can see to the food, for she's a fine cook. But I'm looking to you to sit at the table with me and tend the other guests.'

'And what would your father say to that?'

'How's he to know? I'm inviting the Cassidys, and Adam, and mebbe someone else to make up the numbers. I have the right to ask you to dine at my house, and you have the right to accept. So we'll have no more argument about it, or I'll be forced to come and escort you there myself.'

She marvelled at his confidence. He was happy in his work, he had a home of his own and his son was with him again. Matt had a firm grasp on the ladder and his feet were impatient on the lower rungs.

As it happened, Rab was in London on a rare visit to the exporters when Matt's dinner was held, so she had no trouble in getting a free evening. She hesitated over her fine new gown, then decided that it was probably too grand, and settled instead for her pink muslin. Mary brushed her hair until it shone and crackled, then pinned it up with nimble fingers, getting a reasonable copy of the style Effie had given her before.

Adam called for her. It had been a hot day, but a pleasant breeze had sprung up by the evening, ruffling the 'Sick' notices on house doors.

'Will the cholera ever go, Adam?' It was becoming difficult to remember a time when it had not been part of the town's life.

'It'll tire of us one day.' He shivered. 'God, this place oppresses me!'

'Why don't you leave?' she asked at once, and sensed his side-long glance.

'You're the only person that knows the answer to that.'

They had reached St George's Place. She stopped by the church railings and turned to look up at him.

'Adam, Helen's contented enough with the life she's got. How can you be sure that she'll want to wed you when the time comes?'

His eyes darkened, his voice was scathing. 'Contented? That shop's like a new toy to a bairn. It's the wrong life for a woman like Helen. She'll find that out soon enough – and I'll be waiting.'

'You still think that all a woman needs in life is a man?'

'I know Helen. Give her a full year and she'll turn to me. Then I'll give her such happiness, such love, that—' his voice sharpened. 'Are you all right, Elizabeth?'

She had never known that emotion could act like a blow. The intensity of Adam's voice and his eyes as he talked about Helen and their future together had made her gasp and clutch at the church railings for support. She felt the blood drain from her cheeks and rush to her heart.

'I'm – a stone moved under my foot.' She

released the railings, walked on, pulling away from the hand he had put beneath her elbow for support. She couldn't bear him to touch her, just after he had mentioned Helen's name with such open passion.

She and Adam were the first to arrive. They went straight to the kitchen, to admire the baby.

'You should marry again, Matt, and give this bairn a mother,' Adam said with the bluntness born of affection. 'You're the sort of man who needs a woman by his side.'

Matt shrugged his broad shoulders, clothed in a smart new dark green jacket. 'I'm too busy to go courting, and I cannae think of anyone fit to take Isobel's place. Look to your own interests – is it no' time you were settling down yourself ?'

His brother smiled enigmatically. 'Mebbe I'm no' the marrying sort. Elizabeth – the gown becomes you, but my Cousin Christian was telling me what a fine lady you were when she dined with my father. I'd hoped to see you in that dress tonight.'

She blushed. 'It's a thing too grand for me. Who's expected, Matt?'

He gave Duncan a final hug and laid him down in his crib. 'The Cassidys and their two daughters, and thon Englishman – Forrest.'

She had no time to say anything. The knocker rattled and Matt bustled out to answer it, leaving Adam and Elizabeth to follow.

The Cassidys, husband and wife and teenage daughters, were all plump and rosy and cheerful. They squeezed up the narrow staircase and flowed into the elegant parlour, fingers fluttering, mouths opening and shutting like fish as they admired the well-chosen and carefully placed furniture, the pale grey wall-paper with its delicate floral pattern, the deep red curtains.

The knocker clattered again and Jeremy was there, in pale blue coat and well-cut grey trousers, his eyes once again searching for Elizabeth and holding her in their gaze.

'I'm indebted to Mister Montgomery for bringing us together once more,' he murmured in a stolen moment together. 'The gown is delightful – paid for or not!'

Over his shoulder, she caught sight of Adam's thoughtful blue gaze on them both.

'Mister Forrest—' She moved slightly so that his body blocked the sight of Adam. 'I'd be obliged if you'd be careful no' to let my employer know that you met me in this house.'

His brows lifted. 'Why should he object?'

Coming from a big city – and another country,

when all was said and done – he could have no understanding of the Paisley ways. Rab had thought to use her to attract Jeremy's business; instead, without realising what she was doing, she had introduced the young buyer to Matt. It was clear to her now that Matt had followed up that first meeting with the intention of obstructing any arrangements between his father and Jeremy's company.

If Rab found out about the part she had played in the affair his full anger would come down on her. But she couldn't begin to explain all this to Jeremy.

'Matt and his father don't get on,' she said, lamely.

Jeremy frowned. 'But surely your employer wouldn't object to you visiting a friend—' he began, then shrugged. 'However, if it's your wish – not a word shall he hear of it, I promise you.'

He left with the Cassidys at the end of a success-ful evening. Adam tossed Elizabeth's shawl care-lessly about her shoulders and the two of them went out into the clear mild night.

'I'd never have known Matt was so good at business if I hadn't seen it for myself,' Adam said after a long silence between them. 'While you ladies were inspecting the bairn after dinner he set about young Forrest with all the skill of a politician – or a surgeon. He's got a sharp brain, and a smooth tongue when he wants to use it.'

'Did he get an order?'

'More or less. I'm thinking that he could be Cassidy's junior partner before he's much older. That'd stick in my father's throat,' Adam said with relish.

Then he added with an abrupt change of tone. 'He's no' for you, Elizabeth.'

'Who?'

'The Englishman. Oh, he's pretty enough, and he has a fine way with him,' said Adam condescendingly, 'but you need someone with more to him than that.'

She felt her face burn. 'Adam Montgomery, are you at your black-footing again? I've told you before—!'

'I know what you've told me. I'm just saying that Forrest's mebbe a bonny diversion, but you'd be well advised no' to let him sweep you off your feet altogether. He's a toy – a plaything,' said Adam, and chuckled when she tossed her head and flounced ahead of him along the path.

Matt, at his parlour window, looked out onto the quiet night long after Adam and Elizabeth had turned the corner and disappeared from sight. He felt elated by the success of the evening and by the business deal he had just snatched from his father's very fingers. He had never realised, during those long dull years in the Montgomery warehouse, how invigorating business could be when a man was given the chance to think, and use his brain.

He sat down, gazed complacently about the room, then got up again at once and began to pace the carpet's length. He tingled with energy and the need to talk, or to work. The housekeeper was a civil soul but useless as far as conversation went. Matt wasn't one to spend his time in local howffs, drinking and gossiping – but tonight he needed company. With a brief word to Mrs Crombie, nodding by the kitchen fire, he went out and began to walk.

As he turned into George Street, with some idea of strolling round the streets before stopping some-where for a drink, a woman hurrying towards him tripped over a stone and the large basket she carried fell from her hand, spilling some of its contents.

Matt was near enough to leap forward and catch her before she fell full-length. She was surprisingly light in his arms, a soft bundle of material and flesh that gave itself to him for safe-keeping then immediately struggled for independence.

'Och, those stones!' said a pleasant voice. 'One of these – it's yourself, Matt!'

He peered through the summer darkness. It was a long time since he had seen Helen Grant, but her wide eyes and red hair were unmistakable.

'It's a while since we've met.' She was upright now, but balanced on one foot, still clutching at his arm. 'Did you see my shoe anywhere?'

He located it, and managed to reach for it. She stuck one shapely little foot from under her skirts. 'Would you put it on for me?'

He obliged clumsily, then the two of them crouched in the dusk, gathering up packages that had spilled from the basket. Helen clucked over each one.

'There's no harm done,' he reassured her as the last parcel was retrieved.

'I had them packed in the right order—' She poked among the collection. 'Now look at them!'

He took the basket from her. 'It's over heavy for you, is it no'?'

'I'm no' helpless!' she said at once, tartly, and he grinned.

'I'm sure of that. But I'd be willing to carry it for you – I've nothing better to do,' he added as she hesitated.

She put her head on one side, considering him,

then said, 'Come on, if you're coming,' and set off without another glance.

For an hour he followed her about the streets, both in the old town and in the new town on the other side of the river. When the basket grew lighter and Helen announced that she could finish the work herself he shook his head. 'It's getting late. I'll see you to the end of this and walk to your father's house with you.'

To his surprise he realised that the restlessness had disappeared, and that he was talking more freely to Helen than he had to anyone since Isobel's death. In return, she spoke honestly about Alec's gambling and the last few months of their marriage. Matt, who had always dismissed her as a frivolous female, realised that under the lovely, cheerful exterior was a young woman of considerable courage and great determination.

On the way home Helen stopped outside the Shuttle Street loom-shop.

'Can I see the cloth your weavers are working? It's been a long time since I was in a loom-shop.'

He led her through the passage, beating a light tattoo on the living-room doorway to let the family know that he was there. His fingers found the candle that was kept just inside the loom-shop door for his regular evening visits.

Light flickered over the looms, casting their shadows grotesquely over walls and ceiling. Then as Matt lit a lamp the room was touched with soft gold and the shadows disappeared. A linnet stirred in its cage and cheeped sleepily. Helen's neat nose flared as she drew in the remembered smell of the shop – yarn, linseed oil, the lingering traces of tobacco smoke, the scent of the flowers on the deep sills.

'It's strange to see looms at rest.'

'It's sad.' Talking about Isobel had set up a keen hunger for her. As he stood there, it ached at his body and his heart and his soul like a rotting tooth.

'It's only sad if there's no work for them. But these looms are resting. There's a waiting about them, a promise for tomorrow. You and me need to know about that, more than most.'

'What was it like, the first six months?' he asked bluntly. The question didn't seem to surprise her at all.

'A terrible loss. I put on a cheery face, and I worked and worked to dull my mind. At night, alone in the shop—' she said softly, remembering '—I'd talk to him, say the things I'd never got round to saying. And I'd cry for him.' She laid a small hand lightly on a loom as though feeling for the stilled life within it. 'And after a long while, I began to discover that I can go on living, even though it's never the same.'

'Aye.' He put his own hand, big and confident in the loom, near hers. The pain began to recede slightly, eased by Helen's understanding.

'You'll do well, Matt.' Her voice fell into the golden stillness of the room; her face was like a water-lily within a pool of red hair. 'And so will I. But for now I'll have to get home, for I've to be up early tomorrow.'

'Do you have many late deliveries?' he asked diffidently when they reached her parents' house.

'Quite a lot.'

'I'll mebbe take a walk round to the shop now and then, to help you with your basket.'

Helen studied him with warm brown eyes, then smiled.

'I'd like that. Good night to you, Matt.'

She went indoors, and Matt strolled home, whistling, and slept like a child till morning.

On the evening before he was due to return to London Jeremy Forrest took a box at the theatre and invited some people, Elizabeth included, to visit the New Tontine Theatre with him.

The play was a melodrama, *The Warlock of the Glen*. The drama and pathos of it absorbed Elizabeth from the moment the curtains swept aside to reveal the castle of Glencairn. She leaned over the edge of the box Jeremy had taken, soaking in every moment of the first act, and when the interval came she was stunned to find herself in the small crowded theatre instead of the Scottish glens.

'It's a lovely story!'

Jeremy smiled down at her. 'I wouldn't know. I'm too busy enjoying your pleasure to listen to mere actors.'

She blushed. 'You should pay heed to what they're saying. At five shillings for the seats it's a waste to sit and look at me!'

'On the contrary, every penny was well spent. I'm sorry to be leaving Paisley, Mistress Cunningham. May I pay my respects when I'm next in the town?'

'You're coming back?' The news brought a flutter of excitement to her voice, and she could tell by the lift of his eyebrow that he knew it.

'Certainly. I've bought goods from the Cassidy warehouse and I want to see more of their work next year.'

She felt her heart sink. 'You didnae buy from Mister Montgomery?'

'I'm sorry to disappoint your employer, but I must spend my father's money where he can be sure of the best return. I'm impressed by Matt

Montgomery, and grateful to you for introducing us.' Then his eyes lifted from hers and moved to a spot behind her. 'Isn't that his brother?'

Elizabeth turned. People were beginning to take their places for the next act. There were a few men standing in the box opposite and Adam was among them, watching Elizabeth and Jeremy. He bowed and she saw, quite clearly, the mocking lift of his dark brows as his eyes met hers.

She pinned a bright smile on her face, inclined her head graciously as she had seen Christian do, and turned back to Jeremy, laughing up at him and chattering about the play.

It would do Adam good to see that his opinions about Jeremy mattered not one jot to her.

Jeremy Forrest went back to London and Rab grew more morose with each day that passed. Although she could no longer find a shred of liking for her employer, Elizabeth pitied him. She heard the rumours that were floating from mouth to mouth, whispering that the Montgomery warehouse was failing, the work no longer satisfactory, buyers going elsewhere because of Rab's churlish behaviour.

When Matt crowed to her about his success in

snatching the Forrest business from under his father's nose, Elizabeth's pity for the old man made her say hotly, 'Have you no feelings at all? He's alone now, with nobody to turn to!'

But Matt had learned to be hard.

'He's alone because he drove everyone from him. His new foreman's a dishonest fool and his designer's no' much better,' he said shortly. 'Let him suffer – it's no' before time!'

Only Christian stayed true to Rab, visiting him several times a week, even although the only time she could be sure of finding him at home now was to call late in the evenings.

Elizabeth welcomed those visits. Rab still insisted on her presence in the parlour after supper and she hated every silent moment of it, the old man sunk in his thoughts in one chair, while she sat stitching or knitting in another.

But even Christian could do nothing with Rab.

'Sell off the business and be done with it, man!'

He stood before the grate, glass in hand, and glowered down at her. 'I'll be damned if I will! I've given twelve years of my life to that warehouse and I'll no' let it go now!'

'You've as much money as you'll ever need. You should settle down and enjoy the time that's left to you.'

He gave a harsh bark of laughter and drained the glass.

'There's nothing else that'll interest me. Talk sense, woman! Elizabeth – more whisky!'

'And that's another thing—' Christian nagged as Elizabeth obediently laid down her work and scurried to the kitchen '—you drink too much. One of these days you'll do for yourself. As for talking sense – I never stop, but you're too thrawn to listen to me!'

The rumours grew and took on a sinister note. It was being said that the once-proud Montgomery warehouse was indulging in truck trading, the practice disreputable manufacturers had of paying weavers with unwanted goods instead of with the money the weavers needed.

A man who tried to cheat the workers in Paisley only brought down trouble on his own head. Elizabeth couldn't believe that Rab would be so foolish. But there was no denying it, once the word ran like wildfire through the town, from one coffee house to another, from the Cross to Broomlands, and in all the howffs where men gathered to drink.

'They're making an effigy for old Montgomery—' The story spread as swiftly and as dangerously as the cholera.

Elizabeth had never witnessed the weavers on

the march with drum and fifes; even so, her blood ran cold when she heard about the effigy. Everybody in the town knew what it meant.

If a 'cork' – a manufacturer – tried to undercut the fixed price table, or tried in any other way to cheat his workers, the weavers marched to his door at night carrying before them an effigy of the man for all to see.

Manufacturers had been known to flee the town when they heard that their effigies were being prepared. It was a form of condemnation that few could survive.

As soon as the malignant whisper reached her ears Christian swooped down on her kinsman's house. She and Rab had a furious scene when he refused to find some business to take him elsewhere until the matter had been forgotten, and Christian slammed out of the house, thwarted for once.

Rab continued about his business, face closed, eyes cold, apparently oblivious to the stares and the murmurs about him. It was as though he couldn't believe that the weavers would carry out their intention to shame him, the son and grandson of highly respected local men.

Adam's impatient fist thundered on the street door the day after Christian and Rab quarrelled.

He pushed past Elizabeth without a word and strode into the parlour, where his father sat at his supper.

'It's tonight,' he announced crisply. 'The men are going to march – and it's your door they're coming to.'

Rab picked up a piece of bread, broke it, and dropped the fragments into his broth. 'Get out of my house.'

'For pity's sake, man, are you deaf?' his son asked impatiently. 'Do you think you can take on the whole town and win? I'm no' here for your sake, mind. I wouldnae let Christian come back to face you. Will you do as she says and go off to Helensburgh or some such place till the thing's died down? I can have her carriage here in minutes.'

Rab looked up, his eyes malevolent. 'I'll run from nobody, let alone ragged wastrels with a wooden doll!'

'You're whistling in a gale – there's nobody left to admire your bravery!' Adam shouted at him, enraged beyond endurance. When Rab said nothing, and picked up his spoon to continue eating, the younger man turned on his heel, brushing clumsily past Elizabeth. His face was black with rage.

'Adam—' She hurried after him, caught at his sleeve.

'Let the old fool be shamed before the whole town,' he gritted at her. 'I've done as Christian asked, and I'll do no more!'

Then the anger faded and his eyes focused on her.

'Come with me to Christian's house – you and the lassie. You shouldnae be exposed to such ugliness – not you, Elizabeth.'

There was a look on his face that she had never seen before. It was as though he was seeing her clearly for the first time.

'I've told you before – I cannae just leave him.' Her voice trembled on the last few words. Adam cupped her face with one hand, and without thinking she put her own hand over his, holding it against her cheek.

'By God, Elizabeth—' he said softly, with wonder. 'I've never met your equal. If it wasnae for—' Then he stopped as his father bellowed her name from the room behind them. The hard warmth of Adam's palm left her skin, the door opened and she was alone, her heart crying out for him.

'Tell the lassie to get to her bed – and away to your own room,' Rab ordered harshly when she went to him.

'You've still to take your meat.'

He pushed his half-empty plate away. 'I'm no' interested in food. Just get yourself and the girl out of my sight for today!'

The weavers came later that night, as Adam had said. Lying awake, listening for them, she heard the chant of voices in the distance, the piping of fifes, the deep boom of the district drum.

She slipped out of bed and stood at the window. The street outside was narrow, and her attic room only allowed her a view of the attics and roofs of the houses opposite. Even so, she could imagine the scene below as clearly as though she was watching.

There would be torchlight flickering eerily on walls and turning the men's faces into grotesque, open-mouthed masks. The street would be filled, from house-wall to house-wall, with folk drawn from hearth and howff to watch the spectacle. There would be a taggle of bare-footed, ragged children and noisy, excited drawboys, and there would be the effigy, the centre of attention.

The noise swelled, and she knew that the marchers were outside Rab's front door. Jeering voices floated up to where she stood shaking with cold and terror. She was vividly reminded of the day when the coffins had been dug up and Matt's wife had died, and she listened for the crash of breaking glass and splintered wood.

But the angry weavers had no intention of breaking into the house. There was a sudden cheer, then the voices began to ebb, the drum gave out a final hollow note, and the fifes piped once more then fell silent. The marchers went home, their work done. There wasn't a sound anywhere in the house.

Elizabeth dozed through the long night and was up early in the morning. Even so, the outside door was swinging on its hinges when she reached the bottom of the stairs, and Rab's hat, stick and coat were missing.

She went to close the door then stopped, staring, one hand at her mouth to stifle the scream that came to her throat. For a terrible moment, she had thought that it was Rab Montgomery himself who dangled against the house-wall across the street, hanging on the end of a strong rope that had been thrown about a chimney.

The effigy had been made by someone with a clever talent for detail. In height and breadth it was identical to the man it represented. The men had even managed to get their hands on clothes very like Rab's – dark tailcoat, fawn trousers, a white shirt with a black silk band about the high collar, a top hat on the lolling head.

The mask they had put on it for a face was a parody of Rab's square, ruddy features, and the sightless eyes gave it a ghoulishly human appearance. There was no need to read the label pinned to the figure's breast to tell who it portrayed. A few early risers were standing staring at the hanging creature. Attracted by movement at the door they turned and gaped at Elizabeth, and it seemed to her that their eyes held the same round blankness as the effigy's.

Her empty stomach heaved. She slammed the door and sank down into a heap against it, her knees like water.

She was still there when fists pounded at the wood and Mary came running, sleepy-eyed and frightened from the kitchen.

With the girl's help Elizabeth got up and opened the door, her eyes averted from the wall opposite.

The white-faced man panting on the step was Rab Montgomery's new foreman. He had been the one to find his employer in the vast, half-empty warehouse, hanging from a sturdy beam, with a length of good strong Paisley yarn about his neck.

XI

It was as though the town felt that Rab Montgomery had paid sufficiently for his misdemeanours. Even though he was a suicide, he was given a brave funeral, with a long train of sober-faced men following his coffin.

Matt and Adam led the mourners. At first Matt had strongly resisted his brother's efforts to get him to attend.

Elizabeth, still stunned by the horror of the effigy and the shock of Rab's death, was in Christian's drawing-room when the brothers faced each other, both determined.

'It would be hypocrisy if I was seen there,' Matt said scathingly. 'And to tell the truth, Adam, you'll be a hypocrite yourself if you go!'

Adam gave him an icy blue stare. 'Has the man no rights at all? We owe him some courtesy – family quarrels have no place at a time like this, with the whole town looking on!'

'What's all this noise?' Christian interrupted sharply from the doorway, and the brothers had the grace to look embarrassed as she came to stand between them.

She had acted with her usual efficiency when she heard of Rab's death, sending Adam to the house to bring Elizabeth and Mary back to Oakshawhill with him, seeing to it that a place was found for the maid with friends of hers. Now, Elizabeth thought, the older woman was beginning to show the strain. Her black dress highlighted her pallor, her face was drawn, her eyes blank. But her spine was as ramrod straight as ever and her voice had a bite to it.

'Of course you'll walk behind your father!' she snapped at Matt. He flushed, but shook his head.

'Not even to please you, cousin. There was no love lost between the two of us, and everyone knows that. I've got more to do than stand arguing about it!' he said, and walked out.

'Leave him be!' Christian raised a hand and Adam stopped on his way to the door, his face like a thundercloud.

'Christian, it would be best if we just had a quiet burial, if it's leading to trouble between Matt and me. Who's going to care anyway?'

Small though she was she seemed to expand with sheer rage.

'Who's going to care, is it? Who's going to care? You impertinent upstart,' she flared at him, while he and Elizabeth stared at her in astonishment. 'I'm going to care, that's who! My own kinsman – your own father. He'll go to his final resting place in style supposing I'm the only mourner—'

'You know fine it's not done for a woman to attend a funeral,' he interrupted, but her voice rose above his.

'Don't you presume to tell me what I should do, Adam Montgomery! I'm head of this family now that—' she choked slightly '—now that Rab's gone. If I want to hire the militia band and bury the man with my own two hands I'll do it without interference from the likes of you! He'll have a fitting burial, and you'll be there – and you'll mourn him!' she finished on a note of fury, and swept from the room, leaving Adam and Elizabeth in total bewilderment.

'I pity Matt when she gets to him,' Adam said at last.

But when Christian rattled loudly on Matt's fine door-knocker she discovered that her errant cousin had changed his mind about the funeral. Cheated of her victory, Christian never found out that it was

Helen who had changed Matt's view during one of their walks by the river at night, when the town was settling to sleep and the long working day had finished for them both.

'You'll do what you think's best, Matt,' she said quietly in the near darkness. 'Just remember that you've a son of your own now. Would you want him to see you to your grave when the time comes?'

Suddenly it made sense to Matt, viewed from that angle. He had grown dependent on those meetings with Helen; her easy relaxed presence and tidy, practical mind had helped him to solve more than one problem. With her help he was becoming used to life without Isobel. And still nobody knew about those meetings, which made them all the more precious to him.

After the funeral Christian invited Elizabeth to stay on in her home, as her companion.

'It's lonely now that Adam's found that wee place in Barclay Street. I got used to having someone else around – and after all didn't Rachel, God rest her, mean you to be a companion anyway?' she said sensibly.

Adam had set up his sign at a tiny surgery not far from Helen's sweet shop, and had found himself rooms nearby. The house in High Street was up for sale.

Even in the turmoil of Rab's death Elizabeth found time to wonder over that brief moment when Adam had cupped her face in his hand and looked at her with a new awareness. She hadn't seen that look since, for he was too busy with the funeral and his moving to be more than courteous to her when they met.

Christian insisted on taking Elizabeth off to Edinburgh for a few days to choose new gowns.

'I couldn't be doing with those dull dresses Rab expected you to wear day in and day out,' she said as the carriage jolted over the roads. 'No point in having some bonny young thing about the house if she's wearing dull clothes. Besides, you've more chance of catching Adam's eye with better clothes.'

Elizabeth gaped at her and the older woman chuckled, delighted with herself.

'Did you think I never saw the way you brighten up when he walks into a room? Don't look at me like that – the man has no idea of your feelings for him. Montgomerys were always slow on the uptake when it came to romance. But it's my belief that you'd make a fine wee wife for a young surgeon.'

'Mistress Selbie! I'm a person, no' a cow for sale in the market! And anyway I'd never be Adam's preference.' Elizabeth swooped from indignation to gloom as she finished. Christian clucked her tongue.

'I'm no' talking about his preference, but about what's good for him. And it's my opinion that you're the right lassie.'

'He might have other views.'

'Not at all,' Christian said, so sweepingly that Elizabeth knew she had no idea about Helen. 'You're the one, and the sooner he finds that out the better.'

'If you tell him I'll – I'll—'

'What in the name of goodness do you think I am?' Christian asked, innocently. 'Not a word he'll hear from me.'

But the gleam in her eye said that Adam might receive a nudge in the right direction now and then, and Elizabeth was uneasy for the rest of the journey.

Edinburgh swept everything else from her mind. The streets were packed with people, the new town was a wonder of wide roads and elegant squares, and the dressmakers' shops and milliners' shops and hatters' shops and haberdashery shops were palaces compared to anything she had set foot in before.

'It's a relief to get out of Paisley for a day or two,' Christian said on their final evening as she toasted her toes at the fire in their lodgings. 'Especially at a time like this. I'm glad we had a reason to get away.'

'You're going to miss Mister Montgomery.' Elizabeth watched her closely.

'It's a thought when folk you knew all your life go off and die,' the older woman admitted, staring into the flames, her face averted. 'There's never anyone to take their place. He was an old rascal, but I'll admit to having a fondness for him.'

Then, still watching the flames dancing, she added, 'In fact, there was a time when I might have been his wife instead of Adam's mother, God rest her.'

Elizabeth held her breath and let the silence lengthen until Christian broke it again.

'Och – that was when we were too young to have sense. Rab was all for marriage, but my sights were set higher than a weaver in Paisley. And I did what I set out to do, I wed a banker and had more money than Rab could ever have given me. Not that money matters much when you get older and begin to think clearly.'

A smile twisted her mouth for a moment.

'By the time I came back to Paisley as a well set-up widow Rab was married for the second time. And when Rachel died – well, old bodies never talk of marriage, do we? I thought of putting it to him once or twice, plump and plain, that we should visit the minister and get the thing decided. But Rab would never have agreed to that, and I'd my pride. Mind you—' she added after another pause, '—I've been fair tormented by the thought that if I'd pushed him into marrying me, old bundle of bones that I am now, he'd be alive today. Still, we cannae turn the clock back, can we?'

She sniffed, blinked, and smiled at her new companion.

'Just mind this, Elizabeth – when happiness turns up, grip hold of it with your two hands. Never mind your pride. It never yet kept old bones warm.'

'Mind thon white kid glove you misplaced when you visited, a week or two before he—' Elizabeth said hesitantly.

'Aye?'

'I have it back at Oakshawhill. I found it among his possessions when I was clearing the house.'

Christian smiled, a radiant, bright-eyed smile.

'The daft, sentimental old devil!' she said, a youthful lilt suddenly in her voice, though it shook. 'You'll not forget to give it back to me when we get home, will you, Elizabeth?'

*

The High Street house was sold and the money split between Adam and Matt. Matt bought a partnership with Cassidy, and persuaded the old man to take over the Montgomery warehouse in Forbes Place. He paid a swift visit to London and came home filled with enthusiasm.

'I met up with Jeremy Forrest,' he told Elizabeth on a rare visit to Christian's house. 'He asked after you, and hopes to visit you when he comes to Paisley next.' His eyes twinkled. 'I told him what a fine young lady you'd become – and how bonny you've grown.'

Adam, sprawled over a chair, said nothing, but his eyes caught and held Elizabeth's, and she heard him say, as clearly as if he had spoken aloud, 'He's a toy – a plaything.'

She flushed and wrenched her gaze back to Matt, who had gone on to talk about the work he'd won for the new partnership among the London markets.

The cheerful, rather placid young man who had wooed and won Isobel Gibson had become an adventurer, a gambler with a sane streak that ensured the success of his gambling. Cassidy was trusting enough to let Matt have his head, and the new partnership was thriving from the start.

'You're like a coachman with a team of horses, every one of them going its own way,' Adam told him. 'You know what happens then – the coach ends up in the ditch and the coachman falls into the mire.'

Matt's grin was supremely confident.

'I've got the reins in my hands, and I know fine how to handle them. Besides, if I get hurt, my brother the surgeon can patch me up.'

Throughout October the cholera cases began to decrease at last. At the beginning of November, as the town excitedly prepared for the first municipal election under the new Reform Act, the disease came to a standstill. Well over eight hundred people in Paisley had fallen sick in the previous ten months, and more than half of them, James Montgomery included, had died.

In another month Helen would have been widowed for a whole year, Elizabeth remembered every morning when her eyes opened on a new day. She watched Adam and saw a spring in his step, a squaring of his shoulders, as his long self-imposed silence drew to its end.

Matt decided to put looms into the old Forbes Place warehouse, a move that caused a stir in the town.

'It's the done thing in England now, and it makes sense, having folk working under the one roof,' he argued when Christian criticised him.

'But there's no need for it. It's different in manufactories where there's machinery, like the thread mills at Ferguslie. But looms don't need steam.'

'It'll bring the weavers together instead of having to carry their webs to the looms and carry the work back to the warehouse when it's done. It gives weavers without their own looms a place to work, and it gives me a chance to see that the work keeps on during the day.'

'That's the part of it I don't care for. Handloom weavers have always worked their own hours. As long as the work's done nobody stands over them. Your warehouse is a step nearer the manufactories where women and men and bairns all have to work long hours, with no time to live like human beings.'

His jaw set in familiar, stubborn lines, and once again Elizabeth was reminded of his father.

'I'd never do that. Anyway, times have to change, cousin – and I'd as soon be the man making the changes as the man following along behind, always one step late.'

Then the elections were on them, and for a while nobody thought of anything else. The Paisley folk were highly political, and they had fought hard for the new Reform Bill, which gave them more say in the running of their town. They weren't going to let this election slip past unnoticed.

A day or two after it was all over Matt and Helen swept into Christian's parlour, both bright-eyed and rosy after a walk up the hill on a sharp November evening.

Adam, who was leaning against the mantelpiece talking, looked at once at Helen, Elizabeth noticed. The young widow was a sight to gladden any heart, with her glowing hair offset by a dark green cape and yellow gown.

'Mercy me – here's a surprise.' Christian jumped to her feet. 'Did you two meet on the doorstep?'

'We walked up the hill together.' Helen let Adam take her cape and sat by the fire, her hands held out to its blaze.

Matt stayed on his feet, bathing them all in a wide grin. 'We called at your lodgings, Adam, and your landlady said she thought you might be here.'

He rubbed his hands together, and Christian eyed him closely.

'You've got a plan in your head, Matt.'

The grin almost split his face. 'You could say that.'

She seated herself in her favourite tapestry chair. 'Well – out with it. Is it another new cloth?'

'It's better than that. It's a new wife.'

Elizabeth knew that the shock on Christian's face must be mirrored on her own. Before either of them could move Adam was shaking his brother by the hand, face alight.

'Man, that's the best news I've heard in a while! And I didnae know a thing about it. Well – who's it to be?'

Matt walked to where Helen sat, drew her to her feet, put his arm about her. 'Here she is. We're to be married at New Year,' he said, happiness shining out of his eyes as he looked down at her.

The world stopped. Elizabeth dragged her head round, away from Matt and Helen, past Christian's excited face, until she was looking at Adam. The hand that had clasped Matt's was falling slowly, slowly, to his side. Elizabeth seemed to be deaf, unable to hear anything though she knew somehow that Christian and Matt and Helen were talking all together. In stopping, the world had lost all sense of time. She was able to watch the expressions chasing each other across Adam's face – shock, horror, heartbreak. She was able to stand helplessly and see the colour draining from his features as though a grey veil had been pulled slowly down from hairline to neck.

His step back, away from the happy trio by the fire, was probably swift, but Elizabeth saw it as the languorous movement of a drowned man on the seabed, moved here and there by the tide.

Then all at once the trance shattered; she was back in the parlour, seeing and hearing, and the world was moving at its usual pace again.

'And I hadnae the slightest suspicion!' Christian was quacking joyfully. 'When did this come about?'

Helen's smile was radiant. 'We had no notion of it ourselves until last week. We just met now and again, walking home, and we talked. Then—'

'Then last week,' Matt cut in. 'We just – knew.' He hugged Helen. 'It's mebbe a bit soon, after Isobel and Alec, but we've got bairns to think of, and we're sure of our feelings—'

'Then it's the sensible thing to get wed,' Christian told him briskly. 'Mercy – a wedding, and me with nothing at all to wear—'

It might have been all right if Adam had been left alone to recover from the shock of the news. But Matt left the women to talk about weddings, and turned to his brother.

'Well, Adam – I took your advice. You'll be pleased—'

Even Elizabeth, watching Adam with her heart in her mouth, didn't realise what was going to happen. Matt, one hand held out to his brother, was quite unprepared for the fist that smashed into his face.

Helen screamed as Matt reeled back, tripped over the carpet, and fell against a small table. Wood splintered and glass tinkled as he crashed to the floor.

Adam caught Helen, spun her to face him. 'It's not true!'

She tore herself free and ran to Matt, who lay dazed on the floor. Blood trickled from the corner of his mouth and she used the skirt of her lovely gown to staunch it. Her head turned and her eyes blazed up at Adam.

'Are you insane?' she hissed at him. He moved towards her and she gathered Matt's head in her arms as though determined to defend him with her own life.

'Helen – it was always you and me—'

'Not in many a long year, Adam Montgomery. I'm a woman now, no' a little girl to be owned, can you no' understand that? Your brother can. Leave us to our own lives!'

He stepped back as though she had hit him, his face like marble. When Christian, finding her voice, asked, 'What do you think you're doing? Attacking your own brother, and in my house—' he gave her a strange, formal bow.

'Your pardon, cousin, I'll go before I can offend you further.'

'Adam – wait!' Matt said from the floor, but Helen cut in swiftly.

'Let him go, Matt – let him go away and leave us to our happiness!'

Adam's head came up swiftly at her words but he continued on his way to the door, shutting it with frightening gentleness behind him. Elizabeth wrenched it open, calling his name, and followed him to the front door.

He turned there, his face a mask, his eyes burning.

'You knew! You knew and you didn't tell me!'

'I swear I didn't!'

He walked out, leaving the door swinging. She ran after him and the cold air bit into her at once. Adam lurched onto the road and disappeared into the darkness with long furious strides.

Christian and Effie were in the hall. Christian issued swift instructions about warm water and soft cloths, then turned to Elizabeth.

'Did you know about this?'

She nodded. 'He's hoped, ever since Alec died, that one day she'd turn to him.'

Christian's mouth tightened. 'The daft, mis-guided creature! Did he never realise that Helen needed a man who'd treat her like a human being instead of a kitten? Where are you off to?'

Elizabeth pulled her cloak about her shoulders. 'I'm going to look for him.'

'In every howff in Paisley? That's where he'll be headed. Then, no doubt, he'll pay a visit to the houses by the river.'

The slums by the river were home for local petty thieves and beggars, and for the prostitutes.

'Think on, lass—' Christian put a hand on her arm. 'You'll get no thanks from Adam, you know that well enough. The man's in hell right now, and like as not he'll drag you down there with him.'

'I cannae leave him on his own!'

Christian sighed, and stepped back. 'He's a bigger fool than I took him for, setting his sights on Helen instead of looking closer to home,' she said, and turned away.

There was a rowdy party going on in the ground-floor flat where Adam's landlord lived. The landlady knew who Elizabeth was, and let her go up to his shabby, sparsely furnished room. It was empty.

Elizabeth waited, wandering about the room, picking up books, putting them down again. She managed to get a fire going in the grate, and huddled close to its warmth. The noise of the party floated up through the gapped floor-boards.

After a time she thought that Adam might be in his surgery, and ventured down the rickety stairs. The street was fairly quiet, for most of the towns-folk were in their own homes by that time of night.

She knocked on the surgery door, but there was no answer, and no light showed under the door or at the small window. She wandered on, shivering, joining little knots of children waiting patiently outside howffs for fathers and, in some cases, mothers who were drinking inside. She didn't dare venture in to look for Adam.

A man lurched out of a low, lighted door and into her path. He caught at her to steady himself, then his grip tightened as he bent to peer into her face.

'And what's a bonny wee lassie like yourself doing out at this time of night?' he asked, his voice slurred, whisky fumes almost stifling her.

'I'm – I'm going home to my bed—' She tried to draw away but he pulled her back, close to him.

'Come on, lass – come home to my bed instead.' He began to drag her towards a narrow, dark lane. Struggling didn't help. Instead, she bent swiftly and sank her teeth into the dirty hand that

309

clamped over her arm, biting deep, choking at the sour smell of him.

He yelled and let go. She whirled and picked up her skirts, then ran blindly, gasping open-mouthed for breath, bumping into people.

Someone reeled back with an oath as she crashed into him. Thrown back against a house wall, she raised her hands before her face defensively, but they were dragged down.

'Elizabeth?' Adam stared at her, his face pale in the uncertain light from the street gas lamps.

She was so glad to see him that she could have wept. 'Adam! Are you all right?'

His mouth twisted bitterly. 'No need to let that worry you!' He began to walk away, moving unsteadily over the footpath, and she had to run to catch up with him.

'Where are you going?'

'Down by the river,' he said sullenly. 'To see if there's a kind-hearted lassie and a bottle of whisky waiting for me. Have you any money, Elizabeth?'

He swung round on her, one hand held out.

'I've nothing,' she lied. 'Come back to your cousin's house—'

He laughed. 'After what I did? Mebbe somebody'll give me hosh – hospitality in exchange for my timepiece—'

She caught at his arm. 'There's drink in your room.' When he stared down at her suspiciously she hurried on, 'I took a bottle there myself, for I thought you might be sitting alone.'

Frowning, he considered her, then shrugged and turned back towards the street where his lodging was.

She followed as he climbed the rickety stairs. The party was still going on below. Adam threw the door open and lurched into the room. When Elizabeth closed the door and turned, he was staring blearily around the room.

'Where is it?'

She moistened her lips. 'It – someone mebbe took it downstairs. Adam—' She stood before the door as he moved forward. 'Adam, I knew nothing of Matt and Helen!'

He stiffened and for a moment the effects of drink fled from his face, leaving him clear-eyed and hard as rock.

'I'll thank you no' to mention their names to me – never, do you hear me? Now get out of my way!'

She stood where she was. Some instinct told her that if he went out again, into the dark streets, down to the hovels by the river, he would be lost for all time to her.

'Elizabeth—' he said threateningly, but she was

the one who moved forward, half afraid, half determined, going into his arms, drawing his head down to hers, holding him close.

'Stay with me, Adam—' The words fluttered from her lips, and she saw his dark blue eyes, close to hers, clear again then narrow.

'If I stay – and if I let you stay,' he murmured, 'you know what'll happen. I need a woman tonight – oh, God, Elizabeth, you cannae imagine how much I need a woman with me tonight!'

She felt a trembling in the arms that slowly closed around her, a bruising hunger in the mouth he lowered to hers, and for all her inexperience and fear, she found that there was a hunger in her that matched his, passion for passion.

There was no tenderness in his love-making. He wasn't interested in giving, only in taking. His demands were great, his burning need greater still, but Elizabeth, freed from everything that had happened until that moment, gave gladly, again and again, throwing inhibition to the winds and letting the pure female instincts buried deep within her carry them both on until Adam finally rolled away from her in the narrow bed, and slept.

The party downstairs was over, the house quiet. Elizabeth shivered as the heat gradually ebbed from her and the night air touched her skin. Adam had rolled himself in the blanket and rather than disturb him she got up, moving stiffly, and wrapped herself in her cloak. Then she drew the chair close to the bed and huddled on it.

Her upbringing told her that what had happened was shameful. She had allowed a man to make use of her with no tenderness or care for her at all. She was disgraced.

But Adam's touch had released a deep, hidden instinct within her. In the past hour she had matured, become her true self. She could only be glad, as she shivered in the dawn chill, that it had been Adam, and nobody else, who had brought this gift. If Fate decreed that he was to be the only man, and this was to be the only night, she would accept it and go her own way without complaint.

He woke and rolled over.

'Elizabeth?' He half sat up when he recognised her by his side, then fell back, rubbing a hand over his face. 'God help me – I thought it was all a dream.'

She touched his cheek lightly and withdrew her hand at once, unsure of his mood. 'It's beginning to get light outside. D'you want me to go?'

'You should never have stayed—' said Adam, and reached for her. She let the cloak fall to the chair and moved into his embrace.

This time he showed some compassion, giving her time to match the rhythm of his needs.

He only spoke once. 'I was never a gentle man, Elizabeth,' he whispered, half-apologetically. Then it was her turn to sleep, a deep, sudden sleep that caught her unawares while she still lay with her head on his naked chest.

It was full daylight when she woke and at first she didn't know where she was.

Adam was up, dressed in his trousers, pulling his shirt on.

'You're awake. We'd best go and see my cousin Christian,' he said tersely. She sat up on the cot, and his eyes darkened as they slid over her body. He tightened his lips, but said nothing. Frightened by the look in his face, convinced that in daylight he found her repulsive, she glanced down, and realised that several ugly bruises marred her white shoulders and the soft, youthful curve of her breasts.

As she got up, glad that he had turned away to give her some form of privacy, she winced. She felt raw and stiff. She reached for her shift, then his words made sense.

'Why should you go to see your cousin? I can find my own way back without your help.'

Adam fastened his cuffs, intent on looking out

of the window. 'I can hardly let you go back at this hour of the day without giving her some explanation.'

'I can see to that!'

'Don't be a fool,' he said coldly. 'I have to go to the office for a minute. Wait here. There's no food, but no doubt Christian'll be willing to feed you – though I doubt if she'll feed me.'

'Adam—!'

The door closed behind him. With trembling fingers she finished dressing as quickly as she could, tidied her tangled hair, peered into a cloudy glass, and was glad to see that Adam's passion hadn't marked her face, though she looked like a tinker.

As she scurried down the stairs, anxious to get away before he came back, the landlady was passing through the close below. She turned, looked Elizabeth up and down, and smirked.

Walking was decidedly painful. She moved like an old woman at first, then the pain began to ease and she was able to step out. Even so, Adam caught her when she was only half-way to Oakshawhill.

'I told you to wait for me!' he said harshly.

She turned, glaring up at him. 'And I told you – I can see to myself. Just because—' she stopped short, feeling colour rush into her face. '—you neednae think that you own me!'

His brows knotted between his blue eyes. 'Own you? It's time you stopped reading those romantic novelettes, lassie! Owning's for hounds and horses and cattle, no' for women!'

Nevertheless, he put a firm, possessive hand beneath her elbow and refused to let her go back to Christian's house alone.

Christian opened the door while Elizabeth, grateful for Adam's hand beneath her arm, was negotiating the step.

'Mercy, Elizabeth, where have you been?'

'With me,' Adam said bluntly before she could speak. He bundled her into the house, and headed towards the drawing-room. Christian, mindful of the half-open kitchen door, waited until she had followed them into the drawing-room before she said, 'All night?'

'All night, cousin. It's a pity that I couldnae offer the lassie any breakfast, but I hoped you'd find it in your heart to be kind, and feed us both.'

Christian glared at him. 'My, but you're a cool one, Adam Montgomery.'

He met her look. 'You didn't think that last night. It's thanks to this lassie here that I've got my common sense back. Are you going to feed us, or are you going to throw the two of us out?'

'No need to be daft altogether,' the older woman said crisply and marched out to order food.

'Adam,' Elizabeth said swiftly. 'When you've eaten, will you go to Matt and—'

'No! I don't mind much about last night, but I mind telling you I don't want to hear his name or – hers, again. That's my last word on it!' he said fiercely.

'But you'll meet him again and again. You cannae just pretend he's no' there!'

Adam's chin jutted. 'I'll no' meet him in London. We're going there as soon as I can make the arrangements.'

'London?' So he was going away, out of Paisley, out of her life.

'We?' Christian said sharply, coming back into the room in time to catch his last words. 'What does that mean?'

'It means I'm done with Paisley, for the rest of my life. I'm going to work at St Thomas's hospital, the way I planned before. And Elizabeth's coming with me. Don't fret, cousin, I'll marry the girl and make it all legal.'

Elizabeth turned on him. 'And what makes you think I'd take you for a husband?'

'You'd be well advised to.' His face was

expressionless. 'There can be no love in it, for I've had my fill of such nonsense. But I need a wife, and God knows you need a husband—'

'I can see to myself!'

He ignored Christian, marched over to where Elizabeth stood, and shook her.

'Use your head, girl! If you could see to yourself so well you'd never have allowed yourself to be tumbled into my bed last night!'

'Oh, my!' Christian said from behind him, eyes sparkling.

'And don't tell me that you're used to men, for it was obvious that I was the first. You're so innocent that you'd end up in one of those river houses sooner than see to yourself!'

She tore free, wincing at the pain of her bruises, and fled to her room. If she thought that that meant refuge she was wrong. Feet pounded on the stairs, Adam's voice roared out her name, and the door burst open, slamming back against the wall. He stood in the doorway, glaring at her.

'For the last time, Elizabeth – will you see sense and wed me!'

'Adam Montgomery!' Christian puffed from just behind him. 'Is that any way to propose to a lassie?'

'It's the only proposal she'll get from me,' he

said grimly. 'Go away, Christian! Elizabeth—?'

Christian's bright eyes appeared round the side of his arm. 'Elizabeth – before you say anything I want you to try and mind where you found that fine white kid glove of mine—'

'For the Lord's sake, Christian—' Adam bellowed, rounding on his cousin, 'is this any time to start looking for a glove? Now – out of here and let me and Elizabeth discuss our business in a civilised way!'

With a small shriek Christian disappeared. The door slammed shut, and Adam and Elizabeth were alone.

'Well?'

'What have you to offer me?' she challenged, though now her mind was on that little white glove that had been tucked carefully away in a drawer in his father's room, a symbol of pride and loss.

'Is it not obvious? A good home, comfort, a place in society – independence.'

She tilted her chin. 'I'd hoped for love, one day.'

'You've surely got more sense than that,' he said sweepingly. Then he shrugged. 'Well, if you'd as soon stay here, with Christian, it's your own concern.' He turned to the door.

'Adam—'

He stopped, his back towards her. 'Aye?'

Christian was right. Happiness had to be caught and held. And whatever sort of marriage Adam had to offer, would be better than staying in Paisley, knowing that she would never see him again. Once more she faced bleak choices.

'I'll wed you – if that's what you want.'

He turned, watching her warily. Now it was his turn to be uncertain.

'It has to be your wish too. It's no' a light offer I'm making.'

She nodded, went to him, and felt his arms go round her clumsily, as though he was unsure of his reception.

'It's my wish too,' she said.

XII

The days between Adam's blunt proposal and their marriage passed in a blur of packing and shopping. If it hadn't been for Christian Elizabeth would have thrown her hands up in despair and taken to her bed more than once.

But at last the boxes were packed, and Elizabeth stood by Adam in the minister's parlour, with only Christian and one of Adam's colleagues for witnesses, and promised to live with him as his wife for the rest of her days.

His hands were warm and confident as he slipped the gold wedding band onto her finger. His mouth curved in a brief, reassuring smile as she looked up at him. It was done.

A few hours later they were on their way to London, putting distance between themselves and Paisley with each turn of the coach wheels. Elizabeth hadn't had time to say goodbye to anyone except Christian, and she hadn't seen Matt or Helen at all.

Their wedding night was spent in an inn, a place of stained plaster and shadows in the high corners. While Adam remained downstairs Elizabeth shivered her way into her nightgown and brushed her hair, wondering if any other bride had had to go to her new husband with goose-pimples all over her body. Her teeth chattered with cold and fright. She climbed into bed, at once felt marooned in its icy wastes, and jumped out again, convinced that nasty beasties lurked between the sheets.

Adam found her standing in the middle of the floor when he came upstairs. To her great relief, he didn't laugh when he saw her hopping bare-footed on the wooden floor, shivering and almost in tears.

'It's – cold—' she said, lips trembling, and he reached out his arms and drew her close to him.

'Poor Elizabeth—' he murmured into her ear. 'What have I done, taking you away from the only place you've ever known?'

Then he lifted her and carried her to the bed, where there were no beasties, and his strong body warmed them both. And this time, his love-making was tender and considerate.

She slept contentedly in his arms afterwards, but as they rode into London at the end of their journey her restored confidence began to crumble a little.

She peered, a country mouse, from the windows at the teeming crowds in the capital. The streets seemed to go on for ever, lined with shops and coffee houses. Rows of hackney carriages waiting for custom lined some of the wider roads and there were a number of sedan chairs, each emblazoned with a coat of arms, and heavily curtained.

People strolled the pavements in various stages of elegance. Ragged urchins darted in and out of the crowds, flower girls sat by the kerb in a blaze of colour provided by blossoms that had, like Elizabeth herself, been plucked from rural areas and carried off to the city.

A knife-grinder plied his trade at one corner, puffing serenely at his pipe, gnarled hands insensitive to the showers of sparks that flew about them from his stone. Another man pushing a long wooden barrow was glimpsed as the coach passed, his clothes in rags and his mouth a black hole in his face as he roared out his wares. The coach had left him behind before she could see what he was selling.

Then they were out of the bustle and had turned into the coach station. Adam helped Elizabeth down, but she had little time to look about her before she was being handed into a hackney carriage for the last part of the journey, this time to a graceful quiet road with a tree-lined park opposite long windows.

While she and Christian had been busy buying clothes, Adam had sent word to friends to find a suitable house where he could bring his bride.

To her horror, she saw a small group of servants on the steps outside the high, wide door.

'That's never the house you've taken!' she squeaked in panic to her husband. 'It's too big! And what about those folk – Adam, I cannae look after a house like this!'

The carriage had stopped, the driver was deftly unfolding the steps and opening the door. Adam's hand under her elbow gripped painfully.

'You can and you will. You're my wife, mind that. And smile – nobody's going to behead you!' he added in a steely undertone.

Smiling, panic-stricken, she descended from the carriage.

It was difficult not to burst into tears and demand to be taken home. With growing concern she surveyed the large drawing-room, the lofty hall, the small but imposing dining-room. With each moment that passed Adam, who seemed to be quite at home in his new surroundings, became more of a stranger to her. The warmth he had shown on their wedding night ebbed away as he began to plan ahead to his hospital work.

'There's nothing to be afraid of,' he said a trifle impatiently on their first morning in the house. He leaned against the window sill, studying the street below, and Elizabeth, sipping a cup of hot chocolate, was left alone in the middle of the vast four-poster bed. 'Get dressed and I'll take you to visit the friends who found the house for us. Lucy can tell you all you need to know about life here.'

'I'll learn,' she hurried to assure him. 'With you to help me at first I'll learn—'

'Me?' He laughed shortly. 'My dear girl, don't depend on me for help. I'll have more than enough to do with my own work. Lucy can see to you,' he added carelessly.

Elizabeth was mortified to discover that one of the maids had been detailed to help her to dress. She had been used to fending for herself from the time she could toddle, and in her confusion she made matters worse by trying to assist the girl. Buttons slipped in buttonholes and back out again several times, ribbons were knotted clumsily by two pairs of hands, and hooks simply gave up and refused to co-operate with anyone.

The carriage was waiting and Adam was pacing

the hall restlessly by the time she went downstairs. During the journey he answered her questions tersely, and all she could grasp was that Henry Worthing had been stationed at the army base where Adam's ship called regularly, and he and his wife Lucy now lived in London.

It was obvious by the huge house they went into that the Worthings were moneyed people. Adam handed his hat to the footman and strode into the vast drawing-room without wasting a glance on the magnificent panelling and exquisite furnishings, but Elizabeth stared about her as she followed him, convinced that she had been dropped into some exotic treasure cave.

'Adam! Dear, dear Adam!' Lucy Worthing swooped on him as soon as he appeared.

'What a surprise you gave us!' She kissed his cheek lightly then stood back, to study him, her hands still in his. 'A wife, indeed! And no warning that you'd given your heart away. How dare you keep such a secret from me?'

'I thought you relished secrets. Elizabeth—' He freed his hands, brought Elizabeth forward. 'This is my wife. Elizabeth, may I present my dear friend, Lucy Worthing.'

Lucy was just as beautiful as Helen, Elizabeth noted with a strange, sinking feeling. She had silky fair hair and wide green eyes. Her flawless figure was dressed in a pale green gathered muslin gown that made Elizabeth's pink dress look young and plain.

'Adam, she's lovely!' Lucy's gaze skimmed her face and Elizabeth saw, from the slight tremor of the eyelids, that the other woman had noted the hated scar. 'Come and sit here, my dear, and tell me all about your marriage to this exciting man!'

Her eyes darted from one to the other of them, coquettish when they touched Adam, calculating when they brushed against Elizabeth. It was only natural that Adam's friends would be surprised by his sudden marriage, she thought uneasily as she was led to a satin divan. There was no reason why she should distrust Lucy on such short acquaintance, and yet—

A flibbertigibbet, Christian would have said. She had no time for what she called 'kittens in petticoats'. And Lucy certainly seemed to fit that description.

'I must apologise for the servants – I had little time to find them. I shall find a suitable ladies' maid for you this very afternoon.'

Elizabeth knew sudden panic. 'But I don't need any more servants!'

The other woman's eyebrows arched. 'My dear,

how else are you to see to your hair, and your clothes?'

'The lassie – the girl I have can do it well enough. And I dress my own hair.' Her Scottish tongue sounded heavy and clumsy in this lovely room.

The green eyes swept over her brown hair with a glance that said enough, and roused Elizabeth to defensive anger.

'If I think I need more maids, I can find them myself. Besides, servants cost money, and—'

To her gratitude Adam came to her rescue. 'My wife is quite right, Lucy. Mere surgeons can't afford to run a large household. We don't all come of wealthy stock. Is Henry not at home?'

Lucy's mouth had a downward droop that marked her as a woman unused to being crossed. 'He's making plans in the country with his father. He's to go into Parliament.'

'You didn't travel with him?'

Her nose wrinkled. 'Norfolk in November is dismal. Besides, I wouldn't have been here to welcome you if I'd gone with Henry. Aren't you glad that I stayed here instead, Adam?'

Adam took up a stance before the fireplace. He looked quite at home amid this splendour, Elizabeth realised, although his clothes were plain. 'So – Henry is to go into Parliament?'

'There's nothing else for him to do. It's Parliament or the Church, and of course, I could never be a parson's wife!' Lucy sighed. 'If only he'd left the army before this terrible Reform Bill was passed, he would have had no trouble in getting a seat. Papa says that the Bill will ruin the country, and rob him of all his money.'

'In Paisley—' Elizabeth blurted, then bit her lip.

'Yes, Elizabeth?' her husband asked gently, and she saw the glint of mischief in his eyes. 'You were saying?'

The words came reluctantly. She felt that he was making a fool of her, emphasising her clumsiness before his elegant friend. 'In Paisley, we feel that the Reform Bill will be more just – as you well know, Adam!' she finished with a bite to her voice.

Lucy raised an eyebrow. 'How strange,' she said vaguely.

'You seem to think highly of Mistress Worthing,' Elizabeth said on the journey home.

'She's a charming lady, do you not think so?'

'And very beautiful.'

'Naturally.' There was faint surprise in his voice. 'She was taught to make a career of being beautiful. It's her only asset – that and her father's money. Learn from her, Elizabeth. She'll introduce you to society, and fill your days.'

Elizabeth's days overflowed with Lucy Worthing, and were denied Adam. He became immersed in his work at St Thomas's, spending very little time at home.

Lucy introduced her to crowds of people, took her to the theatre, the opera, dinners, and balls. Sometimes Adam was with them, but more often he excused himself, pleading pressure of work. When Elizabeth tried to turn down invitations, however, he insisted that she go without him.

She quickly realised that Lucy's gossip was almost always motivated by envy and malice. She usually talked about people who had something that she coveted, and as the days dragged on Elizabeth grew to suspect that Adam was one of the items the beautiful woman would have liked for her own collection. She was usually surrounded by young men and her husband, a chinless, silent creature, was quite unruffled by his wife's entourage.

Eventually Lucy's chattering tongue led her to the subject of Caroline, Adam's dead fiancée.

'Such a romantic story – Caroline sailed to join her family in India on the ship Adam served in. And as fortune would have it, he and his fellow officers often paid visits to the area. He was quite besotted with her – I swear I've never seen a young man so in love, before or since.' Lucy's green eyes flicked sideways at Elizabeth. 'We were all in a flutter, preparing for their wedding, when the cholera came. Adam was one of the naval surgeons detailed to work in the district, but of course none of us dreamed that poor Caroline would fall ill. She died in his arms, you know, and he was beside himself with grief. I thought that he would never get over the loss.' Then her voice changed subtly, and she said, in sweet tones that would have made Christian Selbie sniff, 'It gives me such pleasure to see him happily married, after all.'

'Is there nothing I can do with my days? Nothing useful?' Elizabeth appealed to Adam on a rare moment together.

His brows rose. 'You look after my house, you entertain, you lead a busy social life. What more can you want?'

'The housekeeper runs your house. I sit and talk – and talk, and talk. I listen, and I never hear anything worth listening to. And I do nothing useful!' She paced the drawing-room, catching sight of herself in a long mirror – well-dressed glossy brown hair, a neat figure in a stylish dress of deep blue silk, white shoulders bare. 'Can't I be of some use at the hospital?'

Adam sprawled in a tapestry chair, watching

her. 'I couldn't allow you to set foot in the place. It's filled with despair and disease and human misery – can't you see that I need to know that you're here, safe and comfortable?'

She didn't realise until much later what he meant. At that moment she was too wrapped up in her own boredom to weigh his words. 'Surely I could contribute something, even if it was just visiting sick folk, talking to them – helping with their families, mebbe?'

'The women who work in the hospitals are either sisters of mercy or slatterns who sell themselves to patients and doctors alike for the price of drink. You'll not set foot in that place,' he repeated.

'Then what can I do?'

'Lucy seems to be contented enough with her life,' he said, and a curtain came down over his eyes, putting an end to the conversation.

There were happy moments, sometimes whole days when he stayed at home, resting, wanting nobody around but her. On those days he ruthlessly cancelled all her engagements, turning a deaf ear to Lucy's objections. They talked, or explored London in the carriage. They talked about his work, about Paisley, about Elizabeth's opinion of a play she had just seen. They never talked about themselves.

She still had the ability to make him laugh, and he still, when he was relaxed, teased her unmercifully.

In bed, the only place where they could truly be alone, he was sometimes demanding, often courteous and considerate, but always formal. She sometimes wondered, with an hysterical giggle that had to be suppressed, if he was going to call her 'Ma'am' when he made love to her. But he never spoke, and she was oddly shy, too shy to say the endearments she longed to speak aloud.

She loved him deeply, but she wasn't happy. Since it was what he wanted, she worked hard at learning from Lucy. She changed her accent, learned to develop good dress sense, overcame her shyness and mastered the art of polite conversation. She even started giving dinner parties. Winter gave way to spring, and Elizabeth learned to exist within the comfortable glass prison that Adam had made for her.

Christian's letters were a lifeline to her. The older woman wrote every week – a general letter for them both, and a private letter for Elizabeth, which Adam passed to her without comment.

In those private notes she put all the little morsels of gossip that Adam would have frowned on, as well as news about Matt and Helen. Adam knew nothing of their New Year marriage, the Townhead house Helen's father had given them as a wedding present, Matt's continued success, Helen's pregnancy.

'The old warehouse is filled with looms, and every one of them working,' Christian wrote. 'Though I still have my doubts about the whole business, Matt's doing well for himself. I see him very like his father; it's a mercy that he's got Helen to sweeten the hard streak in his nature.'

In April Elizabeth was stunned to see a familiar grin among the throng in the foyer of a theatre. Her hand was seized and shaken warmly.

'Elizabeth! Mistress Cunningham!' Jeremy Forrest's face glowed with pleasure. 'I can scarce believe my eyes! Are you down here on a visit?'

She was so pleased to see him that she could have kissed him in front of all the people. 'I live here, with my husband. I married Adam Montgomery.'

He looked for a moment as though she had struck him, but rallied swiftly. 'I remember him, but I – is he here with you?'

He wasn't, but Lucy swept up to them, eager to find out why her protégée and a handsome stranger had greeted each other so warmly. Her narrowed eyes moved thoughtfully from one to the other, her charm flowed over Jeremy.

'As you and Elizabeth are such – old friends – you must come to a social evening I'm holding next week, Mr Forrest.'

'I accept with pleasure.' His eyes held Elizabeth's. Lucy's beauty hadn't affected him at all. 'Eliz – Mistress Montgomery and I have a great deal to talk about.'

He became a member of the Worthings' circle and life brightened for Elizabeth. He offered sincerity among a sea of false charm, and affection when she felt starved of it.

Lucy saw to it that Adam heard about Jeremy, but he only said casually, 'As I recall, that gentleman was always a particular admirer of Elizabeth's. But not one to be taken seriously.'

When Matt Montgomery came to London on business in June Elizabeth heard of it from Jeremy.

'I'd like to invite yourself and Adam to my father's house for dinner – but Matt tells me that Adam will have nothing to do with him,' he said awkwardly.

'I would be pleased to accept for myself.'

'But you'd not come alone?'

She put her hand briefly on his arm. 'If Matt was to be my escort – oh, Jeremy, I want so much to see him, and I can't invite him to my own home.'

He looked doubtful. 'What would Adam say if he heard that you were dining with us?'

'Adam,' said Elizabeth, 'need never know.'

It was the happiest evening she had spent in London. The Forrests' home was similar to Christian's – large, plain rooms filled with honest, straightforward people. And in their midst, arms outstretched to hug the breath out of her, face split by a huge grin, was Matt.

When he finally released her he stood back and stared. 'My, Elizabeth – you're a lady now!'

'No, I'm still myself. How's Helen?'

'Bonnier by the day, and fairly looking forward to the bairn coming.'

He was Paisley itself. His face, his voice, his very actions transported her back to her home town. She was proud to see how comfortable he was among the English merchants, and how they paid keen attention to his views.

The Forrests and their other guests tactfully left them alone in a corner of the drawing-room after an excellent, plain meal. Questions poured from Elizabeth faster than Matt could answer them.

'Christian writes such news of you, Matt! You're doing well.'

'Well enough.' He hesitated, then broached the subject they had both avoided. 'How's Adam?'

'Working all the time.' She looked down at her hands. 'He seems to like the hospital, though.'

'Does he ever talk of me?'

She shook her head. 'I'd like fine to ask you to dine with us, but—'

'Aye. He must have cared deeply for Helen. If I'd had any notion—'

'You've got as much right to your happiness as he has.'

'And he's got you – what more could a man want?' Matt asked. 'Does Christian ever mention her own health?'

'Never. She's no'—?'

'She's fine. Just a wee turn during the winter. I wondered if she'd told you, that's all. I think she misses you – both of you.'

It was hard to say goodbye to him at the end of the evening. On the way home she made up her mind to speak to Adam, to insist that he invite his brother to his house. She had had enough of the one-sided quarrel and all that it had led to. But Adam was still out when she got home, and he had risen early and gone out again by the time she wakened in the morning.

He arrived home in the afternoon. She was in the drawing-room, alone, when he stalked in.

'Where were you last night?' he asked at once,

and a tremor of fear ran through her. She suppressed it.

'I dined with friends.'

'Indeed?'

'I often do when you're at the hospital.'

'Last night I wasn't at the hospital. I came home because I thought that my wife might like my company at the theatre. When the housekeeper said you had already gone I took it that you had gone on with Lucy. So I followed.'

She moistened her lips.

'Lucy said that she had no idea where you were. Jeremy Forrest was also missing from the group.'

'And Lucy drew that to your attention, I've no doubt. She's over fond of causing mischief.'

'Perhaps – but she has sense enough to know that secret assignations between a man and a married woman are most unwise!'

'You think that I had an assignation with Jeremy?' she taunted, half frightened, half amused. He caught her arms, lifted her out of her chair. His eyes blazed at her.

'Where were you?'

'I was dining at Jeremy's father's house, with Matt.'

The name caught him off balance. He blinked, repeated foolishly, 'Matt?'

'Your brother. He's in London on business, and Jeremy thought that I would like to meet him.'

'You have no right to accept invitations without informing me!' Adam let her go and she stood still, refusing to be intimidated.

'I have every right! Matt's a friend of mine – and so is Helen. It's time you ended this nonsense, Adam. I want to invite your brother here.'

'No!' He swung away from her, almost fell over a small chair, and gripped the back of it. 'I've told you – I'll have nothing to do with him. As my wife, I expect you to respect my wishes!'

'Adam, do you no' see— ' in her agitation her Scottish accent took over '—that as long as you're bitter towards Matt, our marriage is empty? This love for Helen's between us all the time!'

He turned. 'Helen? You think I still love her? You know fine that love has no place in my life – certainly not where Helen's concerned.'

'Without love we have no sort of marriage, can't you see that?'

If he had taken her in his arms then, everything would have been all right. For a breathless moment she thought he might. She moved a step towards him, her heart thumping. But the flicker of doubt in his eyes disappeared and his face was mask-like again as he said stiffly, 'Perhaps you'd prefer to make an end to it?'

'Would you be happier if we did?'

'I made a marriage contract with you,' he said with icy formality. 'I intend to honour it for the rest of my life, if that is your wish. But I must be assured that you'll respect my feelings.'

He strode towards the door, turned as he got to it.

'If you're not prepared to accept those terms, Elizabeth, then you are free to leave. I promise that I'll make no effort to stop you.'

XIII

Elizabeth didn't see Matt again. She and Adam lived for a week in a state of armed truce. He worked long hours at the hospital, came home late, and made no effort to touch her, day or night.

They only spoke when they were with other people. After the first week, life slowly got back to normal, but it seemed to Elizabeth that the pretty glass case she lived in was shrinking and suffocating her.

Three weeks after their bitter quarrel a letter arrived from Scotland, addressed to Elizabeth in a round, unfamiliar hand.

'It's from Helen—' she said without thinking and Adam, sunk in his own thoughts across the breakfast table from her, lifted his head sharply.

'Why would she have anything to say to you?'

'Your cousin Christian's ill.' For the first time in weeks she looked fully at him, and saw how tired and drawn he was. 'It seems that she neglected a chill and it turned to pneumonia.'

He was giving her his full attention now. 'Is she bad?'

Elizabeth's eyes fled along the lines of script. 'She's recovered, but very weak. Helen thinks she'd be the better for seeing us.'

'I have no time to go to Scotland just now,' he said at once. 'But if you want to—'

'Without you?'

'Why not?' He pushed his chair back and stood up. 'God knows we're poor company for each other these days. And it might be as well for you to go where there's no mischief brewing.'

She stared up at him blankly. 'Mischief?'

His mouth twisted. 'You were born with innocent eyes. You know as well as I do that I'm talking of young Forrest and the way he pines after you.'

'How dare you speak like that about my friendship with him? What do you know of him, since you're never with us? I suppose Lucy has been tattling again?'

He ran a hand irritably through his dark hair, now well streaked with grey.

'I've told you before, Elizabeth – he's a pretty enough bauble for you to amuse yourself with, but I have no intention of being cuckolded by a fop!'

Rage brought her to her feet. She faced him across the forgotten meal.

'I'm not a possession to be treated like this!'

'You're a wife,' he told her coldly. 'You made your marriage vows before a minister. And that gives me the right to say what I think about your behaviour.'

She gave a strangled laugh. 'And you made vows on that day too. Why should I remember, when you've forgotten?'

Adam's eyes were narrow shards of ice in a set, pale face. 'I'll not discuss this any further, Elizabeth. Go to Paisley, for that's where your heart is. God knows it was never here, where it should be!'

'Was it ever needed here?' When he said nothing, she swept on. 'And what about my duty as a wife, since you're so set on preaching about it? If I go off to Paisley, who's to see to your comforts and obey your wishes?'

'I'll manage well enough with the servants to look after the house,' he said icily.

'And Lucy to see to your own comforts, as she's always wanted?' she jeered. 'I'm not blind, Adam!'

'I swear that you've dipped your tongue in vinegar. Malice doesn't become you nearly as well as it becomes Mistress Worthing,' Adam told her.

He picked up his blue coat, shrugged himself into it, and began to walk out of the room.

'Adam—' Her voice stopped him, though he didn't turn round. '—If I go to Paisley without you,' she said to his broad back, 'I'll not come to London again.'

Adam adjusted his collar, touched the lace at one wrist.

'I'm aware of that, Elizabeth,' he said, and walked out, leaving her alone.

There was nobody to turn to but Jeremy. She finally found him in his father's warehouse by the docks. Terrified by the bustle of the place, almost knocked off her feet several times as she fought through crowds of burly men carrying crates or rolling barrels to and from the high-masted ships, she almost wept with relief when she saw him.

'Elizabeth!' He caught her by the arm and whisked her out of the path of a trolley. 'This is no place for a woman!'

Her hands were shaking so badly that she could scarcely take the money from her purse. 'I want you to book a seat for me on the next coach to Glasgow, Jeremy. I have to get to Paisley quickly, for Mistress Selbie's ill and needs me.'

'But—' he took the money, perplexed. '—but surely Adam should arrange all that for you?'

'Adam's – he's—' She had intended to say that he was busy, that an urgent message had just arrived from Paisley and she had been unable to trace Adam. Instead the tears that had been unshed during the past terrible weeks broke through, and Jeremy's bewildered, friendly face blurred and disappeared.

He took her into a tiny cubicle where, unseen by anyone, she could cry to her heart's content, wrapped closely in his arms, his fingers stroking her hair. Between sobs, the whole story came out.

'Elizabeth—' he said wretchedly against her forehead, his lips warm. 'How could anyone treat you so badly?'

She mopped at her face, already regretting the words that had spilled out, betraying Adam. 'It's no' the way it seems – he's had so much unhappiness, and I thought I could make up for it. But—'

His fingers brushed her cheek. 'I never thought he was the man for you. When I heard that you'd wed him – oh, Elizabeth, if you'd just waited until I went back to Paisley!'

'Jeremy, you'll help me to get home?' she interrupted, in no state to deal with the declaration of love that seemed to be on its way.

He did everything he could. Elizabeth was put into a carriage and sent back to her house, where she packed a few things and wrote a brief, formal note for Adam. Then she returned to the warehouse, and Jeremy escorted her to the stagecoach depot and saw her on her way back to Scotland.

Her spirits rose as she crossed the Old Bridge on her final lap home. She breathed in the air, devoured the narrow streets and old buildings with her eyes. She was home.

Christian was frighteningly withered and grey-faced, but as full of spirit as ever.

'You should never have come all this way just to see me,' she scolded almost at once. 'Adam has more need of you than I have!'

'He can manage fine for as long as I'm needed here, so that's final,' Elizabeth retorted, and could tell, by the older woman's acceptance of what she said, that Christian was happy to see her.

She slipped back into Paisley life with such ease that after two weeks it seemed that she had never been away. She was busy running Christian's house and seeing to her comfort, and although she sat down several times to write to Adam, she could think of nothing to put on paper. They had said more than enough to each other before she left. That life, the life they had shared uneasily for a short time, was over.

Helen, happily pregnant, welcomed her with open arms.

'I've missed you – and you look so grand! But too pale, you need to get out more.' Her lovely face shadowed. 'Matt says he didnae see Adam at all when he was in London. I wish he'd come north with you.'

'He's too busy just now,' Elizabeth said mechanically, and repeated the words, like a charm to hold Adam's presence at bay, each time she was asked about him.

Christian's health improved from the moment Elizabeth arrived, and three weeks later she was her old self.

'You've a natural healing way with you, lass, but I'm vexed with myself for keeping you from Adam for so long.'

Elizabeth concentrated on the rose she was embroidering. 'He's too busy to miss anyone.'

The cloth she was working on was whipped from her hands.

'I'm not a fool,' the older woman said. 'Adam's too busy to visit his sick cousin, too busy to claim his wife back – even too busy to put quill to paper. What's amiss?'

'You said I'd be welcome here if I found that I'd

done the wrong thing. That's all there is to it.'

'I said you'd be welcome, and I meant it. But I didn't say I'd ask no questions,' Christian said firmly.

It was better to get it over with. Elizabeth gave Adam's cousin a brief, crisp outline of her disastrous marriage, ending with, 'And I'm not going to discuss it with anyone.'

'Except Adam.'

'As he'll never come here to speak to me, I'll never be able to discuss it with him.' Elizabeth said shortly, and reached for her sewing.

'So—' It was warm and still in the garden where they sat. Bees murmured round a flowering bush, a butterfly investigated Christian's patterned dress then moved on, disappointed. 'You just left him in London, did you? With that empty-headed trouble-making minx?'

'If that's what pleases him—'

'Tush! You know fine and well you should never have given her the satisfaction of seeing him deserted by his own lawful wife!'

'I'll not discuss it!' Elizabeth snapped, and accidentally drove the needle into her finger. At least it gave her an excuse for the tears that had arrived in her eyes.

At the beginning of August Jeremy Forrest came

back to Paisley on business. Although there were only two months to go before Helen's baby's birth, she and Matt entertained often, and so Elizabeth and Jeremy met several times.

'That young Englishman's fair taken with you,' Helen remarked when she and Elizabeth were alone in the Townhead house. 'He's gentleman enough to try to hide it, but it's there for a sharp-eyed woman like myself to see.'

'He's just—' Into Elizabeth's mind floated a well-remembered voice, saying '—a toy, Elizabeth.' She pushed it out of the way. 'He's just a dear friend.'

'Is he now? Elizabeth, would I be right thinking that you're in no hurry to go back to Adam, and he's in no hurry to come and seek you out?'

She looked up at her friend's compassionate eyes. 'There's no sense in denying it.'

Helen sighed. 'I'm no' over surprised. He's a strange man, Adam. I could never have settled with him, and I've no idea why he thought I would.'

'He's an unhappy man, and I was wrong when I thought I could help him.' Elizabeth kept her voice steady.

'If you couldn't, of all people, then he's hard to please. Now – Matt's taking the bairns to the fair on Friday, but I've no wish to go through these crowds like this—' she patted her swollen belly. 'Would you like to go along with them? I'd better tell you that Jeremy's going to be there.'

The first day of the annual fair was given over to the farmers, who crowded the town with livestock, machinery, and themselves. The second day belonged to the people, who flocked in their thousands to St James' racecourse to see the stalls and side-shows, the waxworks, and races and Wombell's Menagerie of caged animals.

It took three adults to keep up with young Duncan and Catherine as they scampered through the crowds, demanding to be shown everything. Catherine tackled the merry-go-round and swings with enthusiasm, but Duncan, still a baby and not long on his feet, clutched at his father, wide-eyed with frightened excitement.

The waxworks came next, then the tumblers and the trained pigs and the menagerie. The whole town was in holiday mood and the atmosphere was exhilarating. On the way back to the swings, Elizabeth was side-tracked by a small tent.

'Look – a fortune teller! I've never had my fortune told!'

Matt disappeared through the mob with the children, but Jeremy lingered beside Elizabeth.

'I could tell your fortune for nothing, if you'd listen to me.'

'You've got the gift?' She laughed up at him. The handsome face above hers was serious.

'Enough to know that your happiness lies with a fair-haired Englishman – like me, if you'd only admit to the truth.'

'You're teasing me,' she said swiftly, and turned away towards the tent so that she wouldn't see his expression. 'Oh – my wedding ring – she'll know I'm married.'

'Give it to me, then.' He held out his hand. Elizabeth shook her head.

'I'll no' bother. It'll be a pack of romantic nonsense,' she said lightly, and ran after Matt. She couldn't bring herself to take off the ring Adam had put on her finger. Only one person had the right to do that. Until he did, she would wear it.

'You've never once asked me about Adam,' Jeremy said on his last day, when he came to say goodbye and found her alone. His eyes searched her face intently.

'I have no reason to ask about him.'

'I never see him anyway. Nobody does – and I stopped going to Mistress Worthing's gatherings when you left London. A beautiful woman, but an empty one. Will you write to me, Elizabeth?'

351

'I was never a good hand with letters.'

'Write to me all the same,' he insisted, 'and when I come back we'll talk properly, you and me.'

'Safe journey – mind me to your family.' She held out her hand, but instead of shaking it formally, he used it to draw her into his arms.

She put her hands to his shoulders to push him away, then his mouth was on hers, warm and firm, and suddenly Elizabeth found herself holding him, responding to his kiss eagerly.

They were both breathless when they drew apart. Jeremy's eyes glowed, and he released her reluctantly.

'I wish I had found the courage to do that earlier,' he said huskily.

When she was alone she went out into the garden, stunned by her reaction to his kiss. For the first time in six weeks a man had held her, and her starved body had responded immediately, giving itself away.

It was the underlying reaction that frightened her. She hadn't been satisfied, in those few moments when Jeremy had held her. He had brought her back to life – and had also wakened the deep need for someone with more strength, more vitality, more – arrogance.

She sank down onto a stone seat, staring in

dismay at Christian's immaculate rose-bed. She wanted Adam, she missed him, and her body told her clearly that she would rather be used by him than loved tenderly by a hundred Jeremys.

'God help me!' she said aloud, appalled by her thoughts, and by the tingle that was still travelling along her veins, quickening her pulse, tensing her breasts.

'Why?' said Christian from the door. 'What have you done?'

Elizabeth jumped up guiltily. 'Nothing.'

'Then mebbe He should help you, for you're too young and too healthy to sit about doing nothing,' the older woman said briskly. 'I just met thon Englishman of yours at the gate. He tells me he's away home – but he's coming back. I don't think it's shawls he'll be after next time.'

'What else could it be?' Elizabeth moved about restlessly. Her body was glowing now.

'It's you. He's a nice enough laddie, and moneyed, I hear. What's up with you – you're like a hen on a hot griddle.'

'I'm fine.'

'Aye – well – mebbe he is the right man for you, when all's said and done. Polite, treats a lady like a lady. Whereas Adam—' it was almost as though Christian knew about the torment building up inside Elizabeth '—Adam, now, is no gentleman when it comes to womenfolk. Altogether too conceited, and demanding, and—'

Elizabeth made some excuse and went to the little room where she slept. She threw herself down on the bed, fingers digging into the top coverlet, and whispered Adam's name over and over, consumed by such longing that it hurt.

Adam filled her mind for the next two days. She had become a woman that night in his shabby lodgings, the rowdy party going on below them, but it was only now that she began to mature emotionally, going over their unhappy marriage in her mind, paying attention to small details.

She remembered him refusing to let her work in the hospital, saying to her, 'I need to know that you're here—'

Now she knew what he meant. She had been his hold on reality, his refuge as he worked among suffering and misery. And she had deserted him, knowing full well that his pride would never allow him to ask her to stay.

Who looked after him now? The servants could keep him fed and clothed, but who was there now to share his life and his bed?

With sudden insight, she knew that only she could do that, and that only Adam could ease the ache that had tormented her from the moment she had been in Jeremy's arms.

'I'm going to London,' she said flatly when she and Christian were at dinner. The older woman almost knocked over a glass of water.

'What brought that on?'

'I have to talk to Adam.'

To her surprise, Christian said, 'Are you sure you're wise to rush off like that? Wouldn't you be better to think it over for a week or so?'

'Do you think I'd be doing the wrong thing, seeking him out?'

'I didnae say that. I just think you should turn it over in your mind before you make the move.'

'I've turned it over. I'm expected at a dinner party in Helen's house the day after tomorrow. I'll leave the following morning. I'd best get it over with now I've made up my mind.'

Christian tutted. 'My, Elizabeth, but you're as tender and romantic as that man you wed!'

Although Elizabeth had resolved her marriage in her own mind, she was not at all sure that Adam would agree with her. She steeled herself for a cold rejection, and knew that she might well come back to Paisley in humiliation. But before she did take the journey north again, she vowed to herself, Adam would take the ring from her finger, and she would return as a free woman.

On her second last evening, she stayed up late, stitching at a skirt she was making for herself. Christian and the servants went off to bed, leaving her in peace.

Towards midnight, when she was thinking of giving up the fight to get the skirt finished, someone pounded at the front door.

The material fell to the floor as she jumped up, convinced that there had been some disaster. Or – the thought sent her hurrying through the hall – could it be Matt, to say that the baby was coming early?

She fumbled with the bolts, lifted the latch, and was almost knocked over as a cloaked figure burst into the hall.

It was like taking a step back in time. She wasn't in Rab Montgomery's house, the tall, dark man confronting her wasn't a stranger, his black hair wet with rain; but the scowl was the same. There was even a candle on the stairs, the murmur of sleepy, wondering voices – female, instead of male.

'Adam!' Christian said triumphantly from behind the candle. 'Man, I thought you'd never get here in time!'

'In—?' Elizabeth began to repeat, confused, but Adam's hand closed on her arm, and he steered her to the parlour, saying over his shoulder, 'Get back to whatever you're doing, Christian, and let me talk to my wife in peace!'

He unloosened his cloak, dropped it onto a chair, went to warm his hands at the fire. 'It's a God-forsaken town still. I thought I'd never get an answer at the door. Are you all deaf?'

'They're in their beds, and I was just going to mine,' she said half-apologetically, still unable to believe that he was really here, filling the quiet room with his crackling presence like a thunderstorm.

Then he swung round from the fire and glared at her, brows knotted, and she knew that it wasn't a strange dream.

'In their beds?' said Adam, astonished.

'It's midnight! And this isn't London, remember. Folk here go to their beds at a respectable hour – and rise at a respectable hour too.'

'It's well seen you've settled back in fast enough.' His gaze raked her. He looked thinner, his face drawn, but his vitality was as strong as ever. 'I was right when I said you belonged here.'

'You're always right, are you no'?' They were quarrelling again, not two minutes after he had arrived. All her good intentions and her determination to be reasonable and understanding had

357

flown at once. 'What sort of time's this to arrive on anyone's doorstep?'

'One of the horses cast a shoe and we had to wait until some lazy fool of a blacksmith could be found. Though why I was in a hurry to get here, I cannae think. I'd forgotten about your sharp tongue, woman. Is there any whisky?'

She put herself between the cupboard and his tall, lean body. 'When did you last eat?'

'I've no idea.'

'Then you'd be better with food than drink.' She flounced off to the kitchen, hoping for a few minutes to collect her thoughts, but he followed her, and leaned against the dresser, watching her while she put out bread and meat and ale.

'You've lost none of your skill in the kitchen.'

'It's where I belong,' she said bitterly. 'I leave the drawing-room for fine ladies like Lucy Worthing. She's well, I hope?'

'The last time I saw her, she was blooming.' He pulled out a chair and sat down, reaching for the ale jug. 'You never wrote, Elizabeth.'

'Neither did you. I took it that you were too busy with Lucy.'

Adam eyed her slowly, taking his time, and she felt her skin tingle as though he had touched it.

'Lucy Worthing,' he drawled, 'can be dealt with in only a few minutes of any man's time. It's no wonder that Henry looks as though he's got nothing to do.'

She almost threw the food on the table before him. 'There you are – I'll be getting to my bed now!'

'You'll be sitting down here and keeping me company,' said Adam, nodding at the chair opposite. 'And you neednae look at me like that,' he added as she sat, glaring at him. 'Would you prefer me to lie and say that I'd had nothing to do with the woman?'

'I'd never have believed you, for she was setting her cap at you right under my nose! And men were never any good at resisting temptation!'

'It was Eve that ate the apple, though Adam choked on the core – my namesake, I'm talking of. I was never one to let things stick in my throat. Besides,' he went on with a sudden edge to his voice, 'my own wife had gone off and left me. A man needs a woman around, I'll grant you that much. Come back to your rightful duties, Elizabeth.'

She blinked. There was no pleading in his voice, only an order.

'I will not!'

'You've found someone who can suit you just as well as me?' he asked mockingly.

'I'd no' have to look far to find someone better!'

Adam reached over and took her chin in his hand before she could stop him. He turned her face to the lamplight.

'You don't have the look of a woman who's being pleasured,' he said, and she pulled her face away, blushing.

'There's more to life than a man!'

'There's more to life than a woman – but it's the seasoning that makes the difference at a banquet. It seems to me that we could both do with some seasoning, Elizabeth.'

She got to her feet. 'I'd not go back to you if you asked me on your bended knees.'

He laughed with pure amusement. 'You'd have to wait a long time for that. Now where are you off to?'

'To get some fresh linen. You can have the wee room across the hall.'

'Be damned to that,' said Adam. 'I'll sleep with my wife – the Lord knows I've spent enough time in an empty bed those past weeks.'

She planted her hands on her hips. 'Sleep in my bed? Indeed you'll do no—'

'Hold your tongue, woman,' he said, and pulled

her down onto his knee. Her flailing hand knocked over the ale pot before he managed to capture it and bind it against his chest. She fought against him, then as her lips parted and his tongue teased its way round hers she felt the ache of the past few days dissolve into liquid warmth.

When his arms relaxed their hold she reached up to run her fingers over his hair, stroking the silver above his temples then moving her hand down to hold his face. He was really there, and she was home again. She knew that as surely as the moment she had first realised it, the day Adam held her in Christian's parlour after the cholera riots.

'I love you, Adam Montgomery,' she said, and felt him tense for a moment in her arms. Then he laughed against her hair.

'You drive a hard bargain. But if love's being exasperated with someone till you want to choke her, and if it's wanting to be with her every day, even if it's only to quarrel with her – then I suppose I must love you, Mistress Montgomery.'

It was as much as she could expect from him, and it was enough.

'Oh, Adam—' she sighed, then sat upright on his lap. 'What did Christian mean when she said she thought you'd never get here in time?'

'She's wandered.' Adam reached out for her, but she held him back.

'The truth, now!'

He shrugged, looked slightly guilty. 'She wrote and told me that if I had a brain in my head I'd come up here and talk to you. But I was about to come to Paisley anyway,' he added hurriedly as she opened her mouth to speak, 'for I was going out of my mind in that house without you.'

Then it was his turn to frown. 'I don't know what she meant by me being in time, though – were you planning something?'

'Since you've told me the truth, I might as well tell you. I had a seat booked on the London coach for Friday.'

'So I could have saved myself the bother?'

She struggled to get up. 'Indeed you could not! If you think I was going to come to London just to ask you to take me back, you're—'

His mouth stopped hers. 'D'you want me to help you fetch the linen for the wee room?' he whispered after several minutes.

'The bed in my room's awful narrow—'

'So was the bed in my lodgings, but we managed fine,' he said, and grinned when she blushed. 'And it seems to me that thon big bed in London made us strangers to each other. So—' He stood up, lifting her easily into his arms. '—We'll just have to make the best of that narrow cot, for I've waited long enough to love my own wife!'

She wakened in the morning to find him propped on one elbow, studying her. He bent to kiss her, then drew back again, his eyes warm.

'Now – that's what I'd call the look of a woman who's been pleasured,' he said softly.

'What time is it?'

'Gone nine.'

She sat upright, almost knocking him off the edge of the bed. He recovered, and pushed her back.

'Adam, it's time I was up!'

'You're not a housekeeper now.'

'But what's your cousin going to say to us spending half the day like—' She indicated the tousled sheets, his clothes and hers strewn over the room where they had been impatiently thrown the night before.

Adam was calm. 'We can tell her that we had a lot to discuss,' he said solemnly. 'And now I come to look at you—' his eyes slid over her shoulders, down to the swell of her breasts peeping from the sheet '—I can think of something I'd like to discuss with you right now.'

XIV

Christian was most put out by Adam's refusal to stay in Paisley any longer than he had to.

'Folks are going to be displeased,' she sniffed, but he was unmoved.

'I was never one to let folks get in my way. I've business in Glasgow today, and I hope that Elizabeth and I can be on our way back to London tomorrow.'

'So I'll be expected to travel all the way down there, will I, if I want to have a decent conversation with you?'

He stood before her parlour fireplace. 'Mebbe there'll be no need for that. My business in Glasgow concerns a post in Edinburgh, at the University. Elizabeth, what would you say to living in Edinburgh?'

'Are you not happy in London?'

'Happy enough. But now that the Anatomy

Bill's gone through Parliament and physicians can work with more freedom I've a notion to turn to anatomy. I'd like fine to try to find out what killed folk such as James and Isobel. There's a place for me in Edinburgh.'

Later, when they were alone, he said, 'Come with me to Glasgow.'

'I'd as soon stay here and get ready to go to London, Adam.' She took his hand. 'I'm dining with Matt and Helen tonight. They'll be pleased to see—'

His hand slipped away from hers.

'You know full well that I'll not go with you,' he said coolly. 'I'd be obliged if you'd make your own apologies, and stay with me.'

Her heart sank, taking with it the glow she had been feeling all day.

'So you still care for Helen,' she said dully.

'You can say that to me after what was between us last night? You know very well that it's no' Helen!'

'Matt's your brother! It's time you made your peace with him!'

'Am I to have no understanding from my own wife!' he said angrily. 'Let Matt live here and carry on the family name, and let you and me start our own lives elsewhere, without this nonsense.'

'Not until you face the truth,' she told him steadily. 'You're angry with Matt because, for once, he was the better man. He took what you wanted – and even now you'll not forgive him for it. That's no start to our future!'

'It seems to me that instead of me bringing Helen between us, it's you that's bringing Matt!'

'He's my friend, and so's Helen, and if I can't invite them into my home I'd as soon not share it with you!'

It was hard to understand how a man who had loved her so tenderly a few hours earlier could look at her so coldly now.

'Keep your nose out of this, Elizabeth. It's a family affair!'

He turned away and she caught at his arm and dragged him round to face her again.

'A family affair? Haven't I been part of your family those past three years? Haven't I taken their name for my own, and the worst of them for my husband? God help me, I'm a Montgomery now – and I'll be no party to family squabbles!'

They stood glaring at each other, Elizabeth with clenched fists buried in the skirt of her gown, Adam cold and expressionless, his eyes burning with rage.

'Elizabeth—' he put his hands on her shoulders

'—we're in danger of finishing it here and now.'

It would have been very easy to step forward, towards him. She knew that he wanted to hold her as much as she wanted to be held. But the price was too high. If she and Adam were to take up their marriage again, it must be without any barriers.

'I'm going to Matt's house tonight, as I promised,' she said, low-voiced.

'You'd let him come between us?'

'Matt has no quarrel with you. It's the coldness you feel towards him that'll be the ruin of us. I could never be sure that it wouldn't turn on me one day.'

He stared. 'That's nonsense!'

'It's what I feel.'

'Are you coming to Glasgow with me now?' he insisted.

'No.'

His hands fell away from her shoulders. His face was dark with sudden rage.

'Then be damned to you. You can stay in this town until you rot. I'll go to Glasgow without you – I'll return to London without you – I'll take up residence in Edinburgh without you, and may we never meet again!' said Adam, and slammed out of the room and out of the house.

'Mercy, lassie,' clucked Christian when she

arrived home and heard the news. 'You've driven the man too far this time.'

'I'll not deny Matt and Helen as my friends just to please Adam. That's what was wrong with his father – nobody ever had the courage to make him see his own faults.'

'If you were so set on marrying a perfect man you shouldn't have chosen that one for a start.'

'I never wanted a perfect man!' snapped Elizabeth, and burst into tears.

Helen's bright face clouded over when Elizabeth arrived for dinner on her own.

'We heard that Adam was in Paisley. We hoped he might be with you,' she said hurriedly, delaying Elizabeth in the hall. The murmur of voices came from the drawing room, where the other guests were gathered.

'He was only here on business. He's gone back to London.' Elizabeth's stormy tears had washed her clean, left her feeling very calm, as though she had just been widowed, or was recovering from a long and dangerous illness. She had no doubt that there would be a lot of pain later, but for the moment she felt strangely protected from grief, and apart from other people.

Helen looked at her closely. 'Are you feeling well?'

'I'm fine,' Elizabeth assured her serenely, and swept into the busy room.

She wasn't hungry, but she managed to eat enough to satisfy Helen's watchful gaze. The rest of the night, alone in the great empty spaces of her small bed, loomed ahead, but for the moment she was surrounded by people, and safe from her own thoughts.

Peter Todd trapped her in the drawing-room after the meal so that he could talk at great length about his beloved prize carnations. A stir at the door caught her wandering attention.

Adam, still wearing his dark travelling clothes, stood there.

'Mercy!' Elizabeth thought in a panic, and tried to shrink behind Peter, away from the blue gaze that scissored through the crowd of people between them.

Helen's tawny head swam towards him, followed by Matt's brown mop. Peeping over Peter's shoulder, Elizabeth watched fearfully. If Adam caused a scene in this house, before Matt and Helen's guests, then he would live to regret it, she vowed, swallowing back terror and trying to bolster herself with anger instead.

As though they had met just the day before, Adam shook his brother's hand absent-mindedly, looked down at Helen's lovely face and swollen figure with brief recognition, then his eyes swept up again, scanning the other people there. They found what they sought and he marched across the room just as Peter, suddenly aware that he had lost Elizabeth's attention, turned.

'What's this? Elizabeth didnae tell me that you'd be here, Adam.'

A formal smile flickered about Adam's mouth, and was gone.

'Good evening, Mister Todd. I'll have a word with you before I go. In the meantime—' his hand closed over Elizabeth's elbow, firmly '—I must speak with my wife.'

She was whisked off to the window, pinned against the curtains by Adam's big body, which effectively blocked her way back to the others. Attack was the best form of defence.

'Adam Montgomery, if you make trouble for Matt and Helen and me, you'll live to regret it!'

He glowered down at her. 'Stop clucking like a chicken that's lost its way, woman! I already know that I'll live to regret this evening's work without your threats. I've done as you wanted – I've shaken Matt's hand, and I've come into his house. And you and me leave for London tomorrow morning, if I've to tie you into the stage-coach myself.'

'If Christian put you up to this, you can go back and tell her to keep her nose out of my business!'

He looked as though he would like to shake her hard. 'I've not been to Oakshawhill – I came straight here from Glasgow. I knew fine that my wife would never think of obeying my wishes. Now – we're to take up residence in Edinburgh in six weeks' time, and there's plenty to be done before then, so we'll just get back to Christian's house and—'

'I don't trust you!'

The beginnings of a smile trembled at the corners of his mouth. 'That's the way I prefer it, Mistress Montgomery. I'm going to see to it that this is the last time I dance to your tune. From this night on, you'll do the dancing. Now—' his face softened, his eyes bathed her in their blue light, and her knees weakened at once '—how soon can you and me get out of this place and be alone?'

'Another hour, at least. Folk'll want to talk to you—'

'I'll never be able to keep my hands from you for as long as that,' he said, low-voiced, and she felt her body tighten with desire.

'Adam—'

'Elizabeth—' he said, and the word was a caress that tormented her with its sweet promise. 'To hell with them all. We've travelled a long hard way to find each other. We'll go now and leave them to their own ploys.'

She firmed trembling lips, shook her head. 'We will not,' she said, and the sharpness in her voice was more for herself than for him. 'You're one of them, and they have the right to talk with you while you're here.'

She put a hand on his arm, her fingers keenly aware of the hard, lithe body beneath the cloth, and he sighed and turned so that they faced the room together.

'You're a bully, Elizabeth,' he murmured. 'And you're wrong. I never was one of them. I was always a stranger to this town. Are you willing to come with me and be a stranger here from now on?'

There was no decision to make. Now that she and Adam understood each other, she would be a stranger to any community that didn't hold him.

She pressed his arm lightly, and knew that he understood.

Side by side, they moved forward to make their farewells to Paisley.